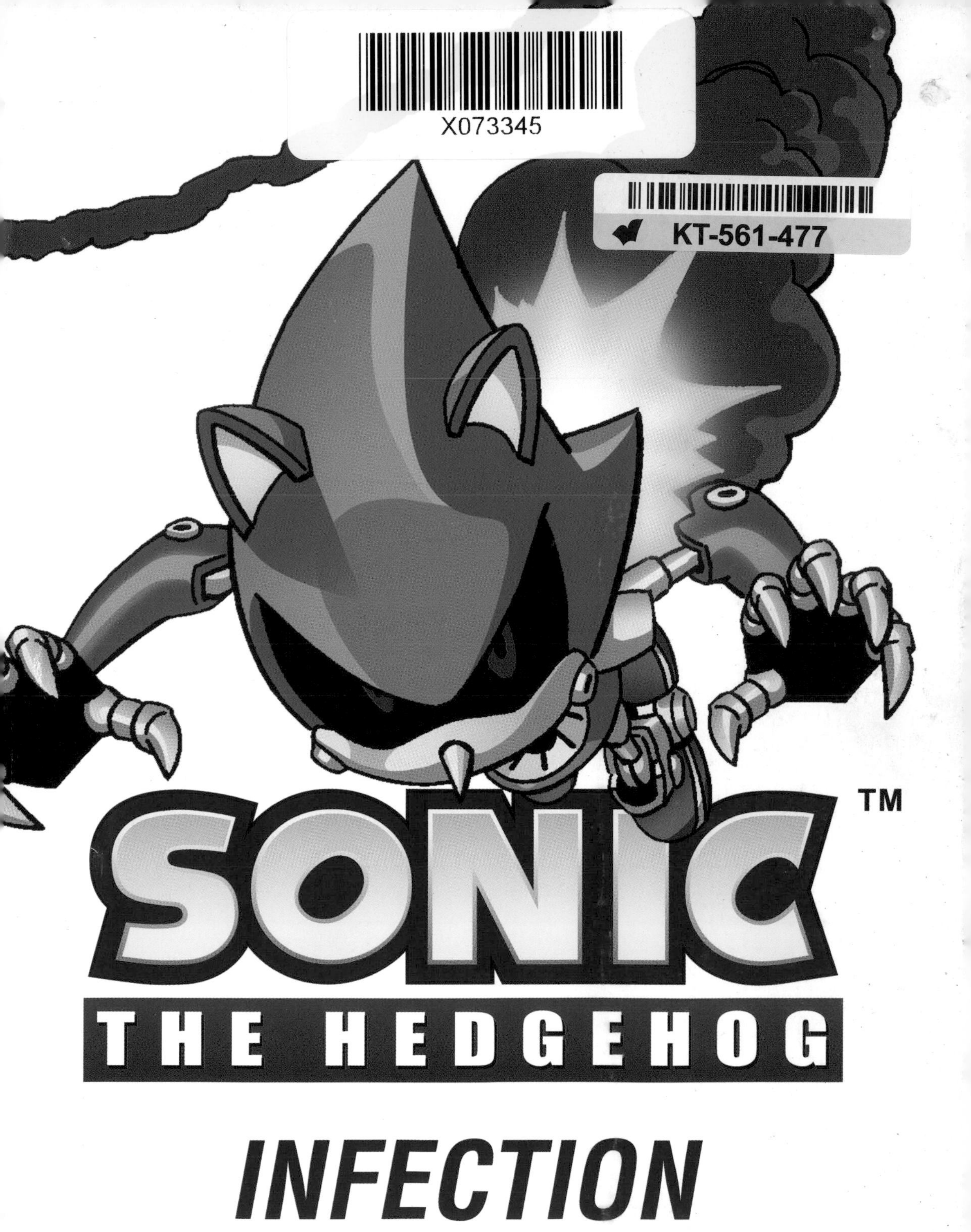

SONIC™
THE HEDGEHOG

INFECTION

SEGA®

Facebook: **facebook.com/idwpublishing**
Twitter: **@idwpublishing**
YouTube: **youtube.com/idwpublishing**
Tumblr: **tumblr.idwpublishing.com**
Instagram: **instagram.com/idwpublishing**

COVER ART BY
JACK LAWRENCE

COVER COLORS BY
MATT HERMS

SERIES ASSISTANT EDITS BY
MEGAN BROWN

SERIES EDITS BY
DAVID MARIOTTE

COLLECTION EDITS BY
JUSTIN EISINGER
AND ALONZO SIMON

PRODUCTION ASSISTANCE BY
SHAWN LEE

ISBN: 978-1-68405-544-9   22 21 20 19   1 2 3 4

Originally published as SONIC THE HEDGEHOG issues #13–16.

Chris Ryall, President & Publisher/CCO
John Barber, Editor-In-Chief
Cara Morrison, Chief Financial Officer
Matthew Ruzicka, Chief Accounting Officer
David Hedgecock, Associate Publisher
Jerry Bennington, VP of New Product Development
Lorelei Bunjes, VP of Digital Services
Justin Eisinger, Editorial Director, Graphic Novels & Collections
Eric Moss, Sr. Director, Licensing & Business Development

Ted Adams and Robbie Robbins, IDW Founders

Special thanks to Anoulay Tsai, Mai Kiyotaki, Aaron Webber, Michael Cisneros, Sandra Jo, and everyone at Sega for their invaluable assistance.

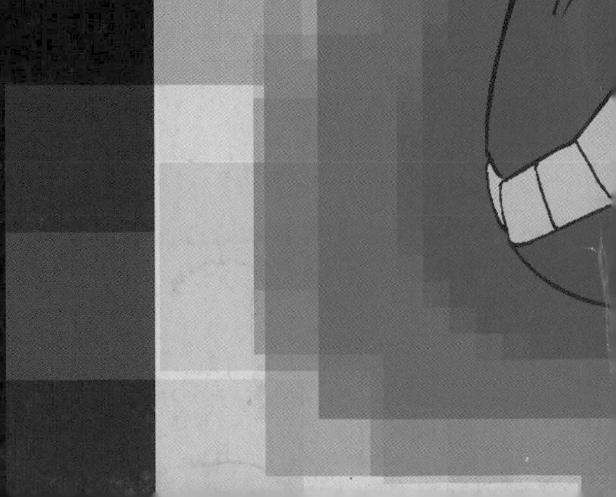

STORY
IAN FLYNN

ART
ADAM BRYCE THOMAS (#13)
TRACY YARDLEY (#14)
JACK LAWRENCE (#15–16)
DIANA SKELLY (#16)

INKS
PRISCILLA TRAMONTANO (#16)

COLORS
MATT HERMS (#13, 15–16)
LEONARDO ITO (#14)

LETTERS
SHAWN LEE

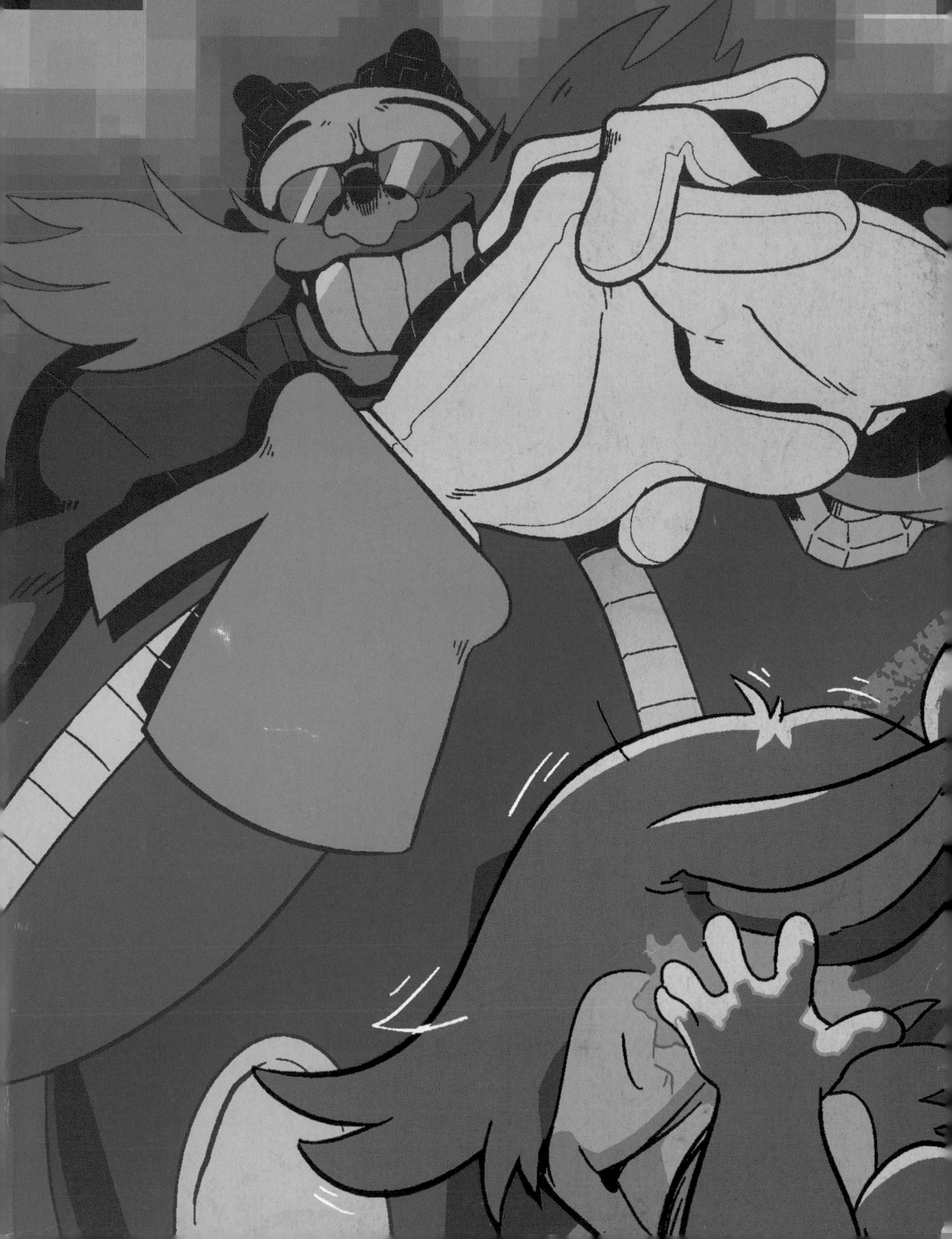

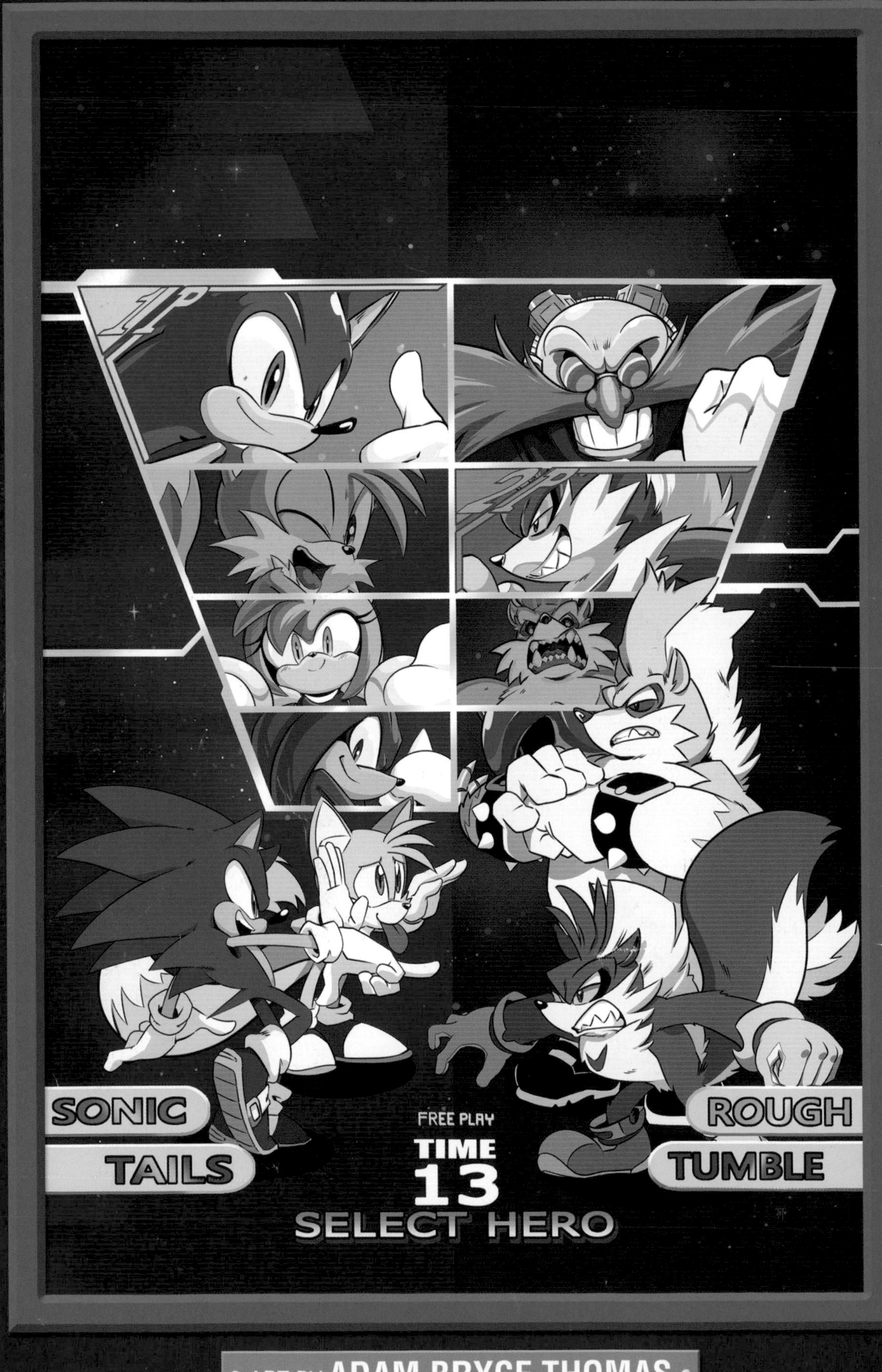
1P
2P
SONIC
TAILS
FREE PLAY
TIME
13
SELECT HERO
ROUGH
TUMBLE

ART BY ADAM BRYCE THOMAS

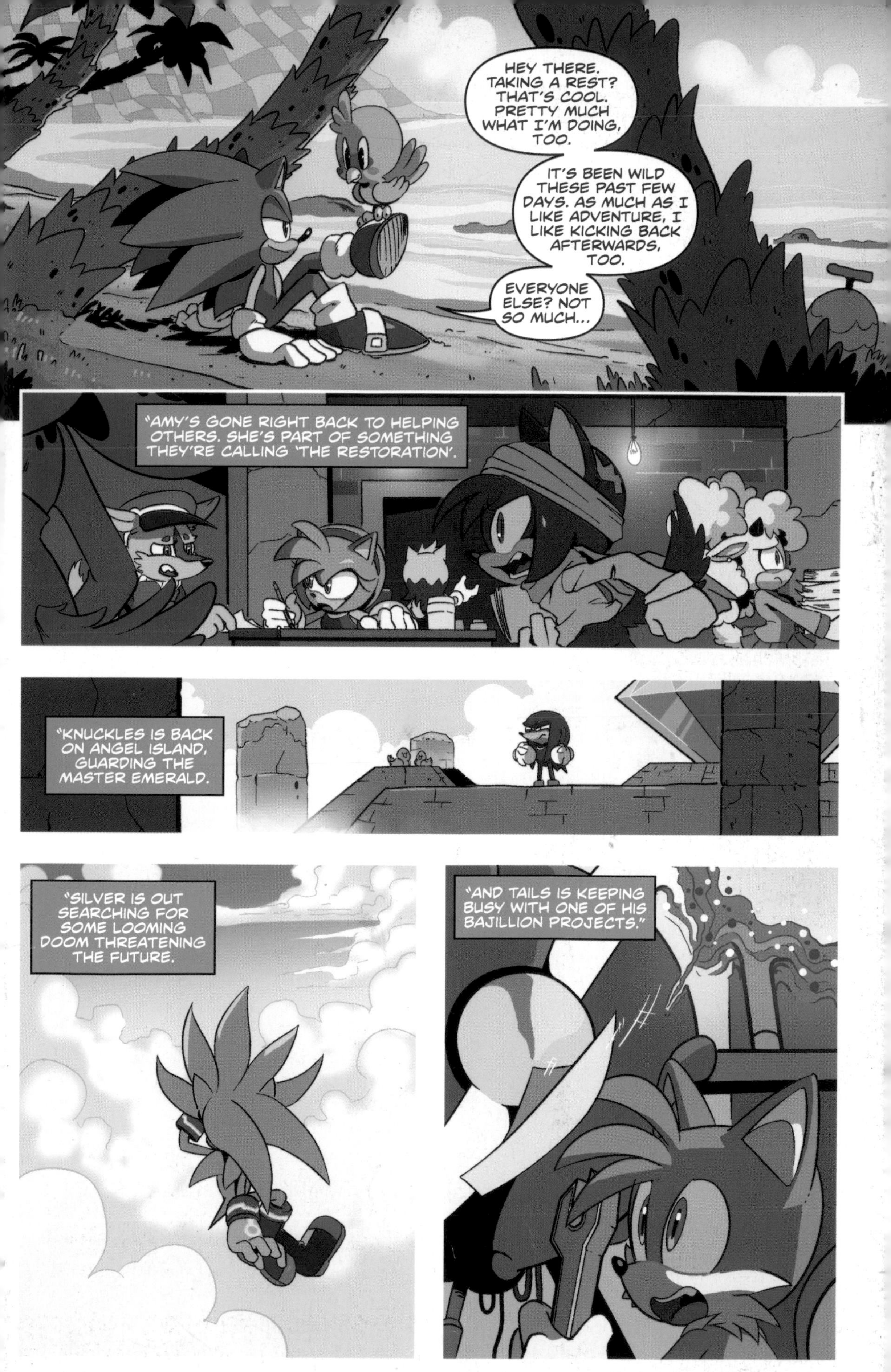
HEY THERE. TAKING A REST? THAT'S COOL. PRETTY MUCH WHAT I'M DOING, TOO.
IT'S BEEN WILD THESE PAST FEW DAYS. AS MUCH AS I LIKE ADVENTURE, I LIKE KICKING BACK AFTERWARDS, TOO.
EVERYONE ELSE? NOT SO MUCH...
"AMY'S GONE RIGHT BACK TO HELPING OTHERS. SHE'S PART OF SOMETHING THEY'RE CALLING 'THE RESTORATION'.
"KNUCKLES IS BACK ON ANGEL ISLAND, GUARDING THE MASTER EMERALD.
"SILVER IS OUT SEARCHING FOR SOME LOOMING DOOM THREATENING THE FUTURE.
"AND TAILS IS KEEPING BUSY WITH ONE OF HIS BAJILLION PROJECTS."

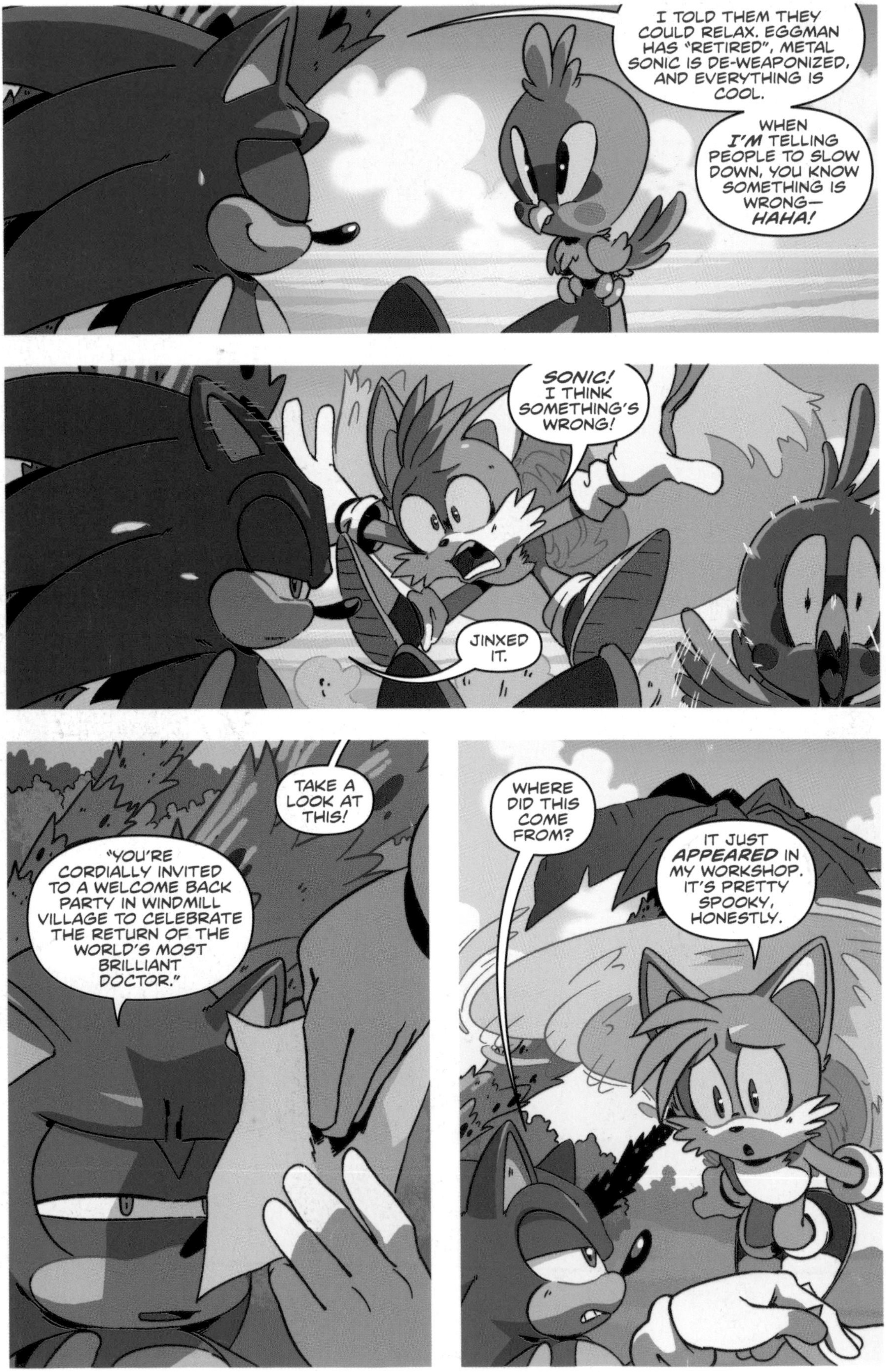
I TOLD THEM THEY COULD RELAX. EGGMAN HAS "RETIRED", METAL SONIC IS DE-WEAPONIZED, AND EVERYTHING IS COOL.
WHEN *I'M* TELLING PEOPLE TO SLOW DOWN, YOU KNOW SOMETHING IS WRONG— ***HAHA!***
SONIC! I THINK SOMETHING'S WRONG!
JINXED IT.
TAKE A LOOK AT THIS!
"YOU'RE CORDIALLY INVITED TO A WELCOME BACK PARTY IN WINDMILL VILLAGE TO CELEBRATE THE RETURN OF THE WORLD'S MOST BRILLIANT DOCTOR."
WHERE DID THIS COME FROM?
IT JUST ***APPEARED*** IN MY WORKSHOP. IT'S PRETTY SPOOKY, HONESTLY.

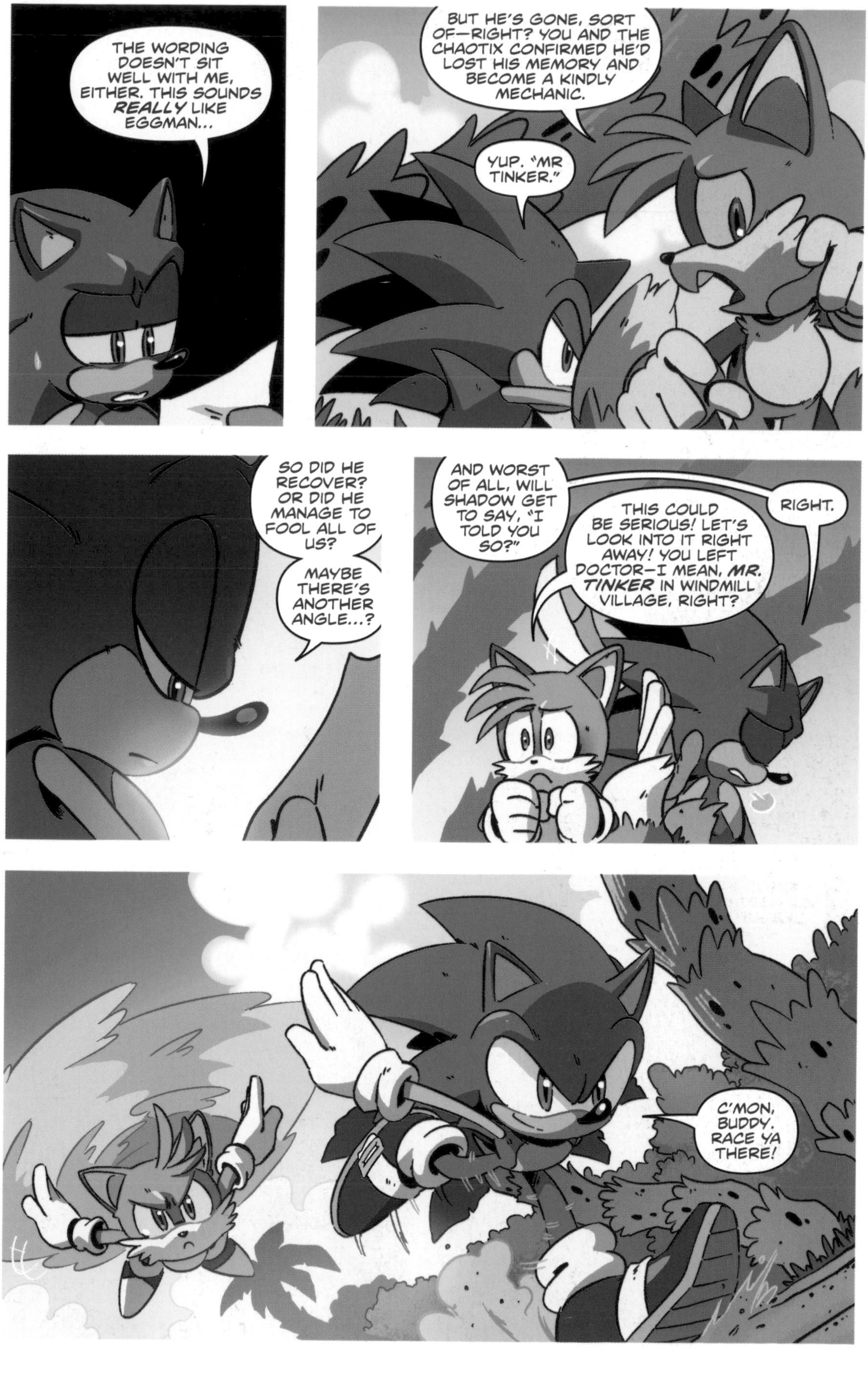
THE WORDING DOESN'T SIT WELL WITH ME, EITHER. THIS SOUNDS *REALLY* LIKE EGGMAN...
BUT HE'S GONE, SORT OF—RIGHT? YOU AND THE CHAOTIX CONFIRMED HE'D LOST HIS MEMORY AND BECOME A KINDLY MECHANIC.
YUP. "MR TINKER."
SO DID HE RECOVER? OR DID HE MANAGE TO FOOL ALL OF US?
MAYBE THERE'S ANOTHER ANGLE...?
AND WORST OF ALL, WILL SHADOW GET TO SAY, "I TOLD YOU SO?"
THIS COULD BE SERIOUS! LET'S LOOK INTO IT RIGHT AWAY! YOU LEFT DOCTOR—I MEAN, *MR. TINKER* IN WINDMILL VILLAGE, RIGHT?
RIGHT.
C'MON, BUDDY. RACE YA THERE!

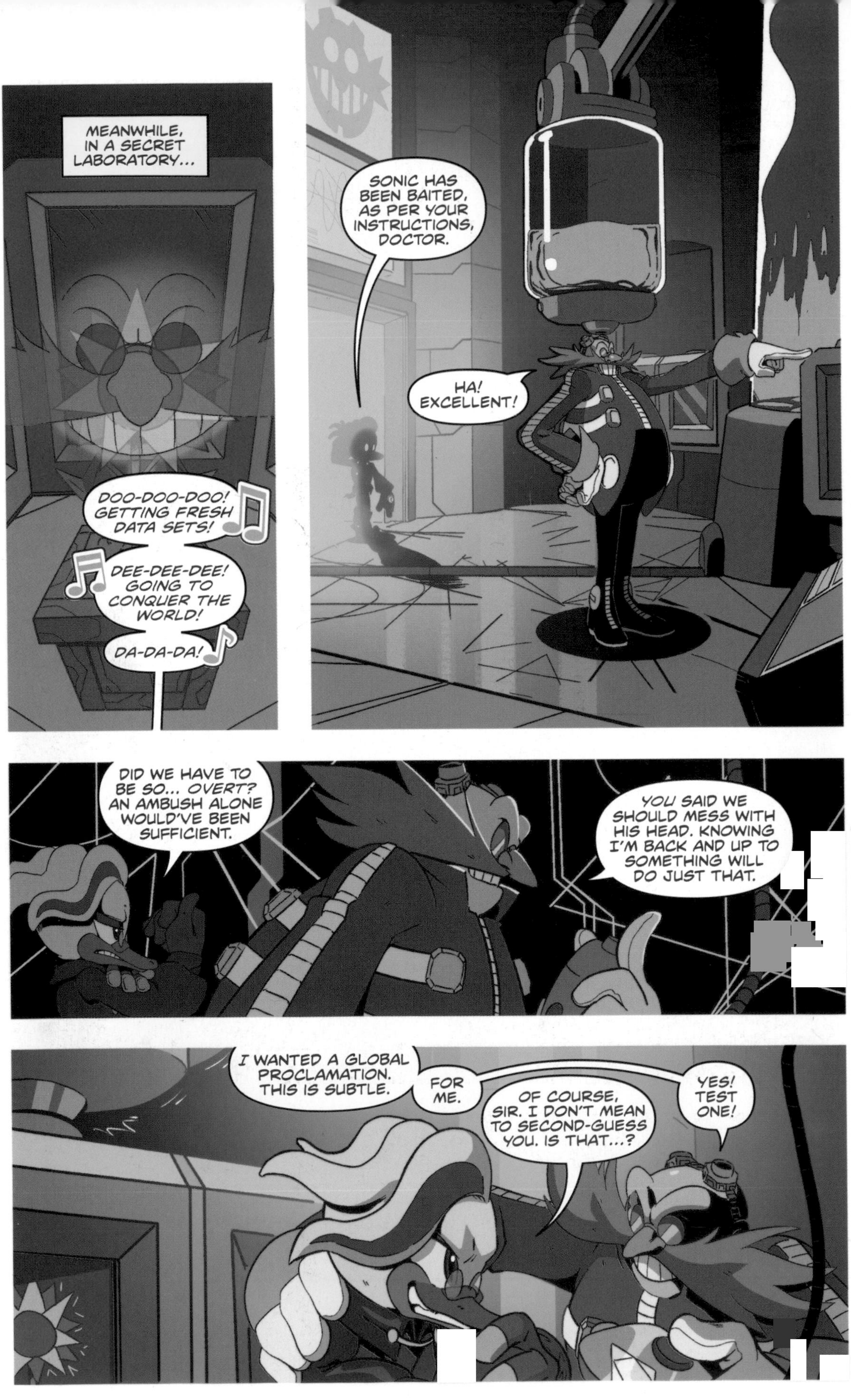
MEANWHILE, IN A SECRET LABORATORY...
DOO-DOO-DOO! GETTING FRESH DATA SETS!
DEE-DEE-DEE! GOING TO CONQUER THE WORLD!
DA-DA-DA!
SONIC HAS BEEN BAITED, AS PER YOUR INSTRUCTIONS, DOCTOR.
HA! EXCELLENT!
DID WE HAVE TO BE SO... OVERT? AN AMBUSH ALONE WOULD'VE BEEN SUFFICIENT.
YOU SAID WE SHOULD MESS WITH HIS HEAD. KNOWING I'M BACK AND UP TO SOMETHING WILL DO JUST THAT.
I WANTED A GLOBAL PROCLAMATION. THIS IS SUBTLE.
FOR ME.
OF COURSE, SIR. I DON'T MEAN TO SECOND-GUESS YOU. IS THAT...?
YES! TEST ONE!

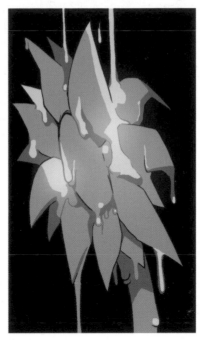

MARVELOUS! TOTAL AND INSTANTANEOUS TRANSMUTATION!

HMM... OF THE ACTIVE PLANT TISSUE, YES, BUT NOT THE PROCESSED WOOD...

I NEED MORE DATA.

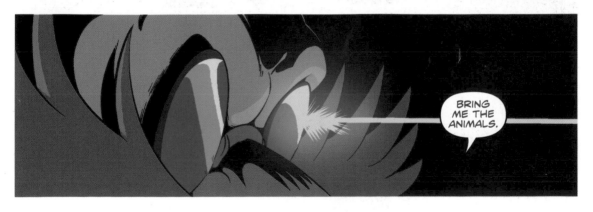

BRING ME THE ANIMALS.

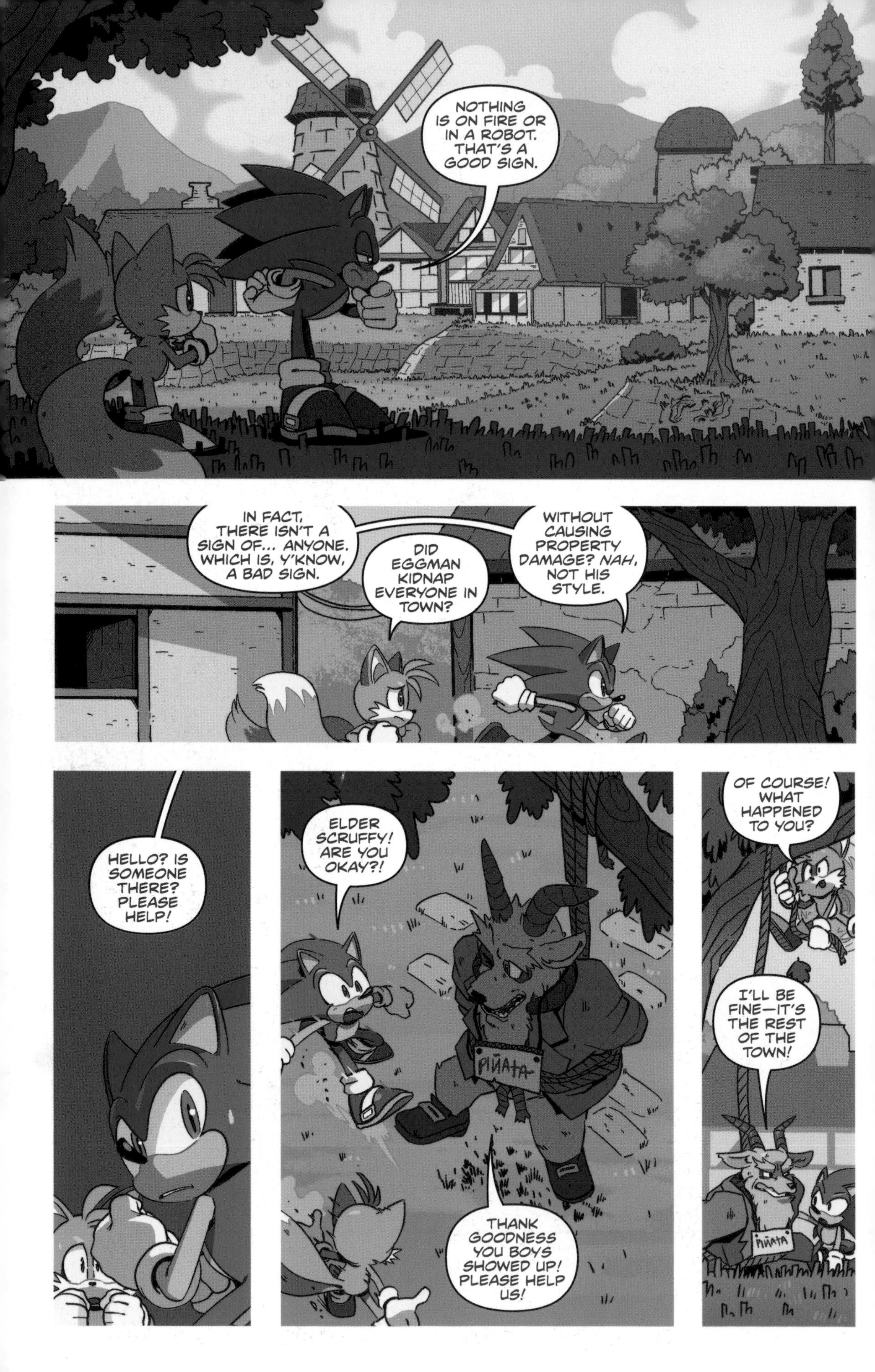
NOTHING IS ON FIRE OR IN A ROBOT. THAT'S A GOOD SIGN.
IN FACT, THERE ISN'T A SIGN OF... ANYONE. WHICH IS, Y'KNOW, A BAD SIGN.
DID EGGMAN KIDNAP EVERYONE IN TOWN?
WITHOUT CAUSING PROPERTY DAMAGE? NAH, NOT HIS STYLE.
HELLO? IS SOMEONE THERE? PLEASE HELP!
ELDER SCRUFFY! ARE YOU OKAY?!
PIÑATA
THANK GOODNESS YOU BOYS SHOWED UP! PLEASE HELP US!
OF COURSE! WHAT HAPPENED TO YOU?
I'LL BE FINE—IT'S THE REST OF THE TOWN!
PIÑATA

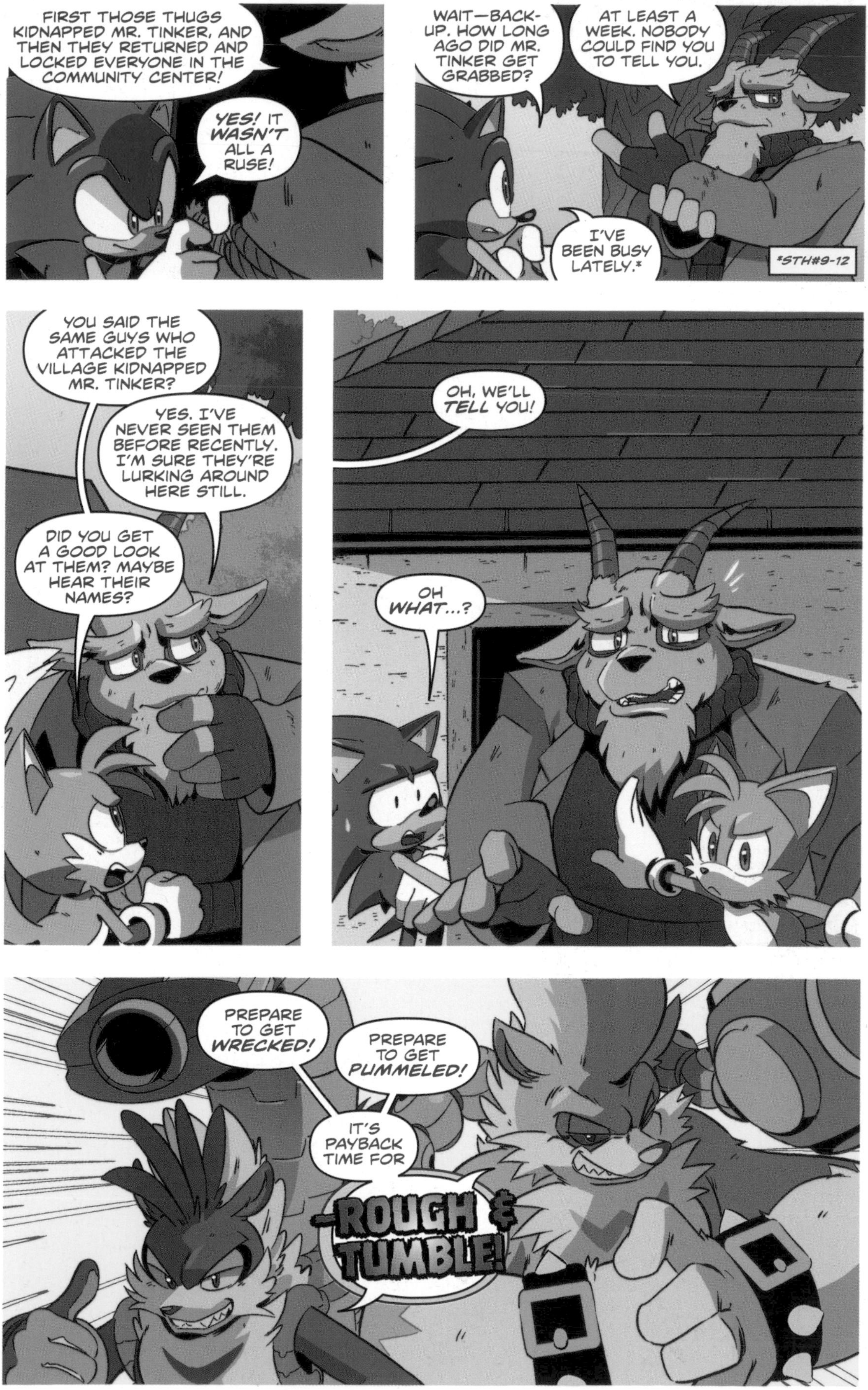
FIRST THOSE THUGS KIDNAPPED MR. TINKER, AND THEN THEY RETURNED AND LOCKED EVERYONE IN THE COMMUNITY CENTER!
YES! IT WASN'T ALL A RUSE!
WAIT—BACK-UP. HOW LONG AGO DID MR. TINKER GET GRABBED?
AT LEAST A WEEK. NOBODY COULD FIND YOU TO TELL YOU.
I'VE BEEN BUSY LATELY.*
*STH#9-12
YOU SAID THE SAME GUYS WHO ATTACKED THE VILLAGE KIDNAPPED MR. TINKER?
YES. I'VE NEVER SEEN THEM BEFORE RECENTLY. I'M SURE THEY'RE LURKING AROUND HERE STILL.
DID YOU GET A GOOD LOOK AT THEM? MAYBE HEAR THEIR NAMES?
OH, WE'LL TELL YOU!
OH WHAT...?
PREPARE TO GET WRECKED!
PREPARE TO GET PUMMELED!
IT'S PAYBACK TIME FOR
ROUGH & TUMBLE!

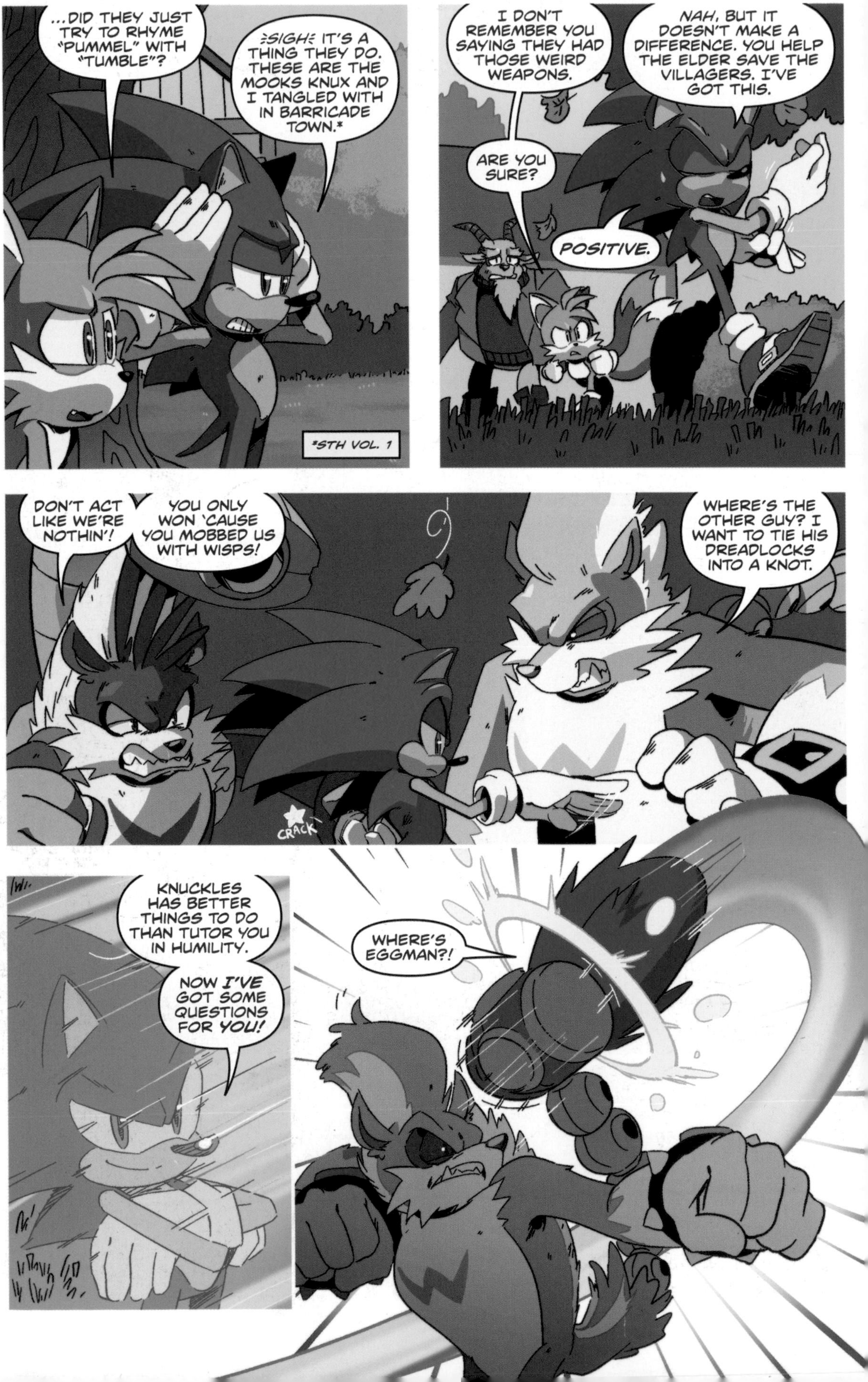
...DID THEY JUST TRY TO RHYME "PUMMEL" WITH "TUMBLE"?
SIGH IT'S A THING THEY DO. THESE ARE THE MOOKS KNUX AND I TANGLED WITH IN BARRICADE TOWN.*
*STH VOL. 1
I DON'T REMEMBER YOU SAYING THEY HAD THOSE WEIRD WEAPONS.
NAH, BUT IT DOESN'T MAKE A DIFFERENCE. YOU HELP THE ELDER SAVE THE VILLAGERS. I'VE GOT THIS.
ARE YOU SURE?
POSITIVE.
DON'T ACT LIKE WE'RE NOTHIN'!
YOU ONLY WON 'CAUSE YOU MOBBED US WITH WISPS!
WHERE'S THE OTHER GUY? I WANT TO TIE HIS DREADLOCKS INTO A KNOT.
CRACK
KNUCKLES HAS BETTER THINGS TO DO THAN TUTOR YOU IN HUMILITY.
NOW I'VE GOT SOME QUESTIONS FOR YOU!
WHERE'S EGGMAN?!

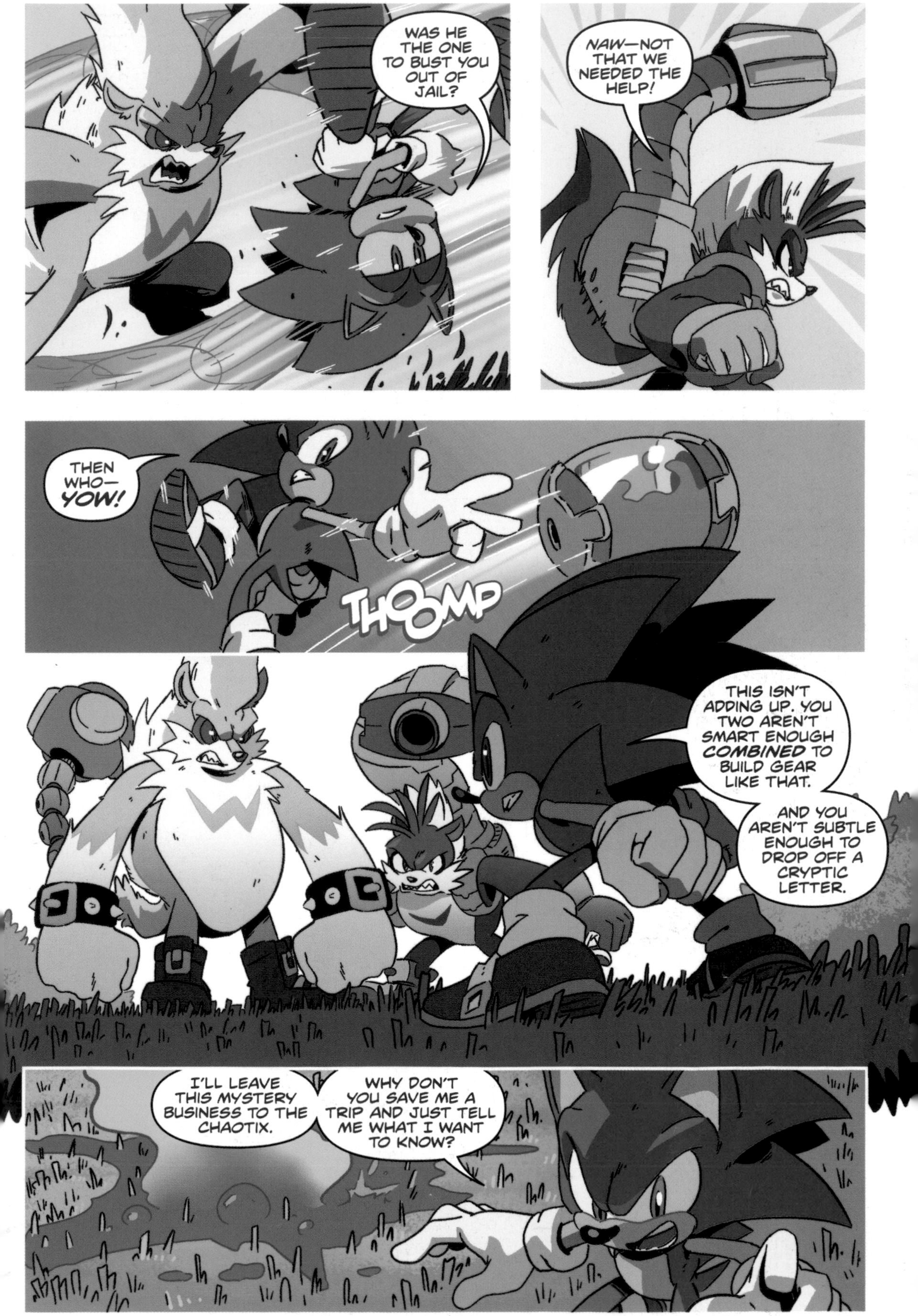
WAS HE THE ONE TO BUST YOU OUT OF JAIL?
NAW—NOT THAT WE NEEDED THE HELP!
THEN WHO—YOW!
THOOMP
THIS ISN'T ADDING UP. YOU TWO AREN'T SMART ENOUGH COMBINED TO BUILD GEAR LIKE THAT.
AND YOU AREN'T SUBTLE ENOUGH TO DROP OFF A CRYPTIC LETTER.
I'LL LEAVE THIS MYSTERY BUSINESS TO THE CHAOTIX.
WHY DON'T YOU SAVE ME A TRIP AND JUST TELL ME WHAT I WANT TO KNOW?

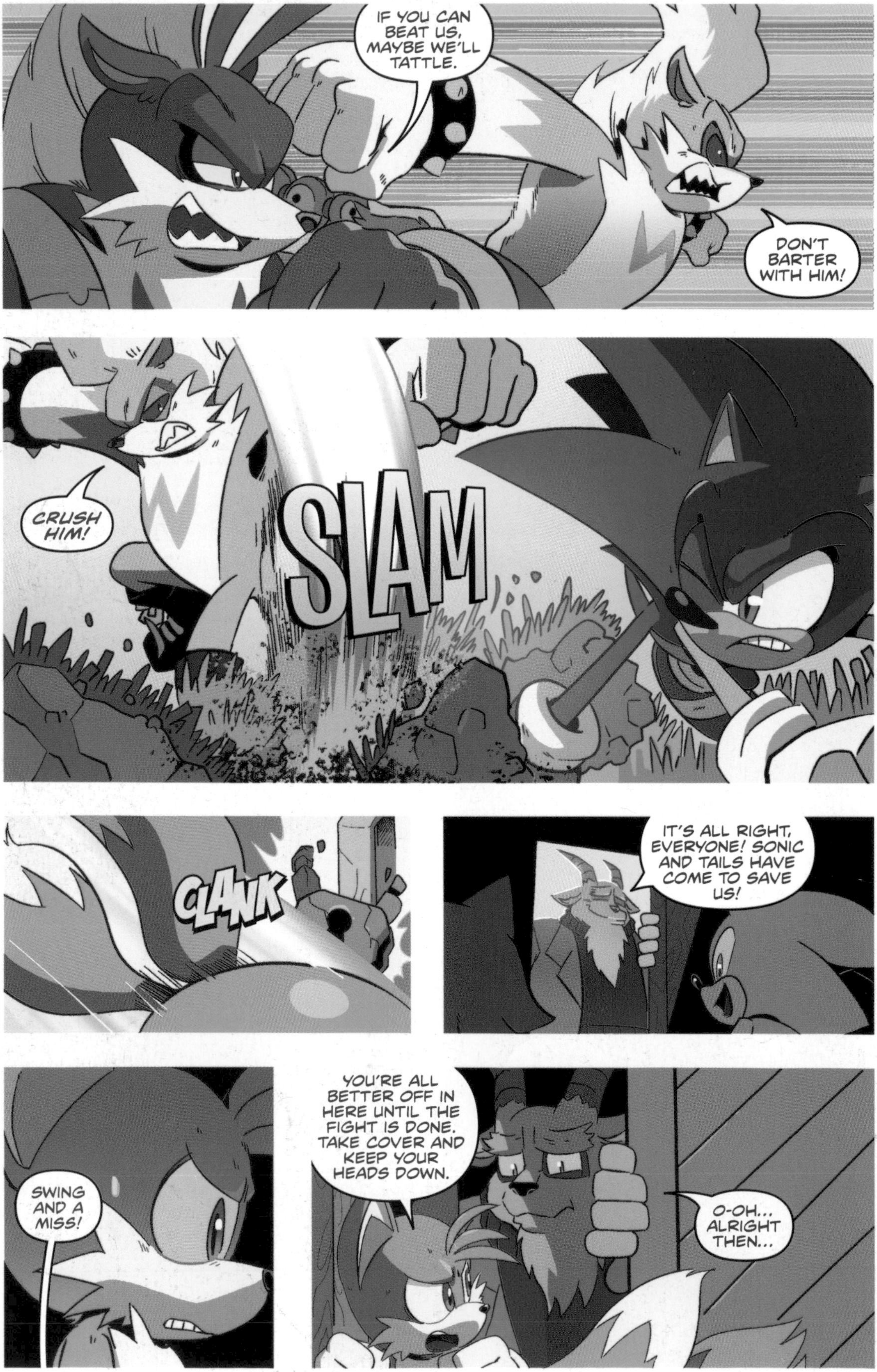
IF YOU CAN BEAT US, MAYBE WE'LL TATTLE.
DON'T BARTER WITH HIM!
CRUSH HIM!
SLAM
CLANK
IT'S ALL RIGHT, EVERYONE! SONIC AND TAILS HAVE COME TO SAVE US!
SWING AND A MISS!
YOU'RE ALL BETTER OFF IN HERE UNTIL THE FIGHT IS DONE. TAKE COVER AND KEEP YOUR HEADS DOWN.
O-OH... ALRIGHT THEN...

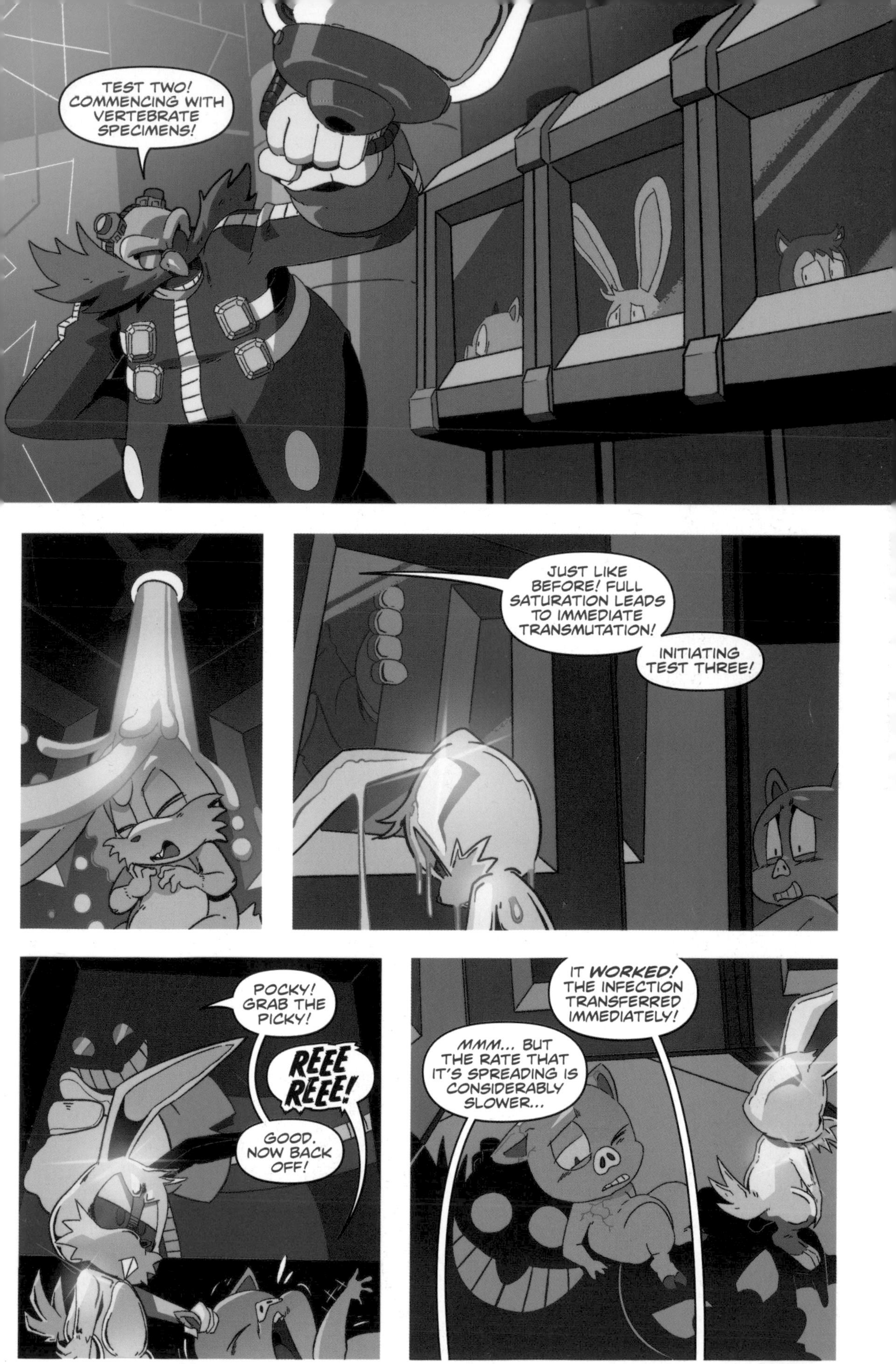
TEST TWO! COMMENCING WITH VERTEBRATE SPECIMENS!
JUST LIKE BEFORE! FULL SATURATION LEADS TO IMMEDIATE TRANSMUTATION!
INITIATING TEST THREE!
POCKY! GRAB THE PICKY!
REEE REEE!
GOOD. NOW BACK OFF!
IT WORKED! THE INFECTION TRANSFERRED IMMEDIATELY!
MMM... BUT THE RATE THAT IT'S SPREADING IS CONSIDERABLY SLOWER...

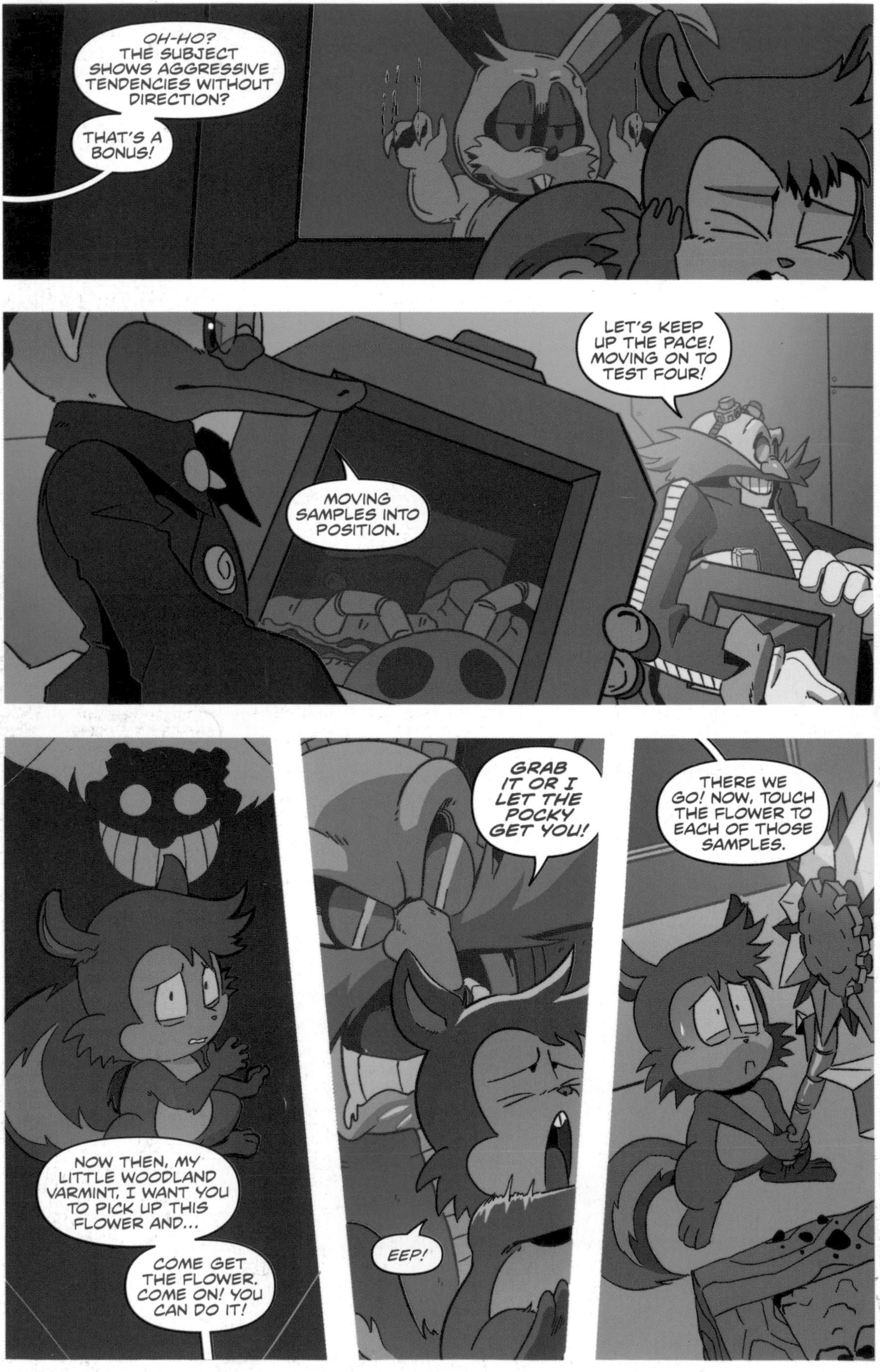
OH-HO? THE SUBJECT SHOWS AGGRESSIVE TENDENCIES WITHOUT DIRECTION?
THAT'S A BONUS!
LET'S KEEP UP THE PACE! MOVING ON TO TEST FOUR!
MOVING SAMPLES INTO POSITION.
NOW THEN, MY LITTLE WOODLAND VARMINT, I WANT YOU TO PICK UP THIS FLOWER AND...
COME GET THE FLOWER. COME ON! YOU CAN DO IT!
GRAB IT OR I LET THE POCKY GET YOU!
EEP!
THERE WE GO! NOW, TOUCH THE FLOWER TO EACH OF THOSE SAMPLES.

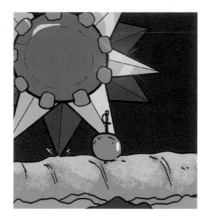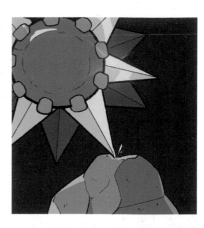

I... DON'T SEE ANY SIGNS OF INFECTION, SIR.

NO, BUT IT *DID* PASS FROM FLORA TO FAUNA. THAT'S TEST FIVE COMPLETE!

MY *METAL VIRUS* IS A COMPLETE SUCCESS!

EVEN WITH THE SLIGHTEST EXPOSURE, MY SYNTHETIC CONCOCTION SPREADS ACROSS ORGANIC TISSUE, CONVERTING IT INTO MY ROBOTIC SLAVE! IT'S AN ARMY THAT BUILDS ITSELF!

INORGANIC OR PROCESSED MATERIAL REMAINS INERT, MEANING MY INFRASTRUCTURE IS SAFE FROM INFECTION OR CORRUPTION!

I'M A GENIUS!

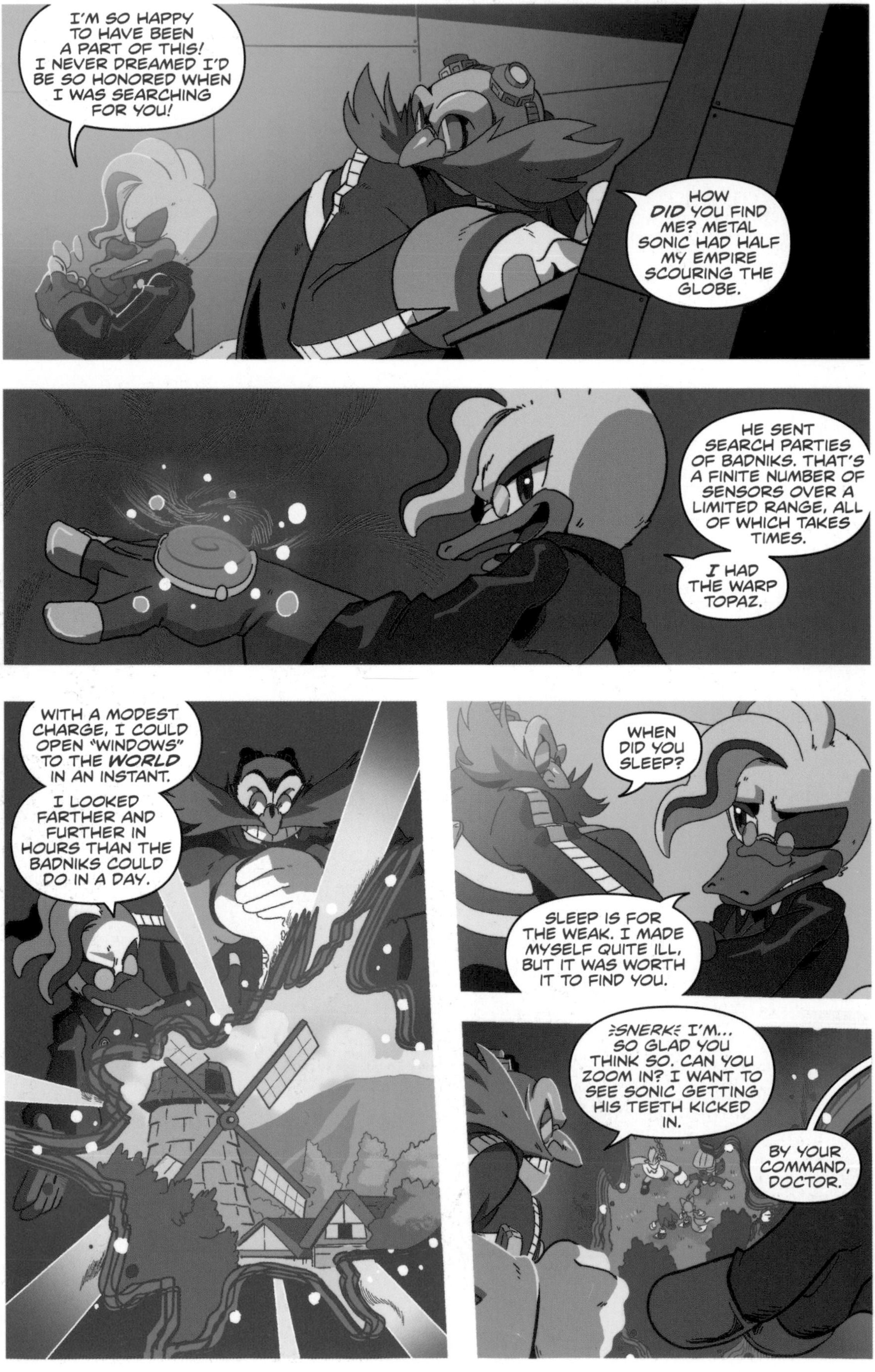
I'M SO HAPPY TO HAVE BEEN A PART OF THIS! I NEVER DREAMED I'D BE SO HONORED WHEN I WAS SEARCHING FOR YOU!
HOW DID YOU FIND ME? METAL SONIC HAD HALF MY EMPIRE SCOURING THE GLOBE.
HE SENT SEARCH PARTIES OF BADNIKS. THAT'S A FINITE NUMBER OF SENSORS OVER A LIMITED RANGE, ALL OF WHICH TAKES TIMES.
I HAD THE WARP TOPAZ.
WITH A MODEST CHARGE, I COULD OPEN "WINDOWS" TO THE WORLD IN AN INSTANT.
I LOOKED FARTHER AND FURTHER IN HOURS THAN THE BADNIKS COULD DO IN A DAY.
WHEN DID YOU SLEEP?
SLEEP IS FOR THE WEAK. I MADE MYSELF QUITE ILL, BUT IT WAS WORTH IT TO FIND YOU.
≷SNERK≶ I'M... SO GLAD YOU THINK SO. CAN YOU ZOOM IN? I WANT TO SEE SONIC GETTING HIS TEETH KICKED IN.
BY YOUR COMMAND, DOCTOR.

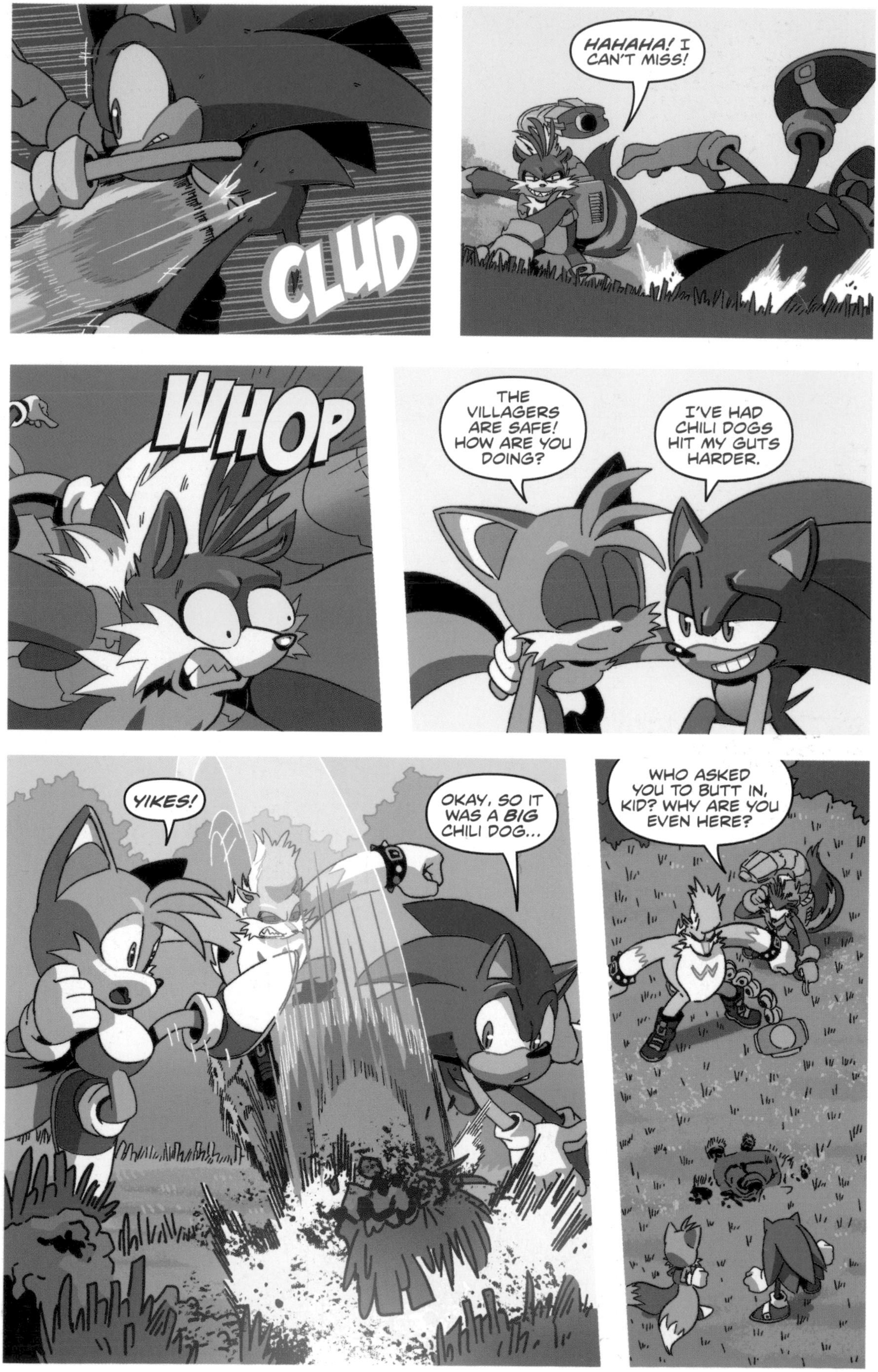
CLUD
HAHAHA! I CAN'T MISS!
WHOP
THE VILLAGERS ARE SAFE! HOW ARE YOU DOING?
I'VE HAD CHILI DOGS HIT MY GUTS HARDER.
YIKES!
OKAY, SO IT WAS A BIG CHILI DOG...
WHO ASKED YOU TO BUTT IN, KID? WHY ARE YOU EVEN HERE?

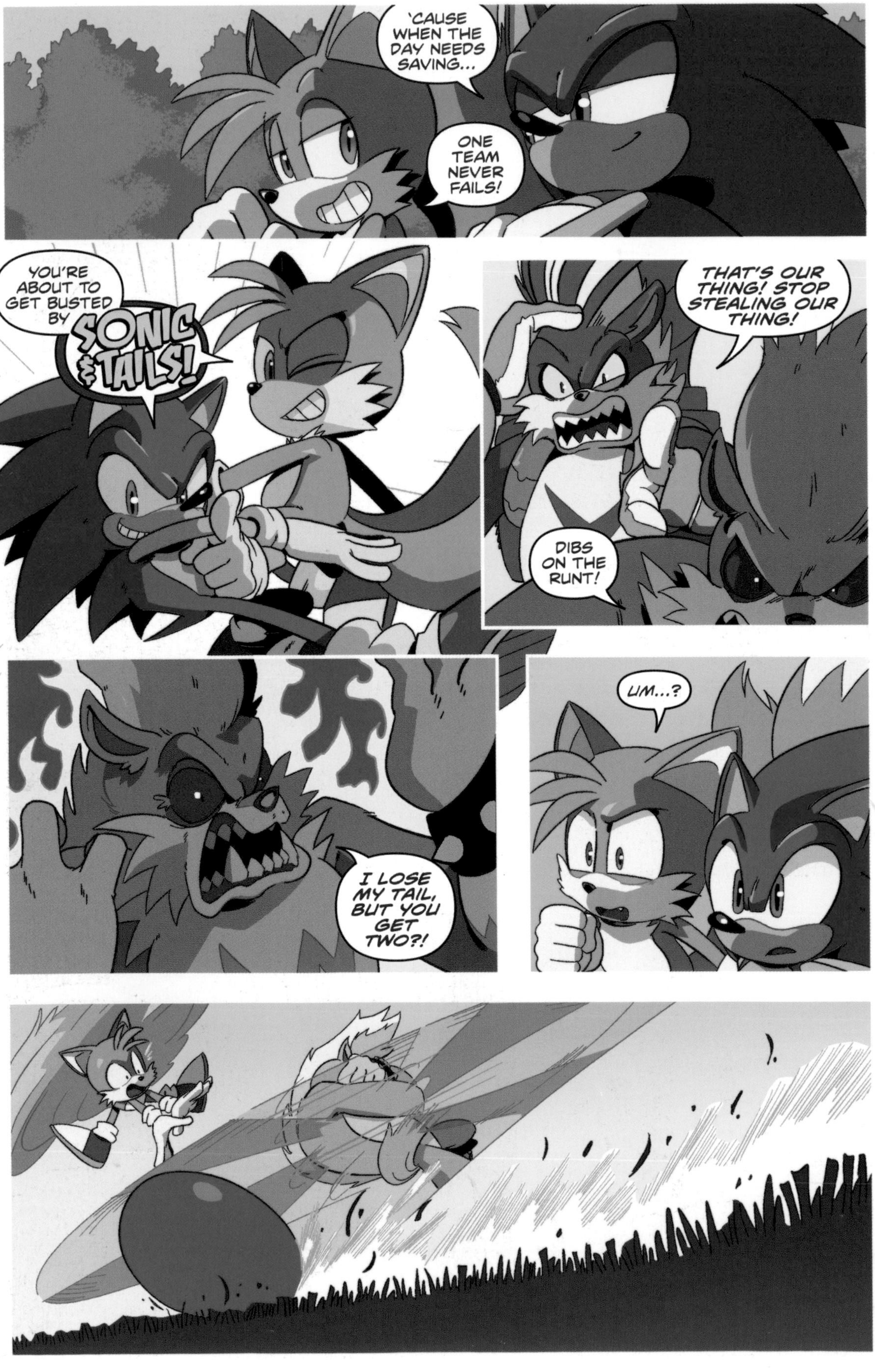
'CAUSE WHEN THE DAY NEEDS SAVING...
ONE TEAM NEVER FAILS!
YOU'RE ABOUT TO GET BUSTED BY
SONIC & TAILS!
THAT'S OUR THING! STOP STEALING OUR THING!
DIBS ON THE RUNT!
I LOSE MY TAIL, BUT YOU GET TWO?!
UM...?

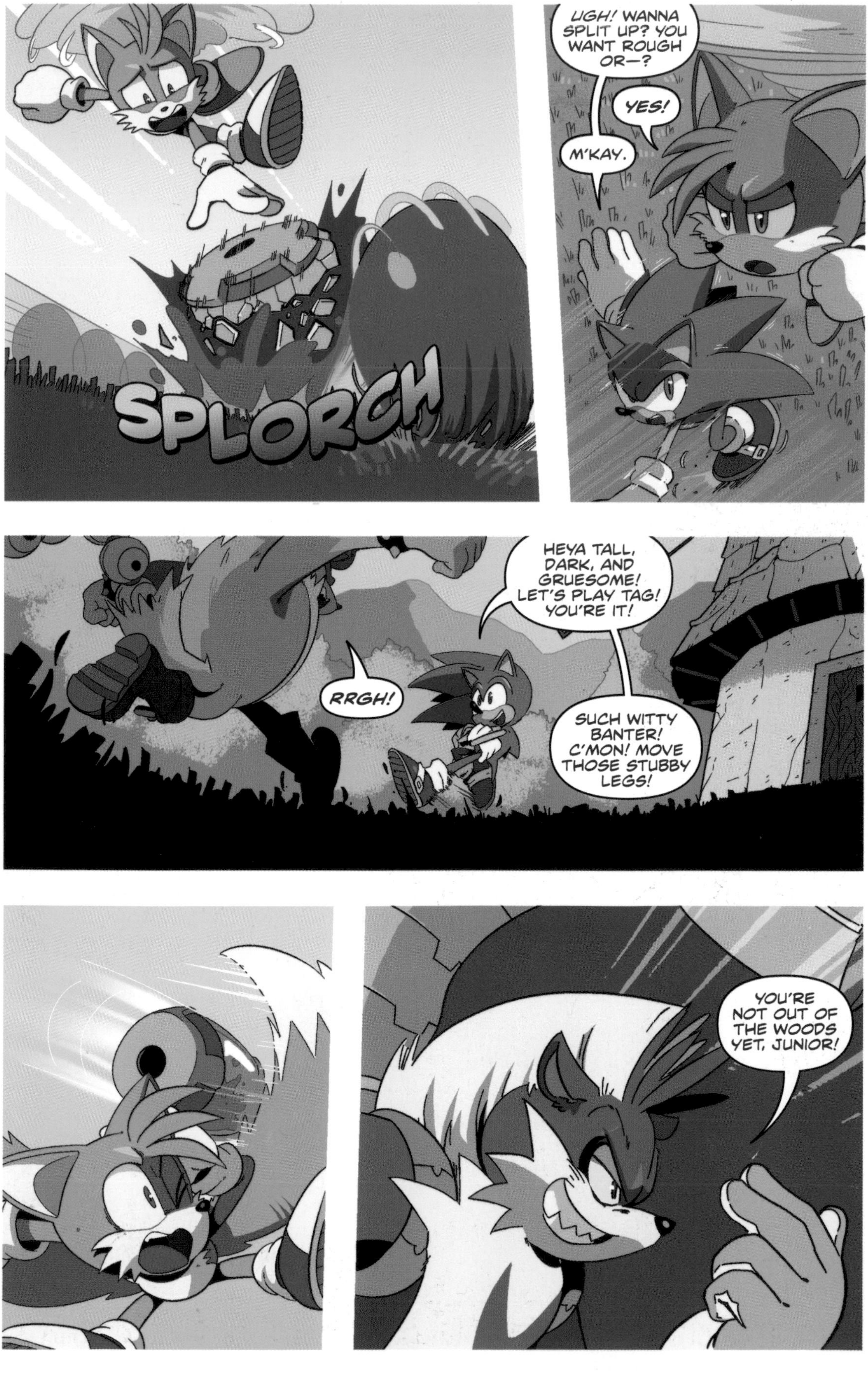
SPLORCH
UGH! WANNA SPLIT UP? YOU WANT ROUGH OR—?
YES!
M'KAY.
HEYA TALL, DARK, AND GRUESOME! LET'S PLAY TAG! YOU'RE IT!
RRGH!
SUCH WITTY BANTER! C'MON! MOVE THOSE STUBBY LEGS!
YOU'RE NOT OUT OF THE WOODS YET, JUNIOR!

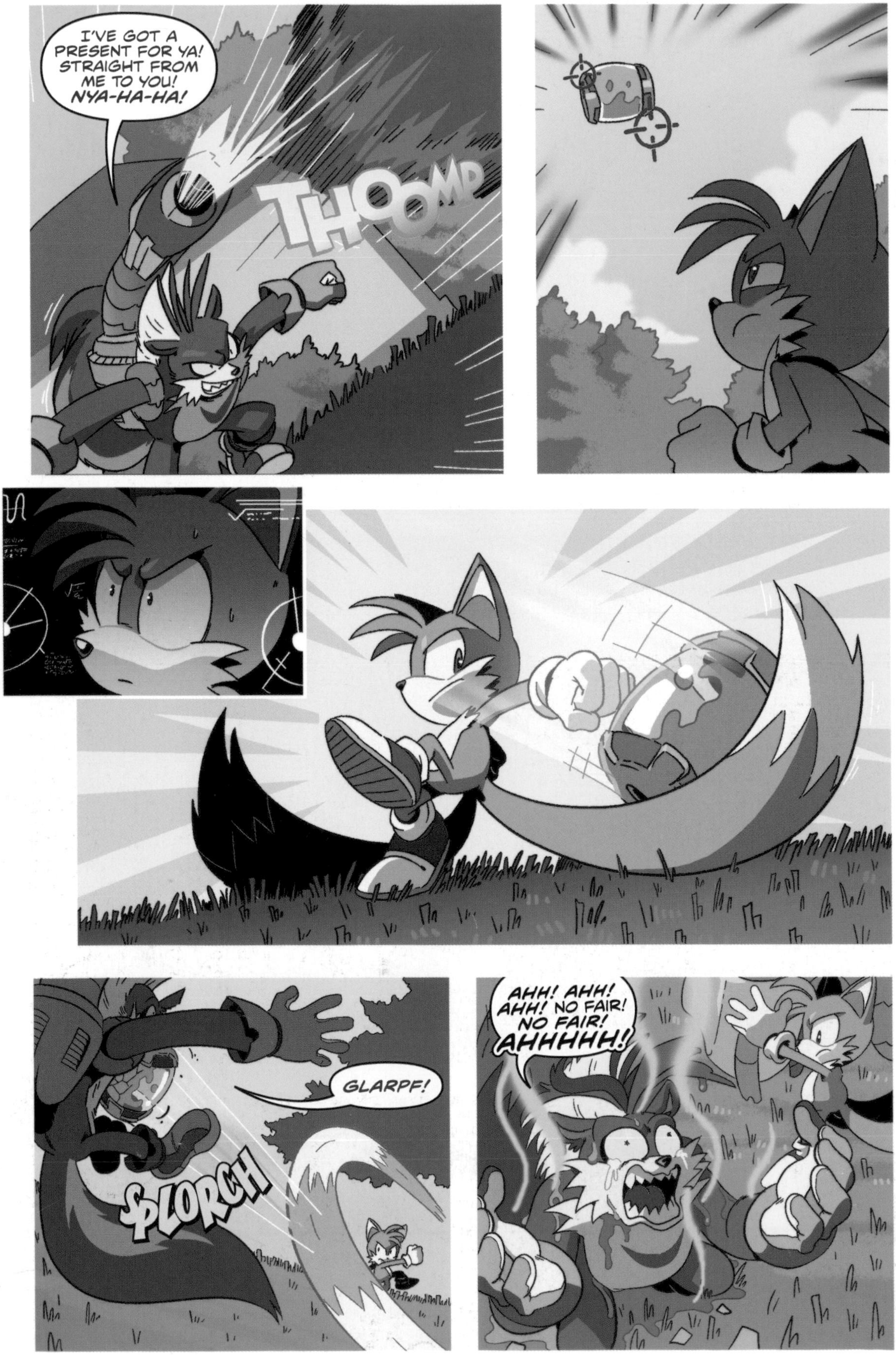
I'VE GOT A PRESENT FOR YA! STRAIGHT FROM ME TO YOU! NYA-HA-HA!
THOOMP
GLARPF!
SPLORCH
AHH! AHH! AHH! NO FAIR! NO FAIR! AHHHHH!

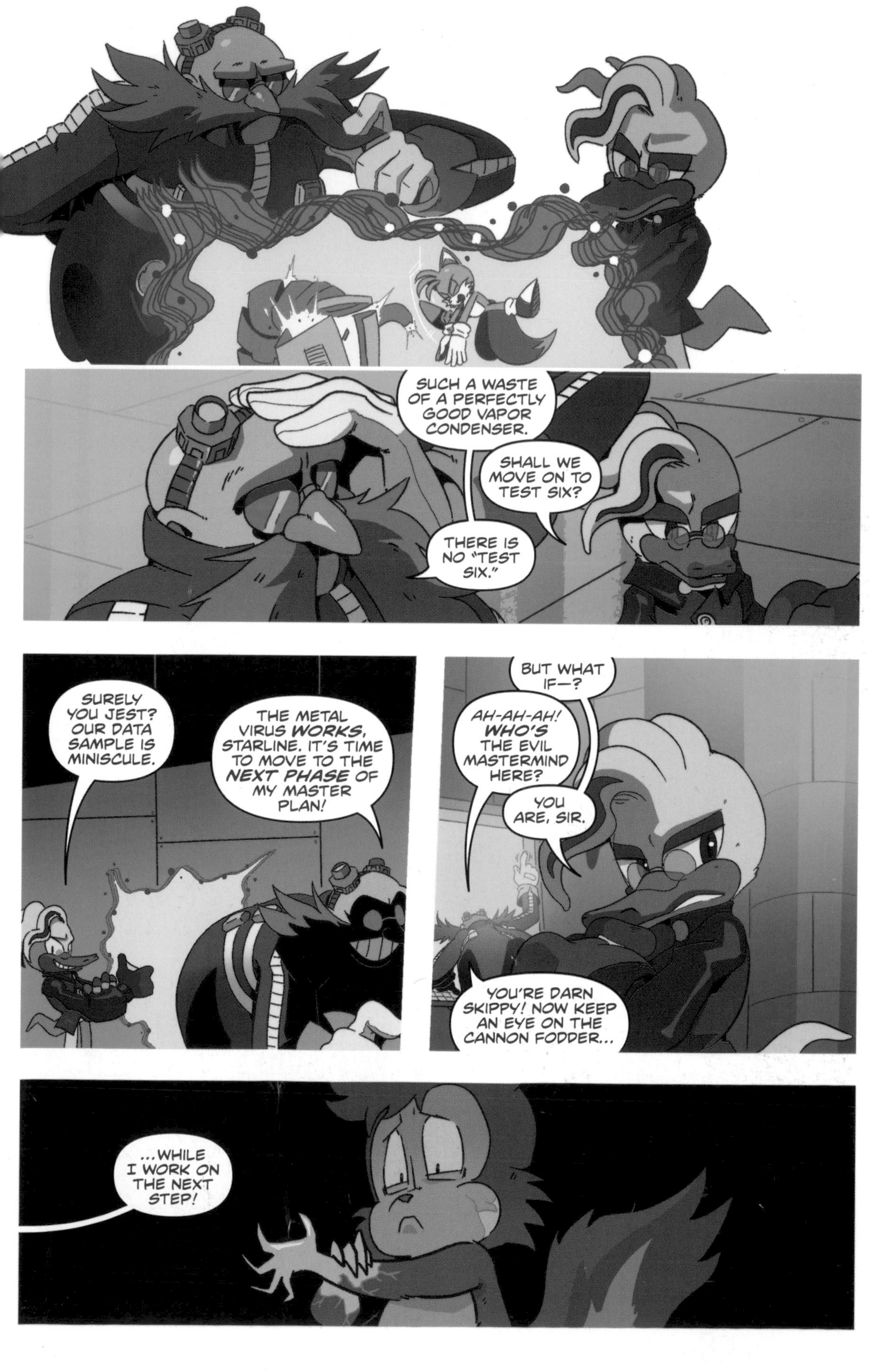
SUCH A WASTE OF A PERFECTLY GOOD VAPOR CONDENSER.
SHALL WE MOVE ON TO TEST SIX?
THERE IS NO "TEST SIX."
SURELY YOU JEST? OUR DATA SAMPLE IS MINISCULE.
THE METAL VIRUS **WORKS**, STARLINE. IT'S TIME TO MOVE TO THE **NEXT PHASE** OF MY MASTER PLAN!
BUT WHAT IF—?
AH-AH-AH! **WHO'S** THE EVIL MASTERMIND HERE?
YOU ARE, SIR.
YOU'RE DARN SKIPPY! NOW KEEP AN EYE ON THE CANNON FODDER...
...WHILE I WORK ON THE NEXT STEP!

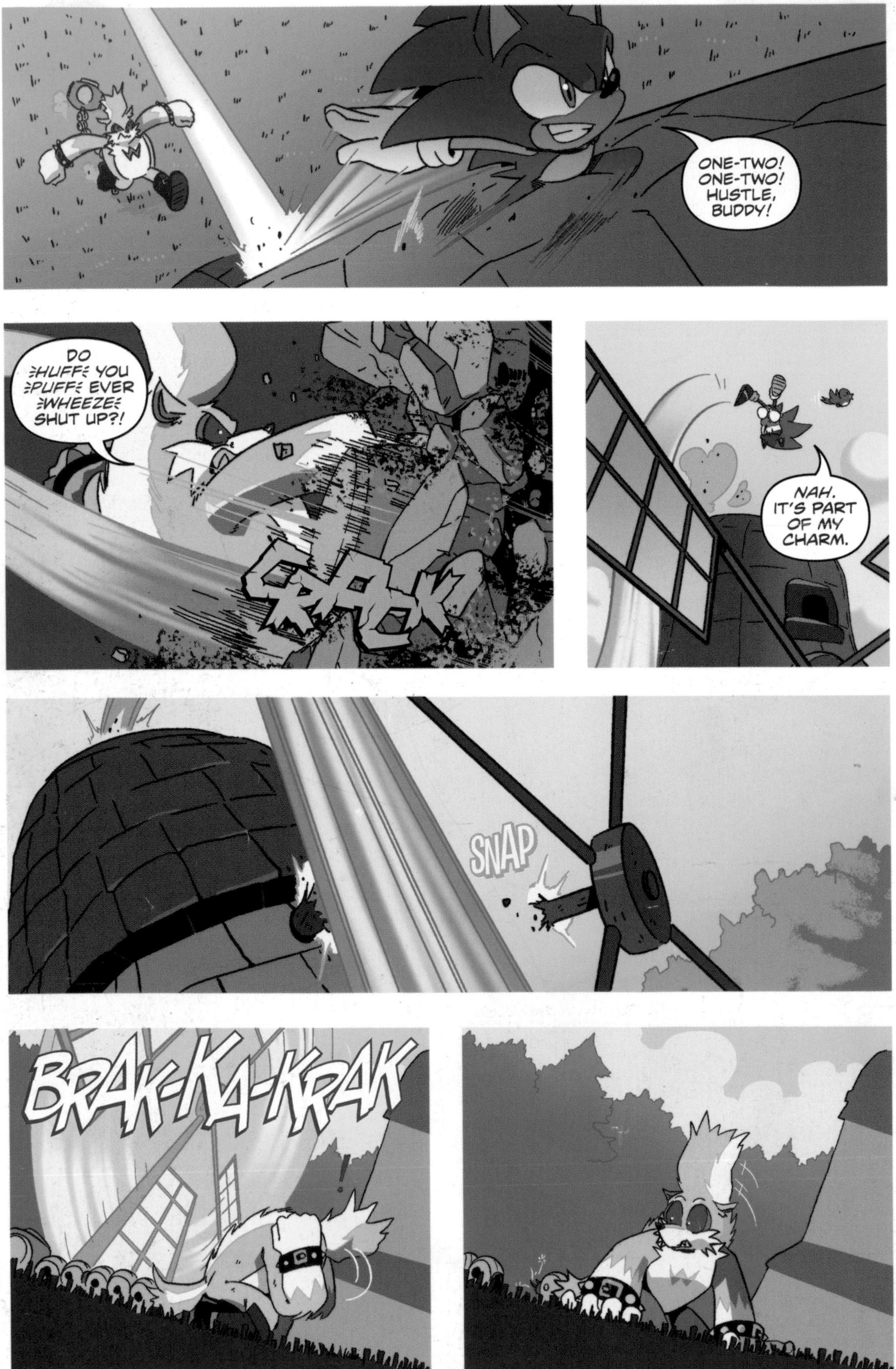
ONE-TWO! ONE-TWO! HUSTLE, BUDDY!
DO ≶HUFF≶ YOU ≶PUFF≶ EVER ≶WHEEZE≶ SHUT UP?!
CRACK
NAH. IT'S PART OF MY CHARM.
SNAP
BRAK-KA-KRAK

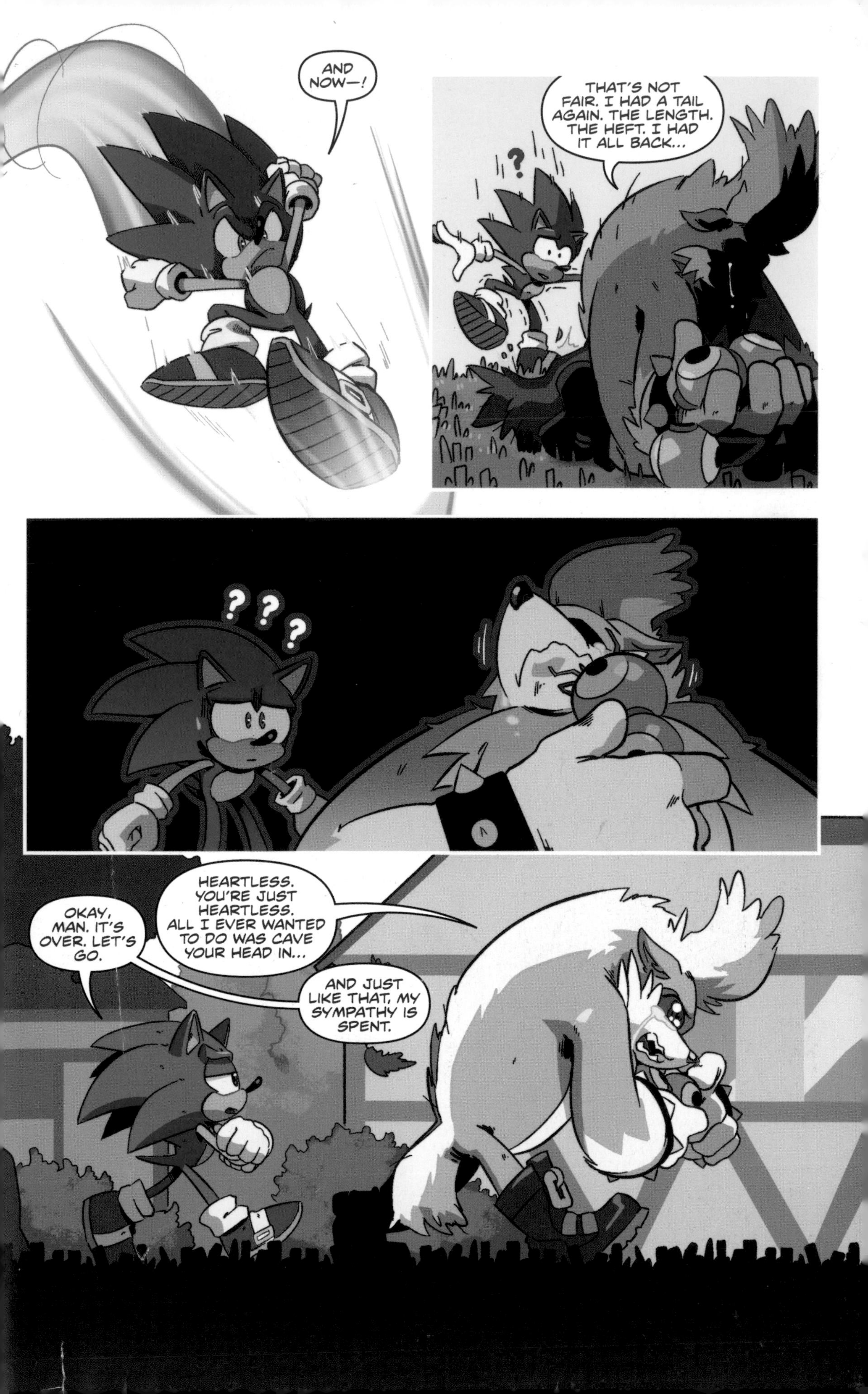

AND NOW—!
THAT'S NOT FAIR. I HAD A TAIL AGAIN. THE LENGTH. THE HEFT. I HAD IT ALL BACK...
?
???
OKAY, MAN. IT'S OVER. LET'S GO.
HEARTLESS. YOU'RE JUST HEARTLESS. ALL I EVER WANTED TO DO WAS CAVE YOUR HEAD IN...
AND JUST LIKE THAT, MY SYMPATHY IS SPENT.

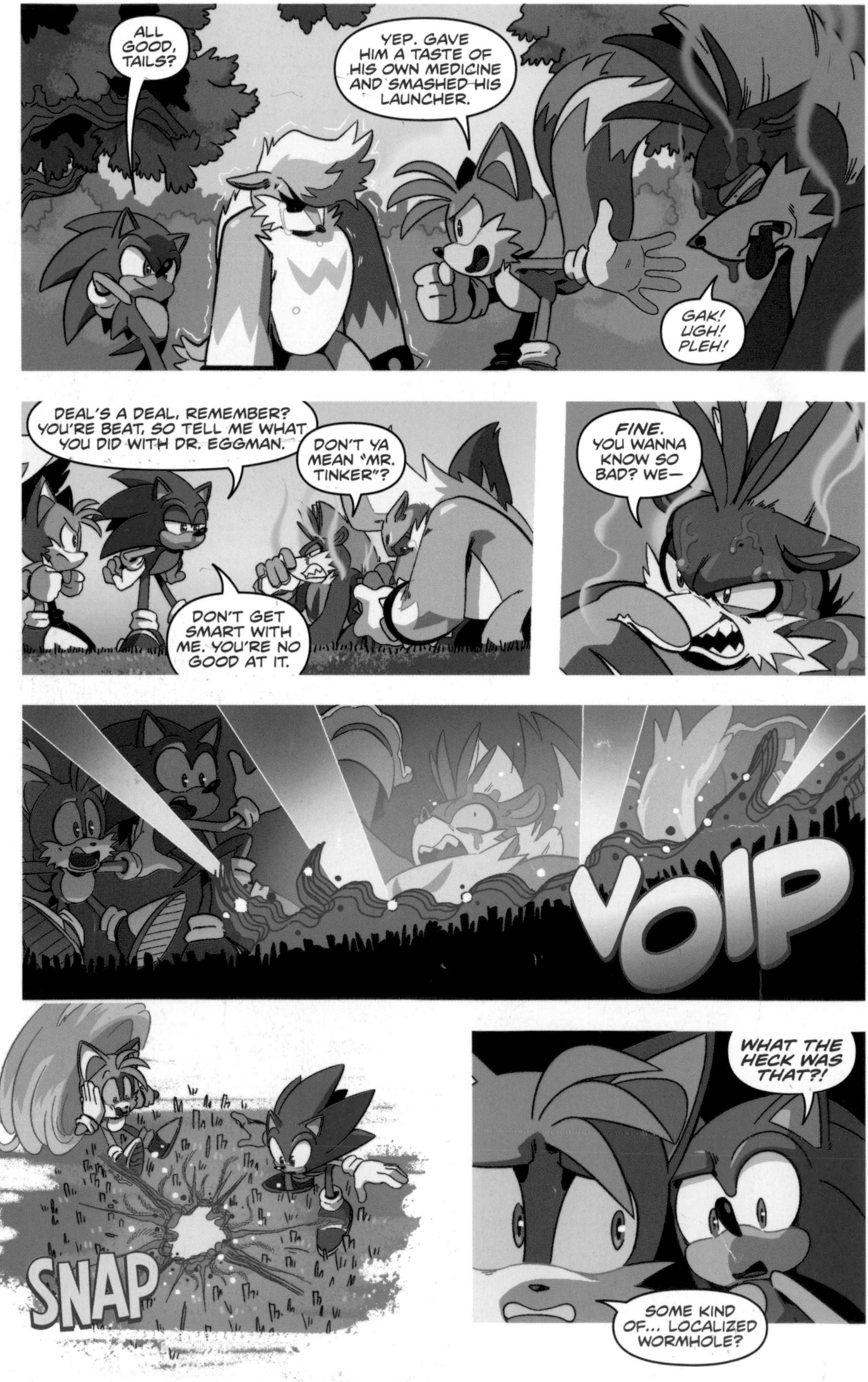
ALL GOOD, TAILS?
YEP. GAVE HIM A TASTE OF HIS OWN MEDICINE AND SMASHED HIS LAUNCHER.
GAK! UGH! PLEH!
DEAL'S A DEAL, REMEMBER? YOU'RE BEAT, SO TELL ME WHAT YOU DID WITH DR. EGGMAN.
DON'T YA MEAN "MR. TINKER"?
DON'T GET SMART WITH ME. YOU'RE NO GOOD AT IT.
FINE. YOU WANNA KNOW SO BAD? WE—
VOIP
SNAP
WHAT THE HECK WAS THAT?!
SOME KIND OF... LOCALIZED WORMHOLE?

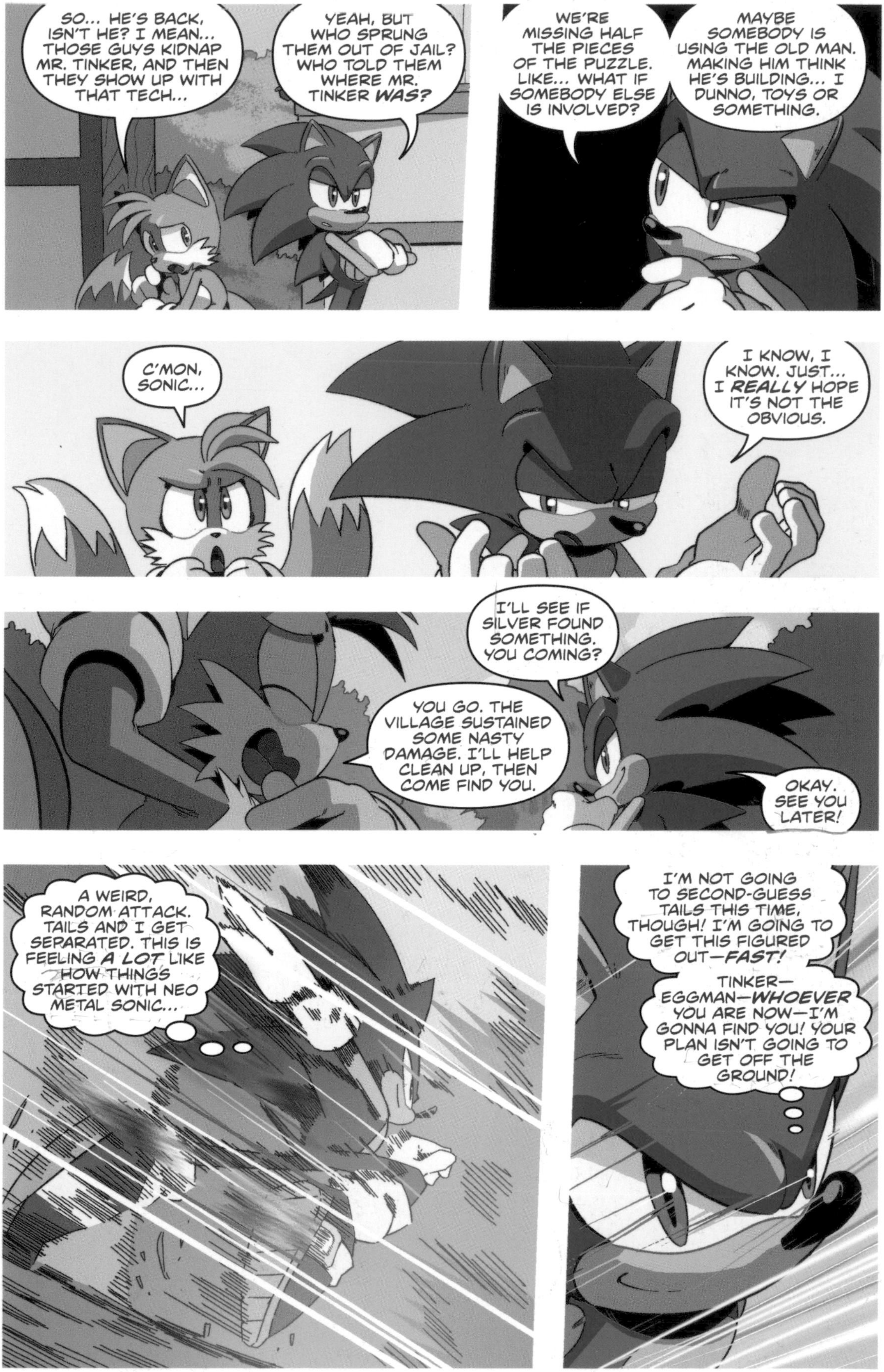
SO... HE'S BACK, ISN'T HE? I MEAN... THOSE GUYS KIDNAP MR. TINKER, AND THEN THEY SHOW UP WITH THAT TECH...
YEAH, BUT WHO SPRUNG THEM OUT OF JAIL? WHO TOLD THEM WHERE MR. TINKER *WAS?*
WE'RE MISSING HALF THE PIECES OF THE PUZZLE. LIKE... WHAT IF SOMEBODY ELSE IS INVOLVED?
MAYBE SOMEBODY IS USING THE OLD MAN. MAKING HIM THINK HE'S BUILDING... I DUNNO, TOYS OR SOMETHING.
C'MON, SONIC...
I KNOW, I KNOW. JUST... I *REALLY* HOPE IT'S NOT THE OBVIOUS.
I'LL SEE IF SILVER FOUND SOMETHING. YOU COMING?
YOU GO. THE VILLAGE SUSTAINED SOME NASTY DAMAGE. I'LL HELP CLEAN UP, THEN COME FIND YOU.
OKAY. SEE YOU LATER!
A WEIRD, RANDOM ATTACK. TAILS AND I GET SEPARATED. THIS IS FEELING *A LOT* LIKE HOW THINGS STARTED WITH NEO METAL SONIC...
I'M NOT GOING TO SECOND-GUESS TAILS THIS TIME, THOUGH! I'M GOING TO GET THIS FIGURED OUT—*FAST!*
TINKER—EGGMAN—*WHOEVER* YOU ARE NOW—I'M GONNA FIND YOU! YOUR PLAN ISN'T GOING TO GET OFF THE GROUND!

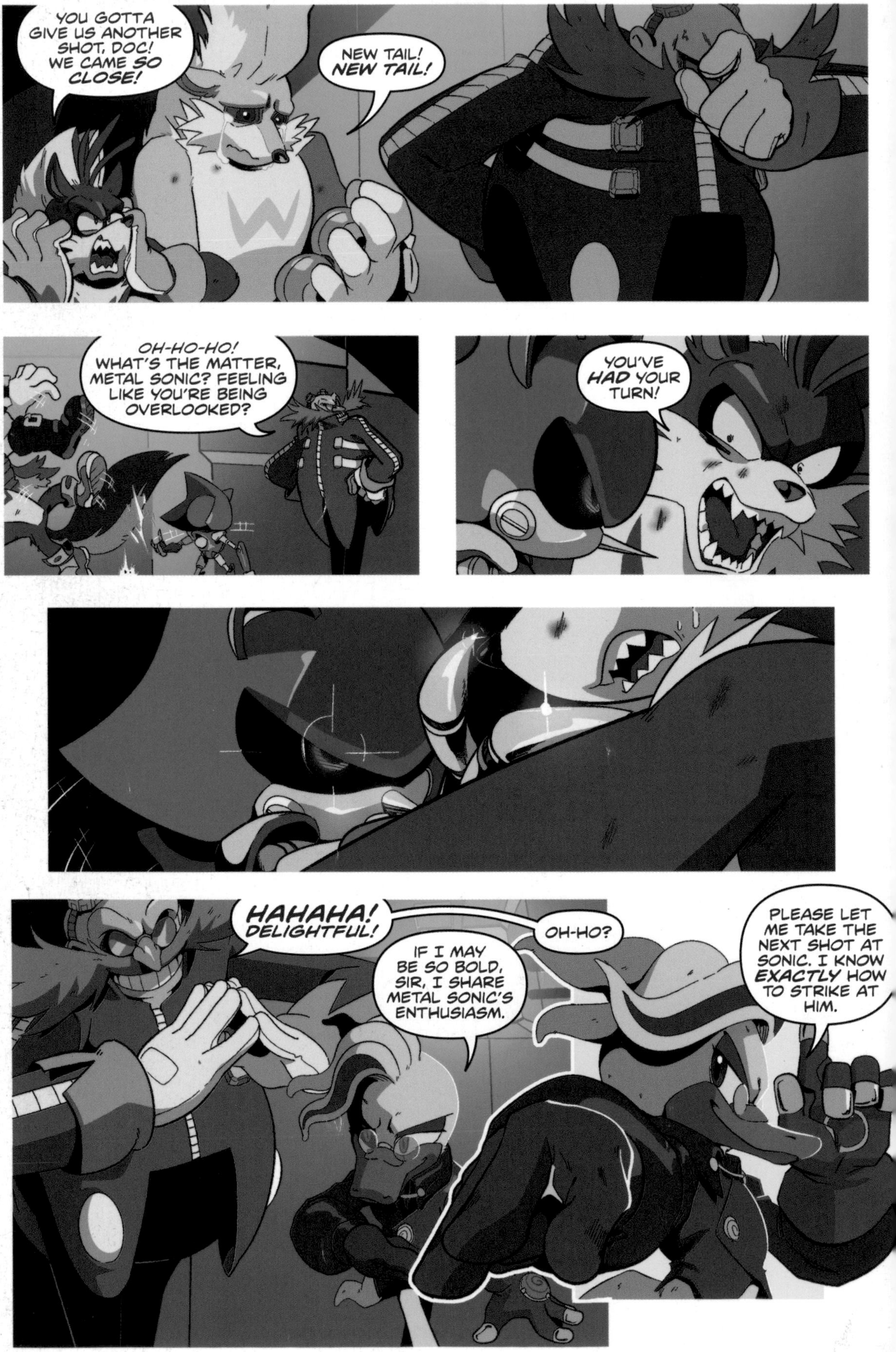
YOU GOTTA GIVE US ANOTHER SHOT, DOC! WE CAME SO CLOSE!
NEW TAIL! NEW TAIL!
OH-HO-HO! WHAT'S THE MATTER, METAL SONIC? FEELING LIKE YOU'RE BEING OVERLOOKED?
YOU'VE HAD YOUR TURN!
HAHAHA! DELIGHTFUL!
OH-HO?
IF I MAY BE SO BOLD, SIR, I SHARE METAL SONIC'S ENTHUSIASM.
PLEASE LET ME TAKE THE NEXT SHOT AT SONIC. I KNOW EXACTLY HOW TO STRIKE AT HIM.

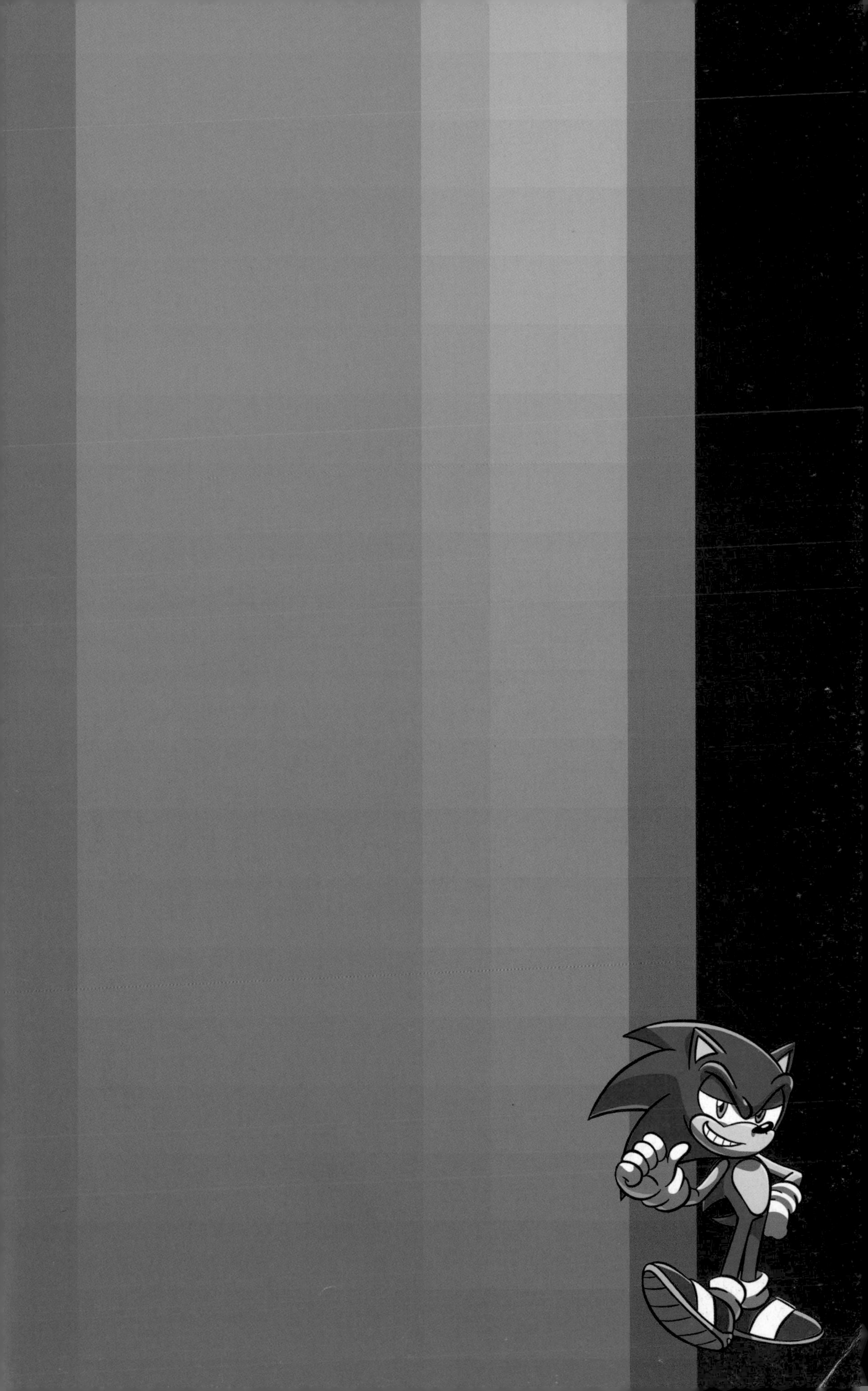

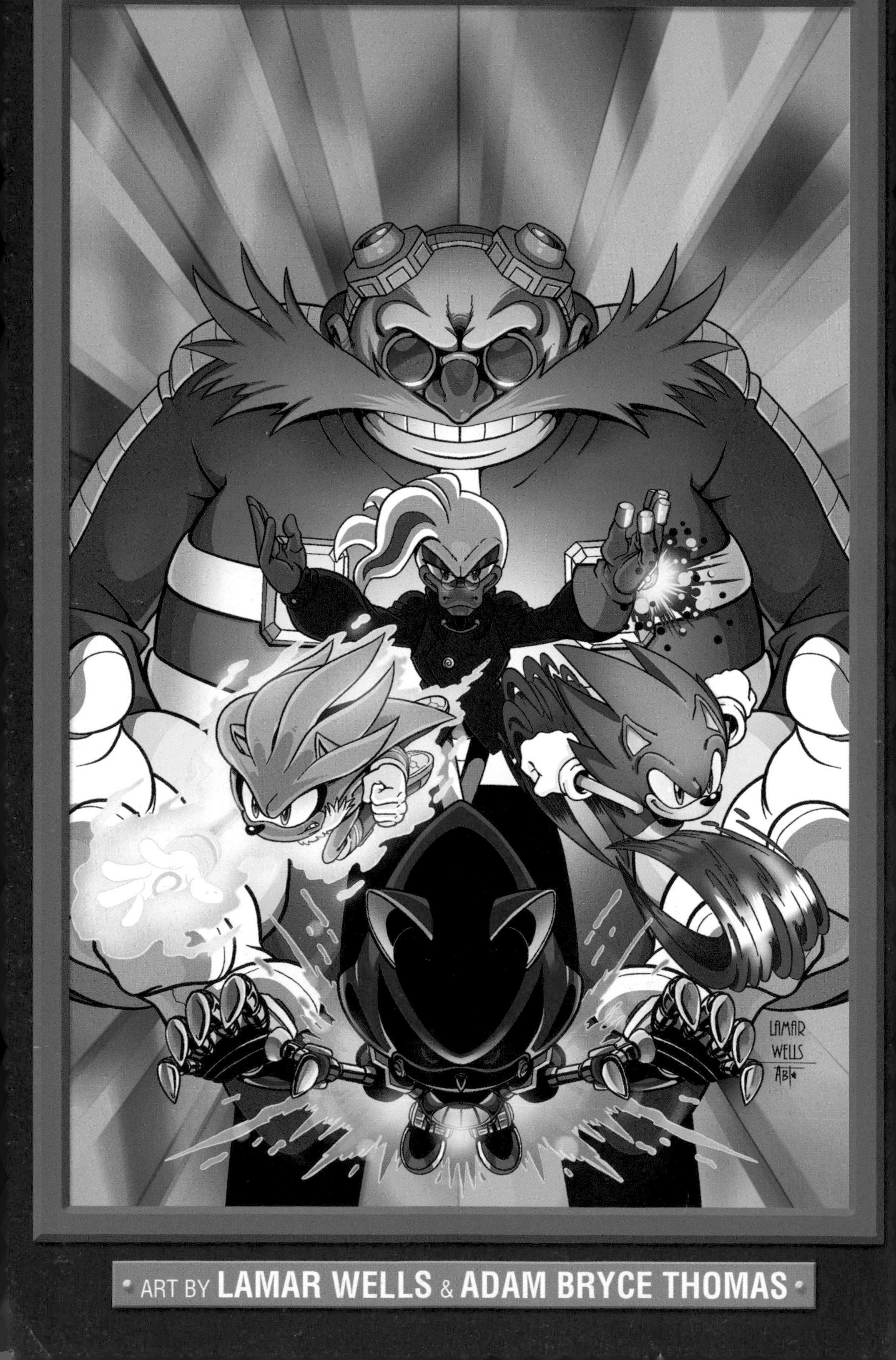
LAMAR
WELLS
ABT

ART BY **LAMAR WELLS** & **ADAM BRYCE THOMAS**

FROZEN PEAK.

YOU'RE SURE THIS IS THE WAY?

THIS IS WHERE THE GUY TOLD ME TO GO.

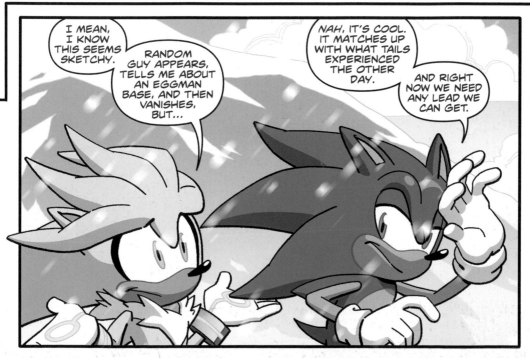

I MEAN, I KNOW THIS SEEMS SKETCHY.

RANDOM GUY APPEARS, TELLS ME ABOUT AN EGGMAN BASE, AND THEN VANISHES, BUT...

NAH, IT'S COOL. IT MATCHES UP WITH WHAT TAILS EXPERIENCED THE OTHER DAY.

AND RIGHT NOW WE NEED ANY LEAD WE CAN GET.

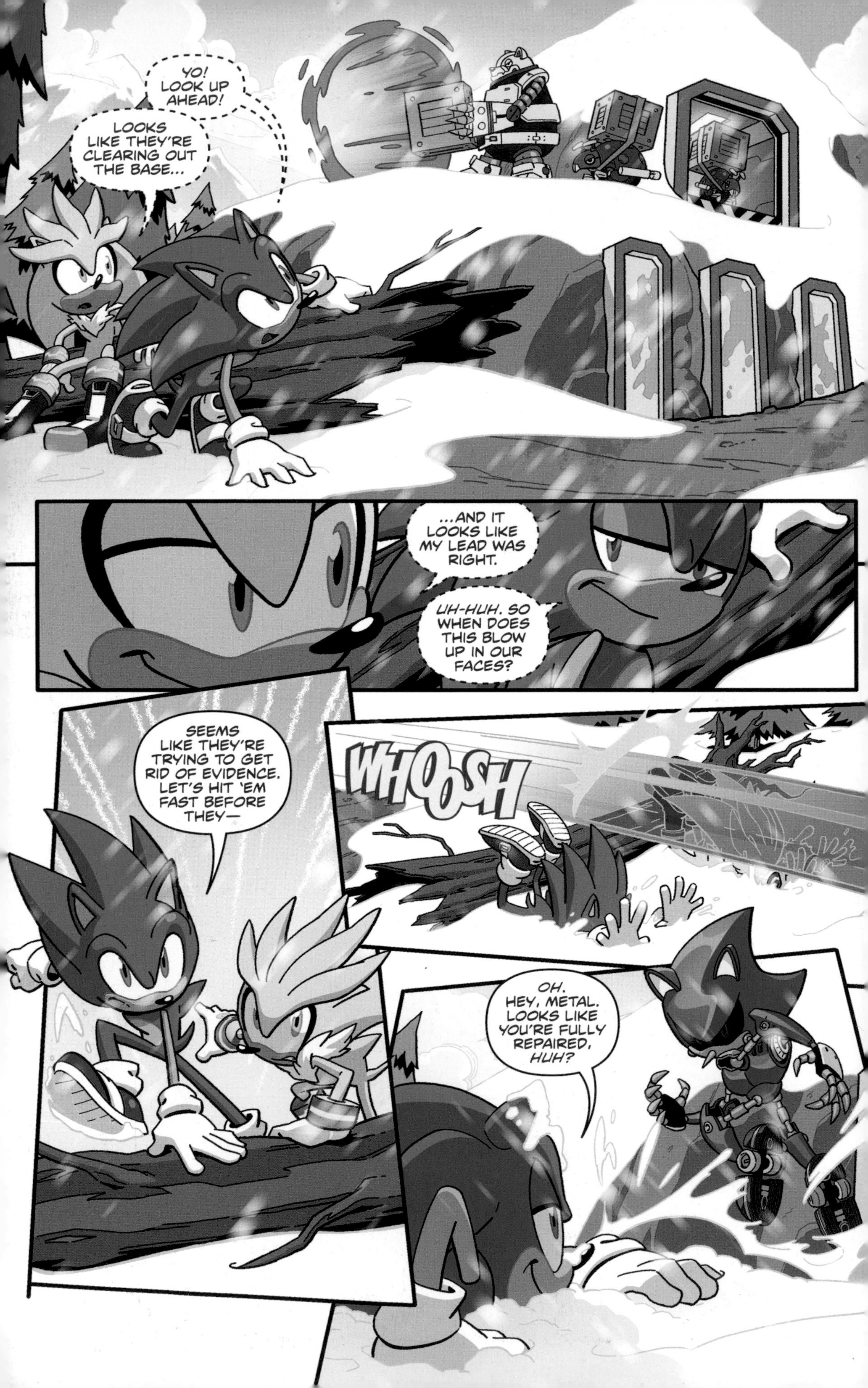
YO! LOOK UP AHEAD!
LOOKS LIKE THEY'RE CLEARING OUT THE BASE...
...AND IT LOOKS LIKE MY LEAD WAS RIGHT.
UH-HUH. SO WHEN DOES THIS BLOW UP IN OUR FACES?
SEEMS LIKE THEY'RE TRYING TO GET RID OF EVIDENCE. LET'S HIT 'EM FAST BEFORE THEY—
WHOOSH
OH. HEY, METAL. LOOKS LIKE YOU'RE FULLY REPAIRED, HUH?

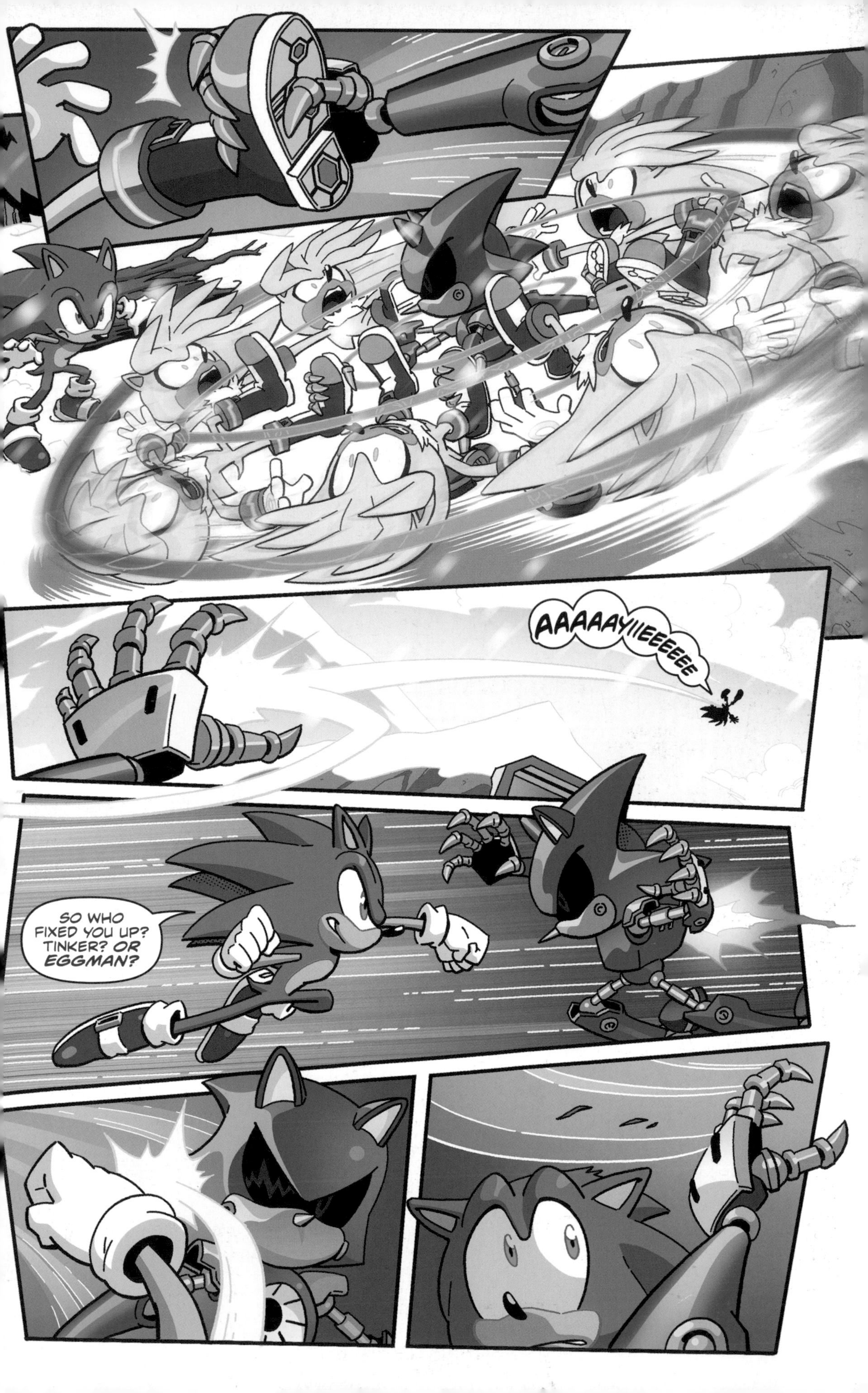
AAAAAYIIEEEEEE
SO WHO FIXED YOU UP? TINKER? OR EGGMAN?

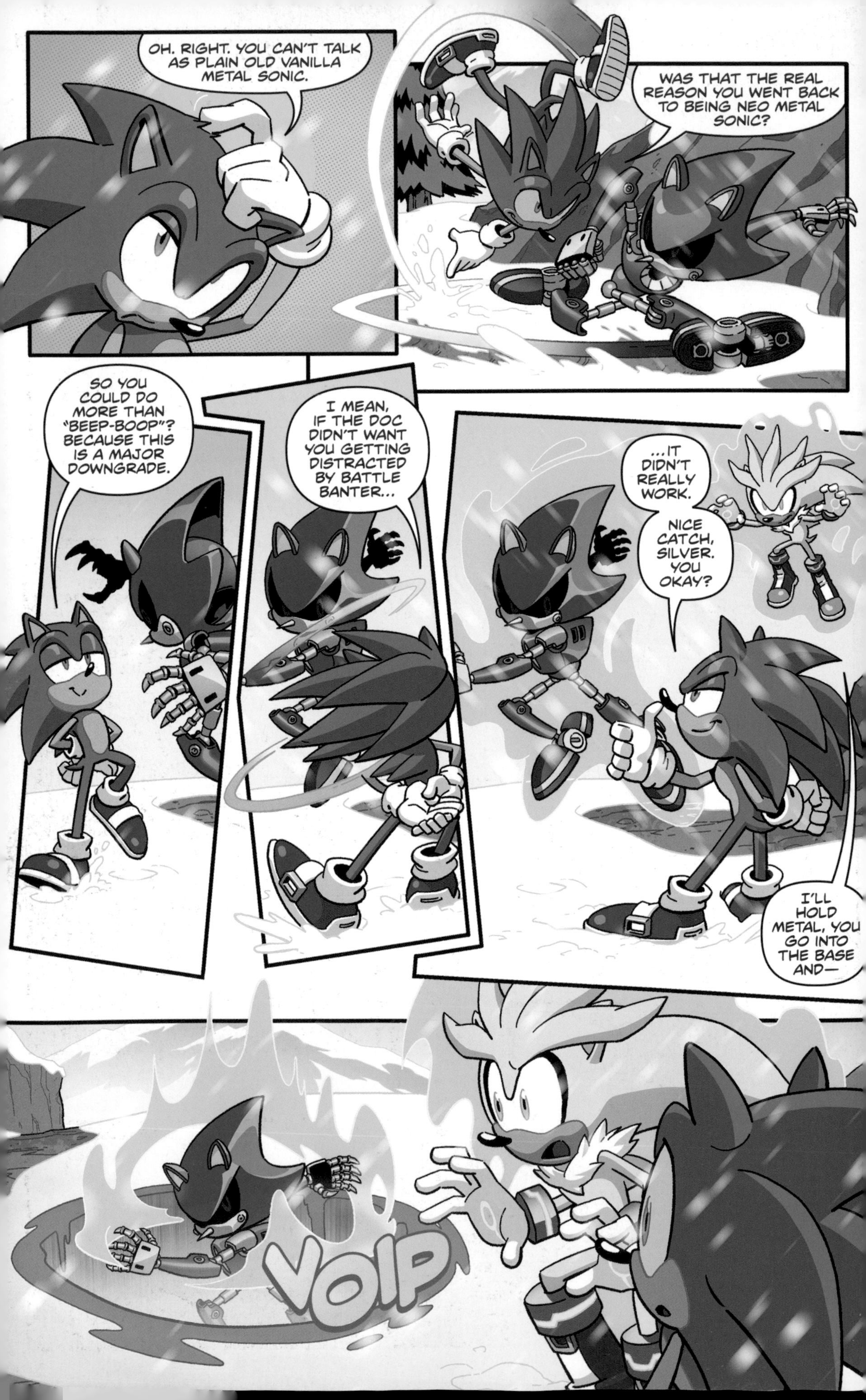
OH. RIGHT. YOU CAN'T TALK AS PLAIN OLD VANILLA METAL SONIC.
WAS THAT THE REAL REASON YOU WENT BACK TO BEING NEO METAL SONIC?
SO YOU COULD DO MORE THAN "BEEP-BOOP"? BECAUSE THIS IS A MAJOR DOWNGRADE.
I MEAN, IF THE DOC DIDN'T WANT YOU GETTING DISTRACTED BY BATTLE BANTER...
...IT DIDN'T REALLY WORK.
NICE CATCH, SILVER. YOU OKAY?
I'LL HOLD METAL, YOU GO INTO THE BASE AND—
VOIP

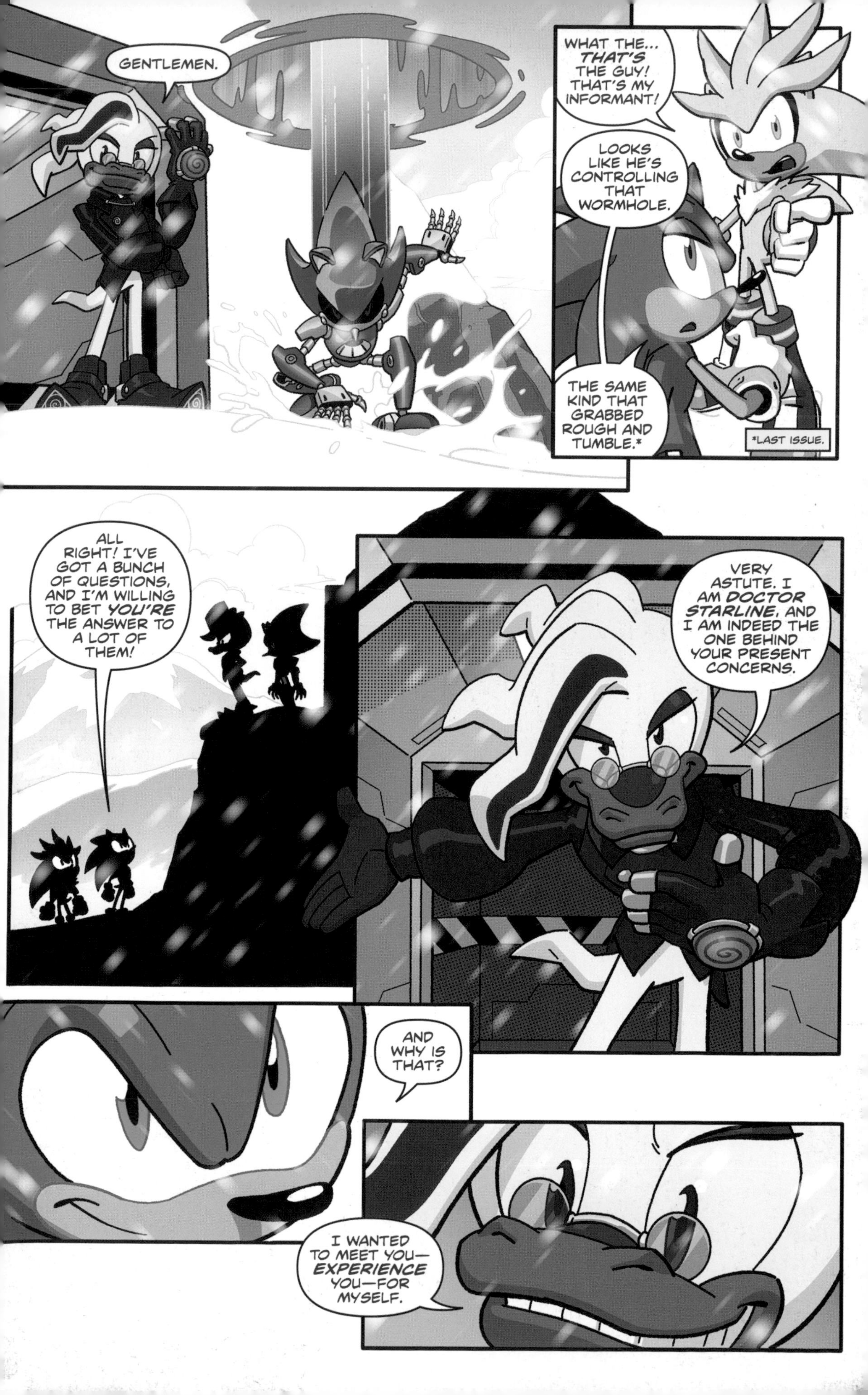
GENTLEMEN.
WHAT THE... THAT'S THE GUY! THAT'S MY INFORMANT!
LOOKS LIKE HE'S CONTROLLING THAT WORMHOLE.
THE SAME KIND THAT GRABBED ROUGH AND TUMBLE.*
*LAST ISSUE.
ALL RIGHT! I'VE GOT A BUNCH OF QUESTIONS, AND I'M WILLING TO BET YOU'RE THE ANSWER TO A LOT OF THEM!
VERY ASTUTE. I AM DOCTOR STARLINE, AND I AM INDEED THE ONE BEHIND YOUR PRESENT CONCERNS.
AND WHY IS THAT?
I WANTED TO MEET YOU—EXPERIENCE YOU—FOR MYSELF.

THE BLUE BLUR! HERO ACROSS TIME AND SPACE! THE ONLY BEING ALIVE TO BE ABLE TO STAND UP TO THE OVERWHELMING MIGHT AND BRILLIANCE OF DR. EGGMAN THROUGH SHEER SKILL ALONE!

CAN I MEASURE UP? CAN I COMPLETE MY OBJECTIVE WITH YOU IN MY WAY? EVERYTHING ABOUT THIS ENCOUNTER HAS BEEN CONSTRUCTED TO BE THE ULTIMATE TEST OF OUR ABILITIES AND WILLPOWER!

HE DID NOT SOUND THIS CREEPY OR CRAZY WHEN I TALKED TO HIM!

AT LEAST YOU'RE GIVING ME STRAIGHT ANSWERS. I'LL ASSUME YOU BUSTED ROUGH AND TUMBLE OUT OF JAIL WITH YOUR SKY-HOLES.

SO TELL ME THIS: WHAT DID YOU DO WITH MR. TINKER?

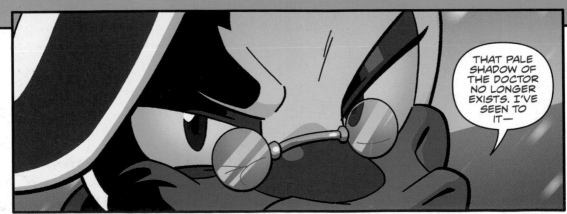

THAT PALE SHADOW OF THE DOCTOR NO LONGER EXISTS. I'VE SEEN TO IT—

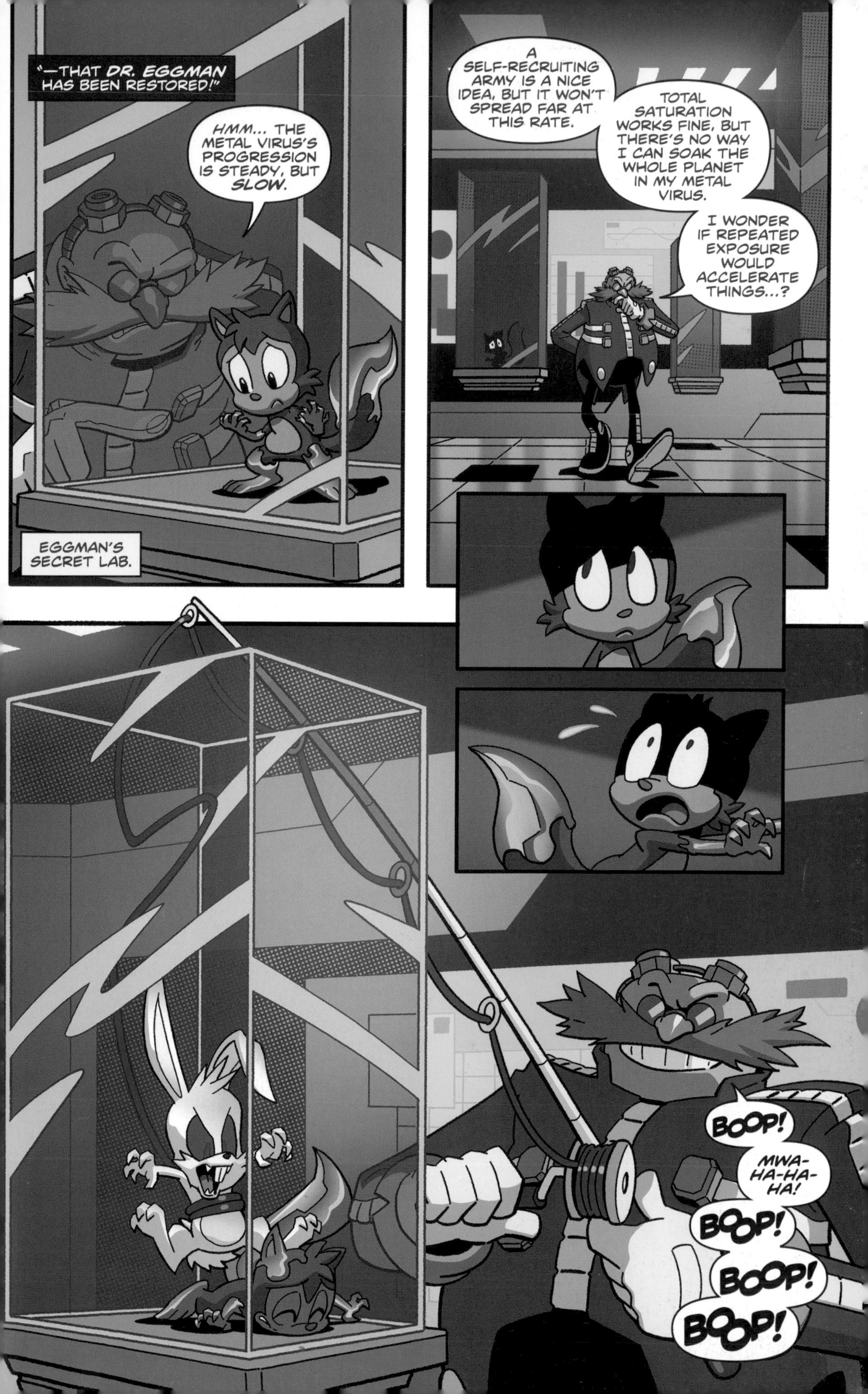
"—THAT DR. EGGMAN HAS BEEN RESTORED!"
HMM... THE METAL VIRUS'S PROGRESSION IS STEADY, BUT SLOW.
EGGMAN'S SECRET LAB.
A SELF-RECRUITING ARMY IS A NICE IDEA, BUT IT WON'T SPREAD FAR AT THIS RATE.
TOTAL SATURATION WORKS FINE, BUT THERE'S NO WAY I CAN SOAK THE WHOLE PLANET IN MY METAL VIRUS.
I WONDER IF REPEATED EXPOSURE WOULD ACCELERATE THINGS...?
BOOP!
MWA-HA-HA-HA!
BOOP!
BOOP!
BOOP!

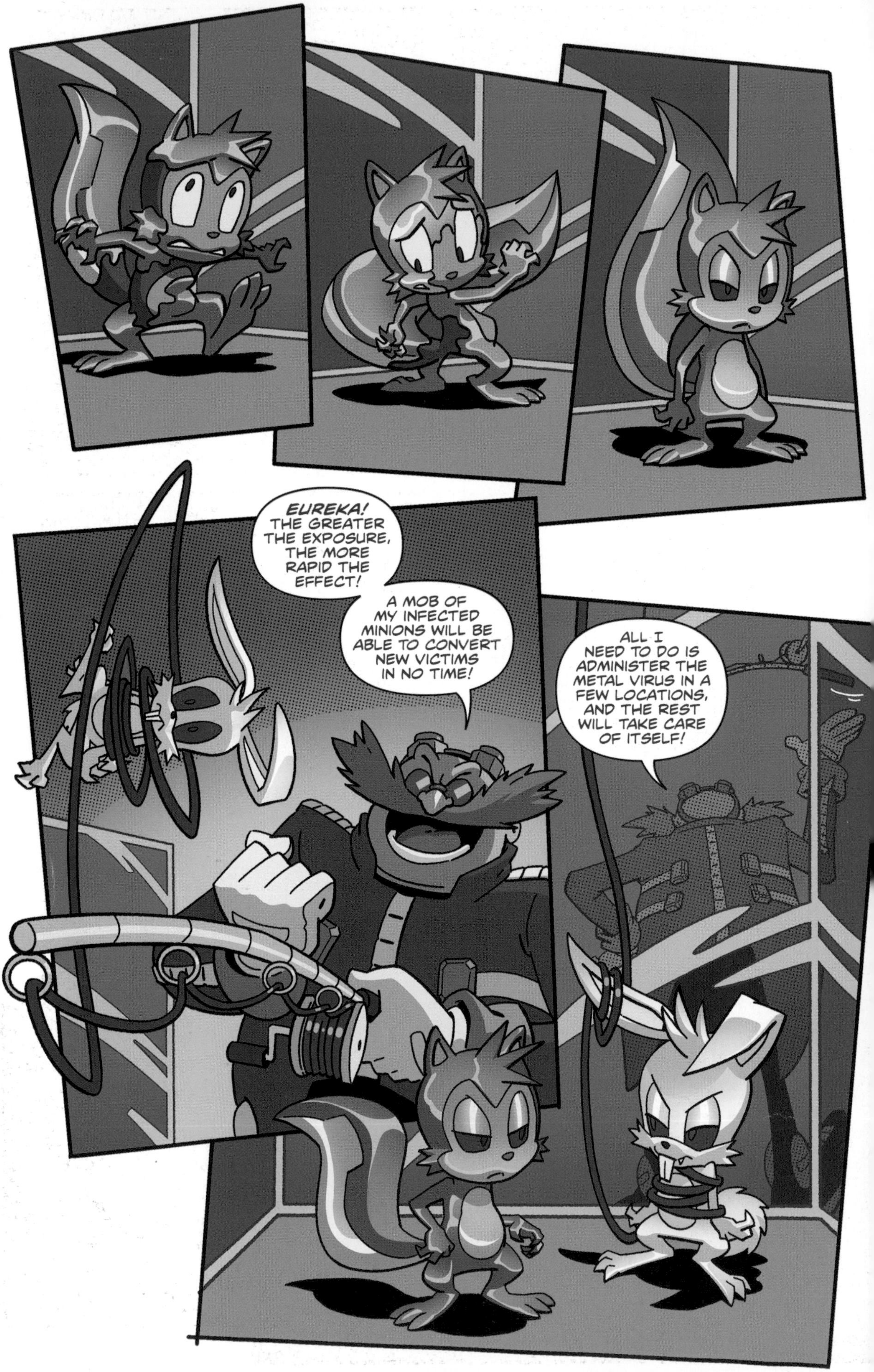
EUREKA! THE GREATER THE EXPOSURE, THE MORE RAPID THE EFFECT!
A MOB OF MY INFECTED MINIONS WILL BE ABLE TO CONVERT NEW VICTIMS IN NO TIME!
ALL I NEED TO DO IS ADMINISTER THE METAL VIRUS IN A FEW LOCATIONS, AND THE REST WILL TAKE CARE OF ITSELF!

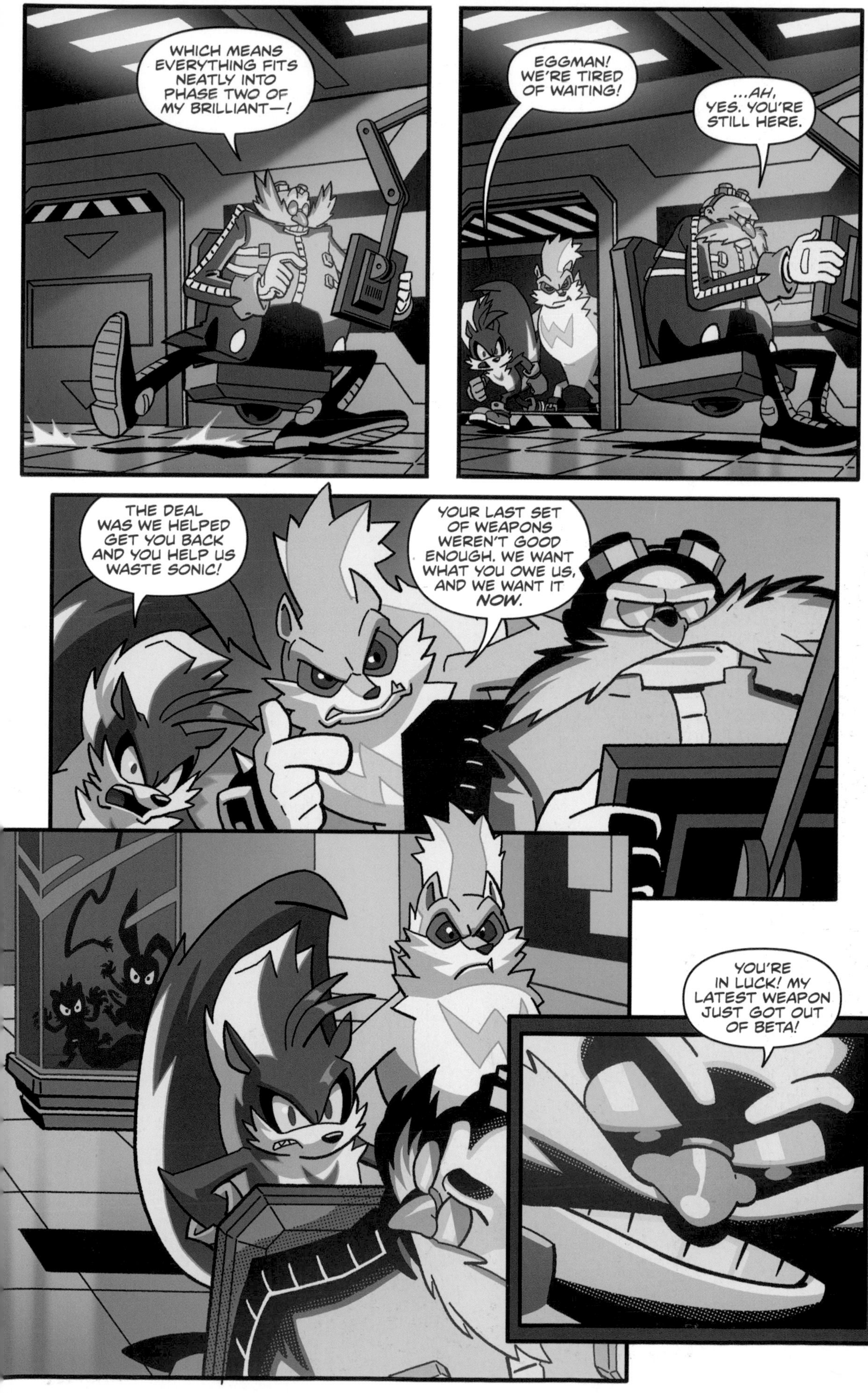
WHICH MEANS EVERYTHING FITS NEATLY INTO PHASE TWO OF MY BRILLIANT—!
EGGMAN! WE'RE TIRED OF WAITING!
...AH, YES. YOU'RE STILL HERE.
THE DEAL WAS WE HELPED GET YOU BACK AND YOU HELP US WASTE SONIC!
YOUR LAST SET OF WEAPONS WEREN'T GOOD ENOUGH. WE WANT WHAT YOU OWE US, AND WE WANT IT *NOW.*
YOU'RE IN LUCK! MY LATEST WEAPON JUST GOT OUT OF BETA!

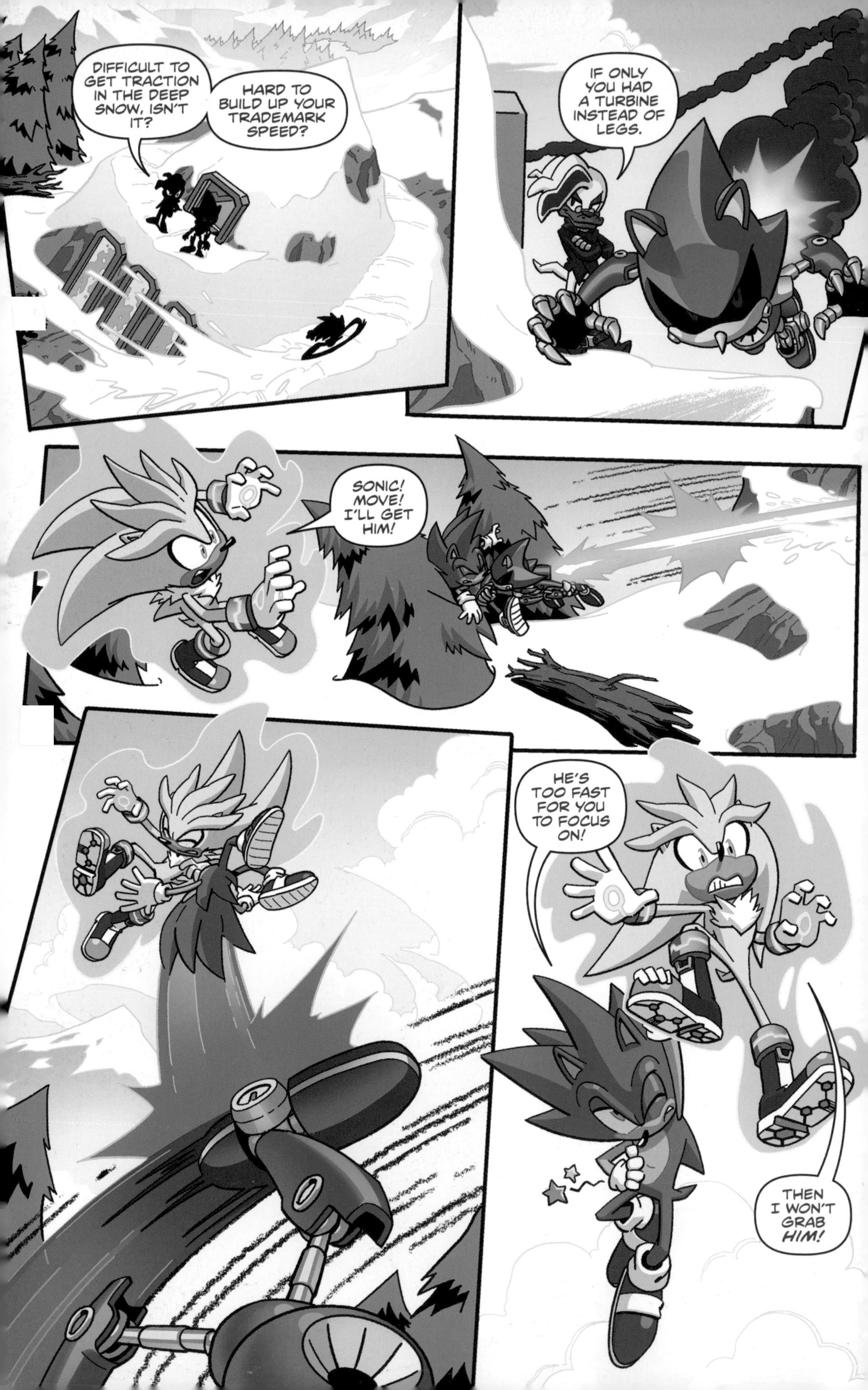
DIFFICULT TO GET TRACTION IN THE DEEP SNOW, ISN'T IT?
HARD TO BUILD UP YOUR TRADEMARK SPEED?
IF ONLY YOU HAD A TURBINE INSTEAD OF LEGS.
SONIC! MOVE! I'LL GET HIM!
HE'S TOO FAST FOR YOU TO FOCUS ON!
THEN I WON'T GRAB HIM!

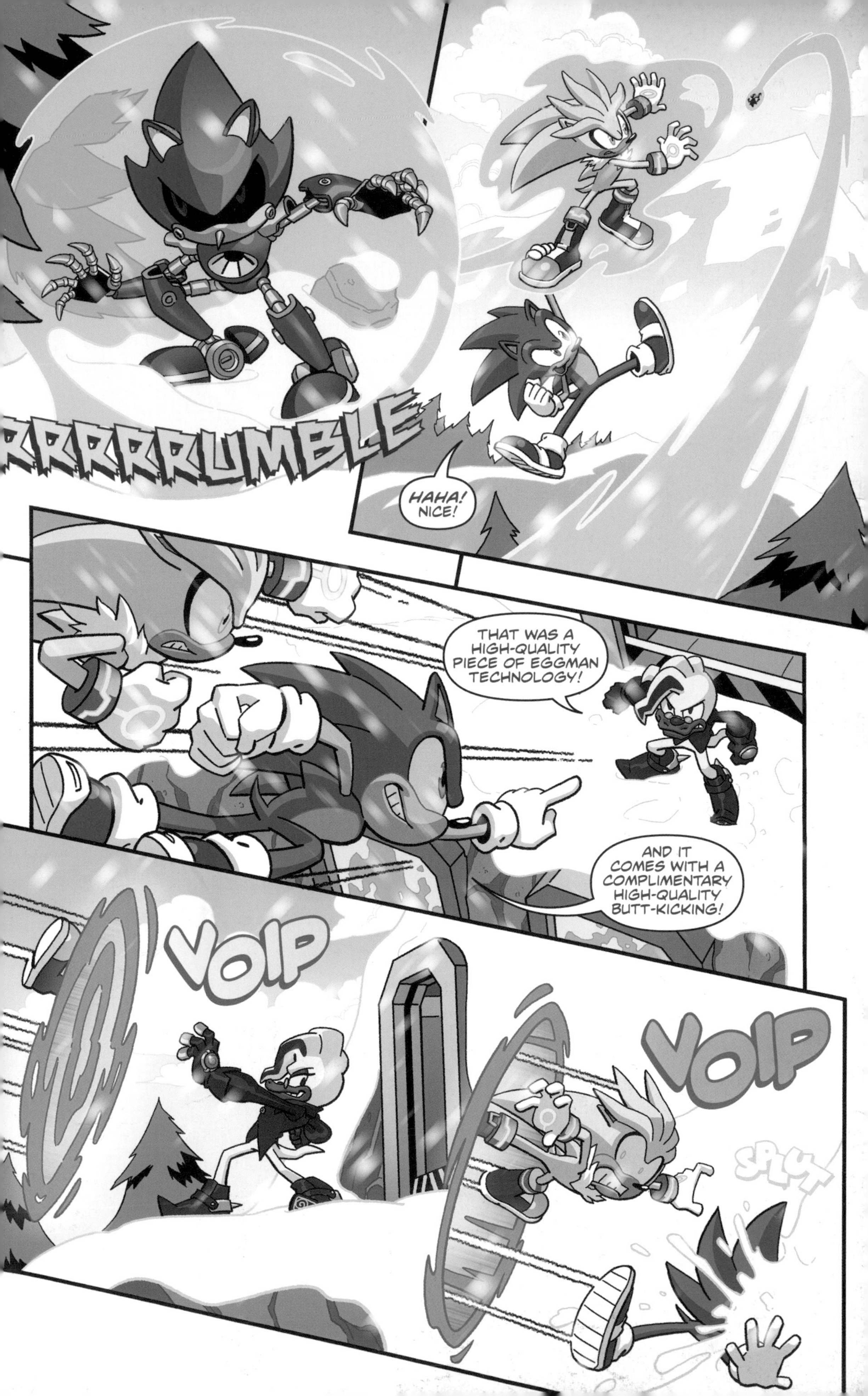
RRRRRRUMBLE
HAHA! NICE!
THAT WAS A HIGH-QUALITY PIECE OF EGGMAN TECHNOLOGY!
AND IT COMES WITH A COMPLIMENTARY HIGH-QUALITY BUTT-KICKING!
VOIP
VOIP
SPLUT

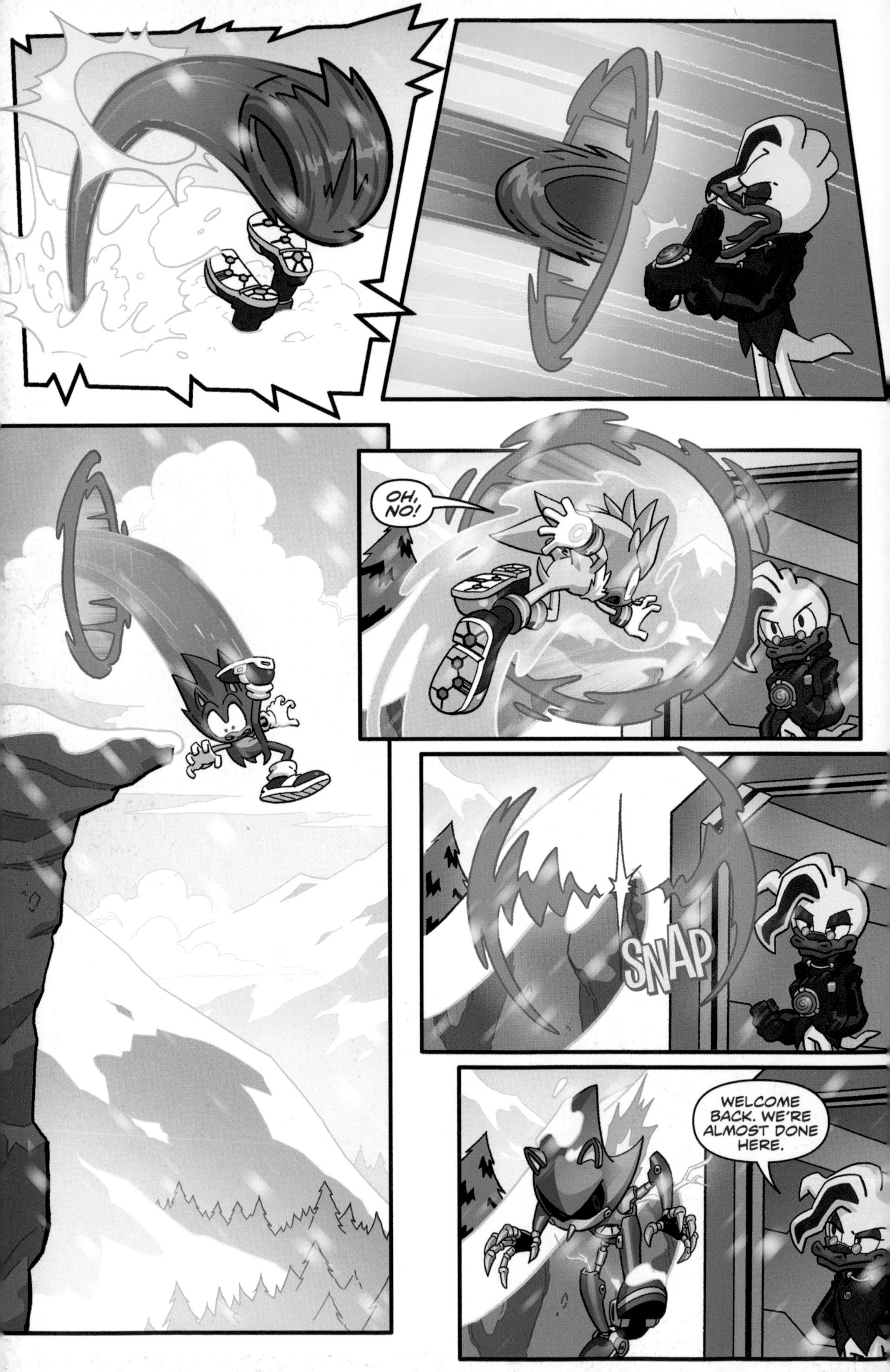
OH, NO!
SNAP
WELCOME BACK. WE'RE ALMOST DONE HERE.

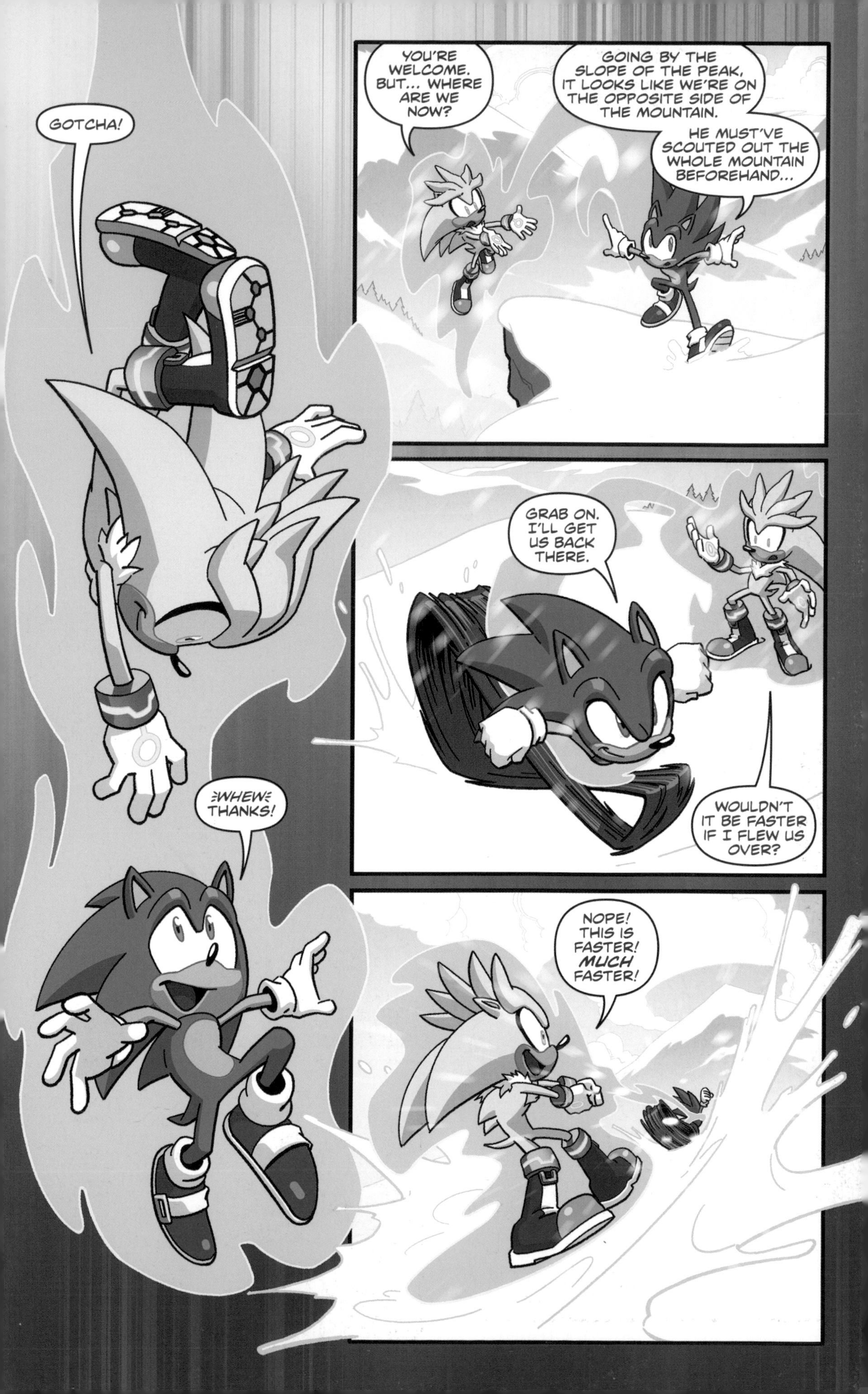
GOTCHA!
≈WHEW≈ THANKS!
YOU'RE WELCOME. BUT... WHERE ARE WE NOW?
GOING BY THE SLOPE OF THE PEAK, IT LOOKS LIKE WE'RE ON THE OPPOSITE SIDE OF THE MOUNTAIN.
HE MUST'VE SCOUTED OUT THE WHOLE MOUNTAIN BEFOREHAND...
GRAB ON. I'LL GET US BACK THERE.
WOULDN'T IT BE FASTER IF I FLEW US OVER?
NOPE! THIS IS FASTER! MUCH FASTER!

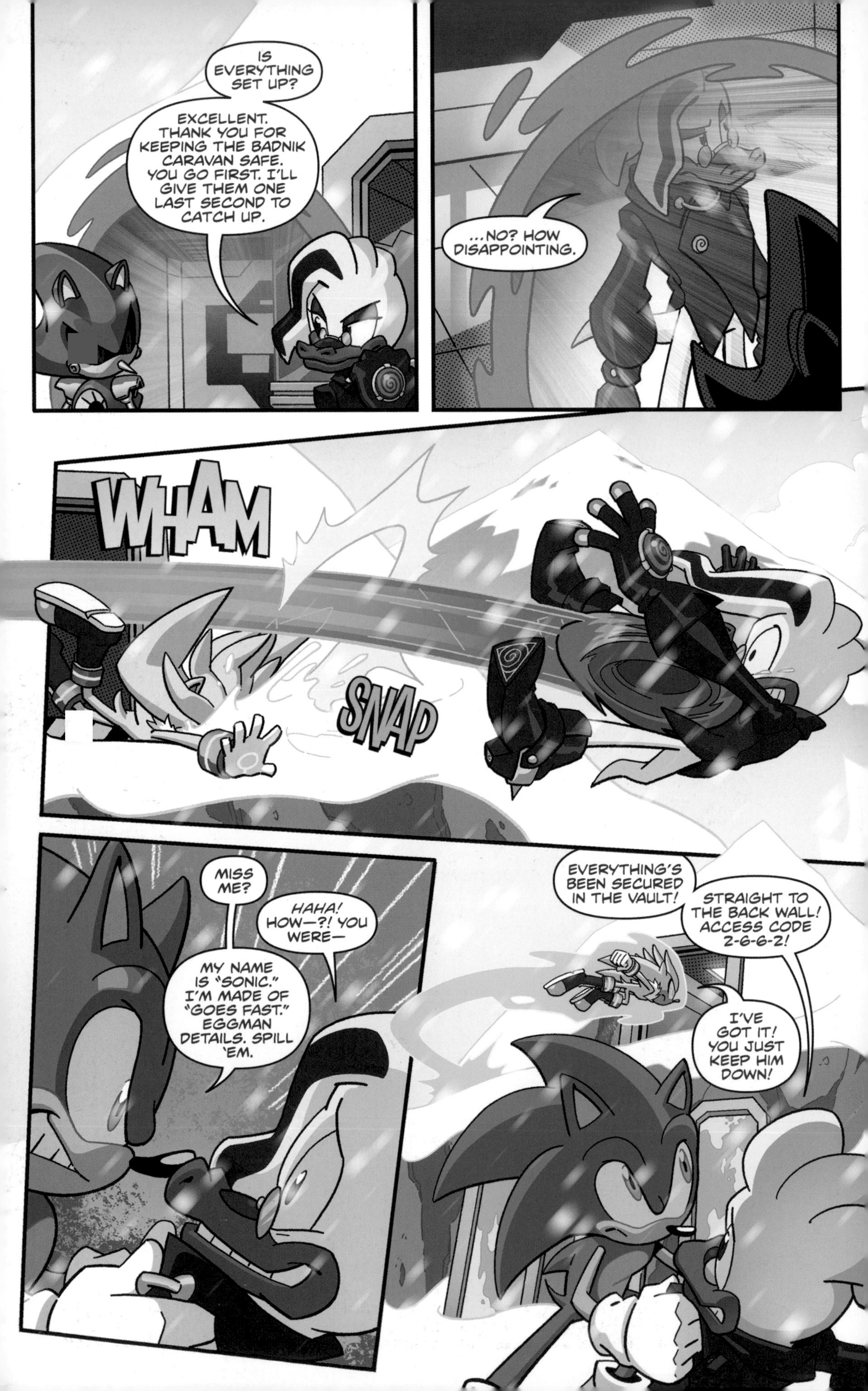
IS EVERYTHING SET UP?
EXCELLENT. THANK YOU FOR KEEPING THE BADNIK CARAVAN SAFE. YOU GO FIRST. I'LL GIVE THEM ONE LAST SECOND TO CATCH UP.
...NO? HOW DISAPPOINTING.
WHAM
SNAP
MISS ME?
HAHA! HOW—?! YOU WERE—
MY NAME IS "SONIC." I'M MADE OF "GOES FAST." EGGMAN DETAILS. SPILL 'EM.
EVERYTHING'S BEEN SECURED IN THE VAULT!
STRAIGHT TO THE BACK WALL! ACCESS CODE 2-6-6-2!
I'VE GOT IT! YOU JUST KEEP HIM DOWN!

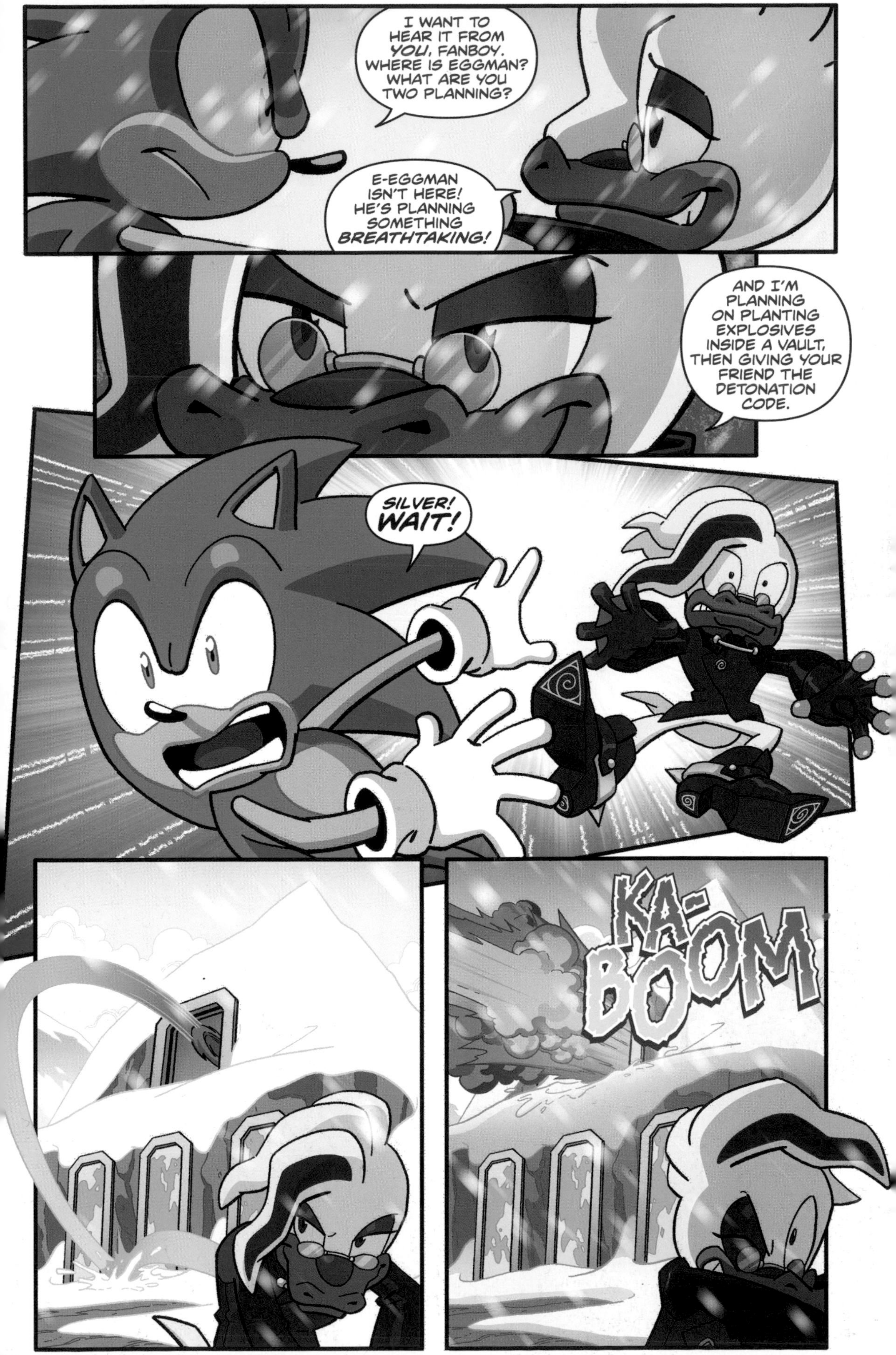
I WANT TO HEAR IT FROM YOU, FANBOY. WHERE IS EGGMAN? WHAT ARE YOU TWO PLANNING?
E-EGGMAN ISN'T HERE! HE'S PLANNING SOMETHING BREATHTAKING!
AND I'M PLANNING ON PLANTING EXPLOSIVES INSIDE A VAULT, THEN GIVING YOUR FRIEND THE DETONATION CODE.
SILVER! WAIT!
KA-BOOM

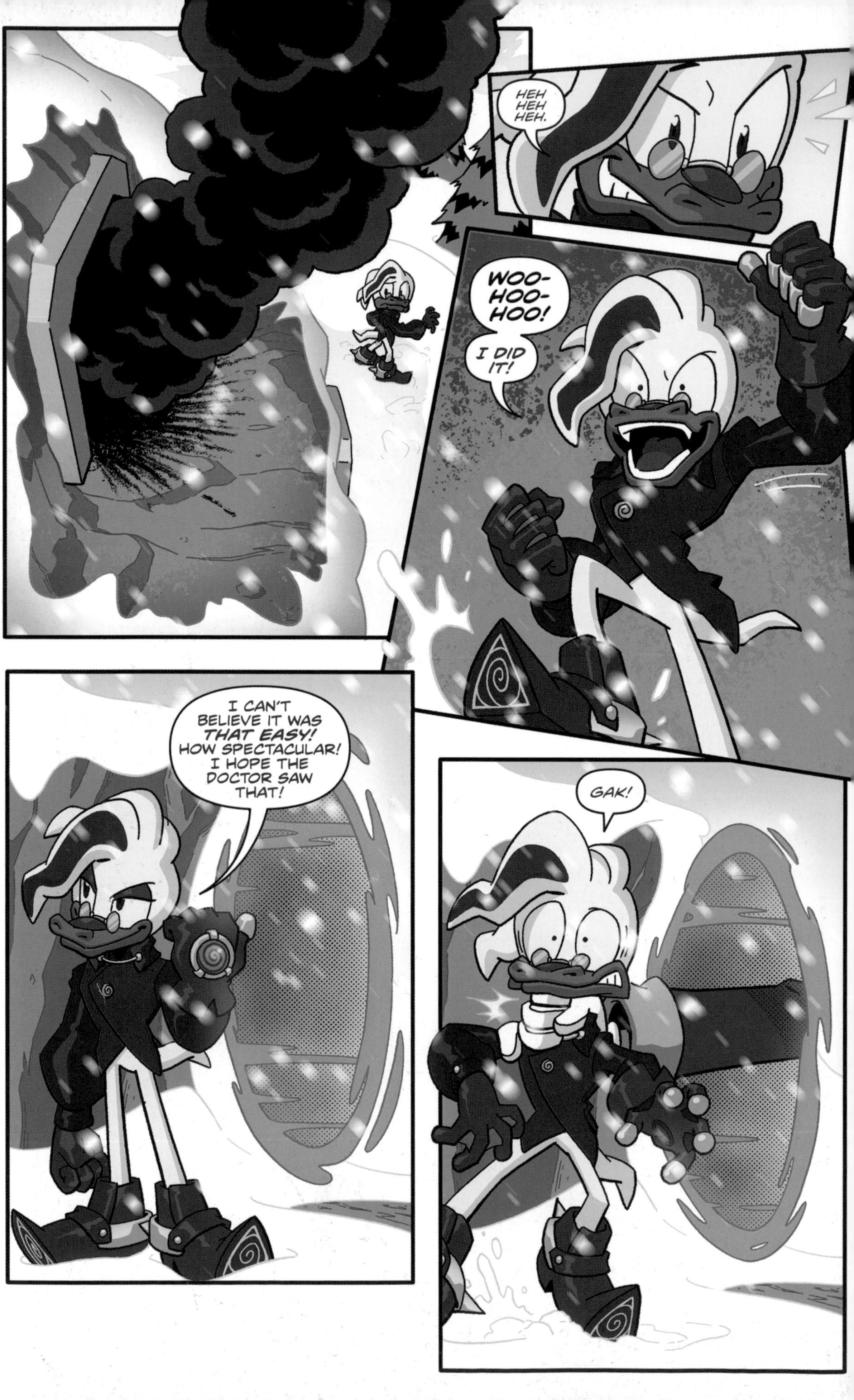
HEH HEH HEH.
WOO-HOO-HOO!
I DID IT!
I CAN'T BELIEVE IT WAS *THAT EASY!* HOW SPECTACULAR! I HOPE THE DOCTOR SAW THAT!
GAK!

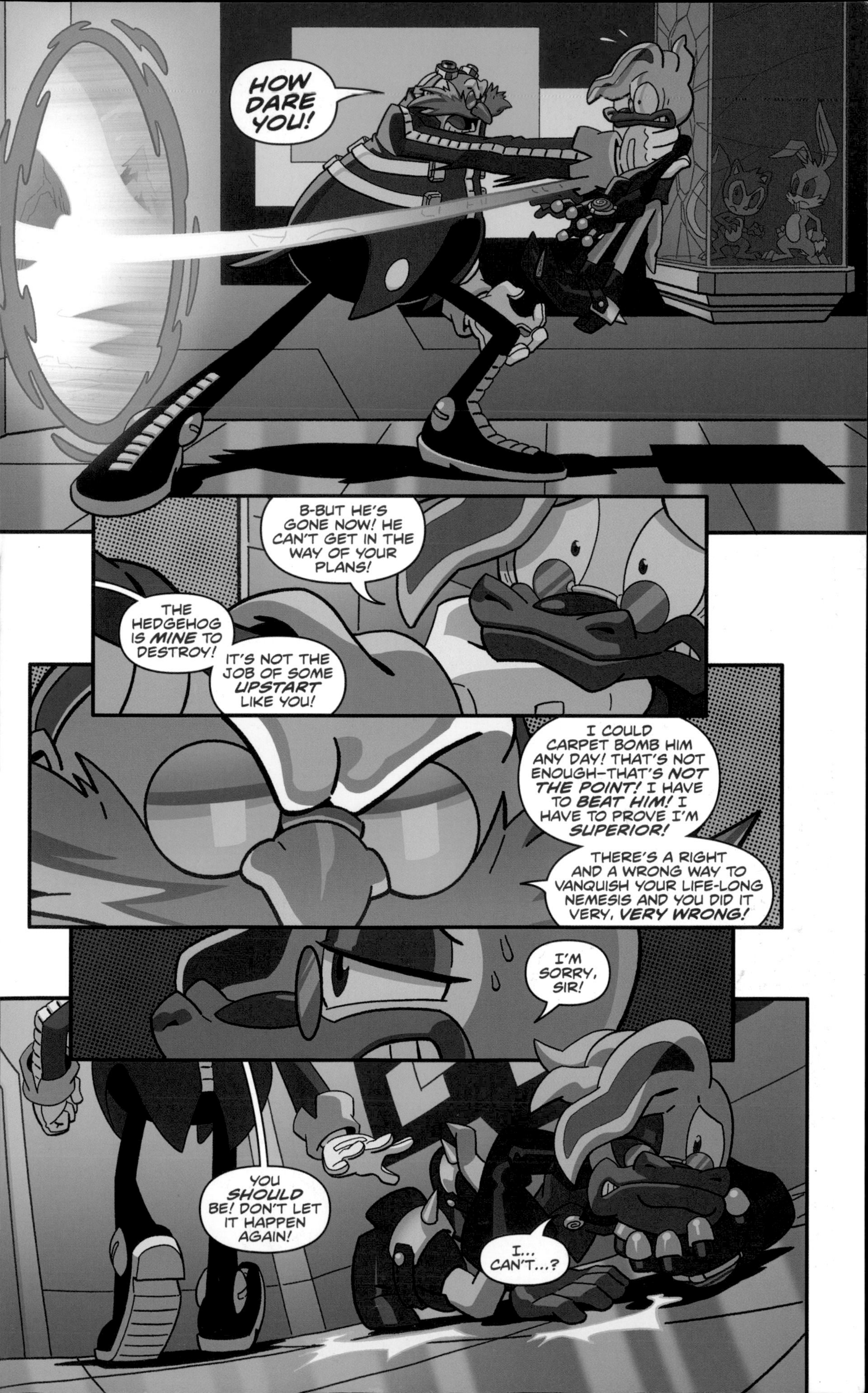
HOW DARE YOU!
B-BUT HE'S GONE NOW! HE CAN'T GET IN THE WAY OF YOUR PLANS!
THE HEDGEHOG IS MINE TO DESTROY!
IT'S NOT THE JOB OF SOME UPSTART LIKE YOU!
I COULD CARPET BOMB HIM ANY DAY! THAT'S NOT ENOUGH–THAT'S NOT THE POINT! I HAVE TO BEAT HIM! I HAVE TO PROVE I'M SUPERIOR!
THERE'S A RIGHT AND A WRONG WAY TO VANQUISH YOUR LIFE-LONG NEMESIS AND YOU DID IT VERY, VERY WRONG!
I'M SORRY, SIR!
YOU SHOULD BE! DON'T LET IT HAPPEN AGAIN!
I... CAN'T...?

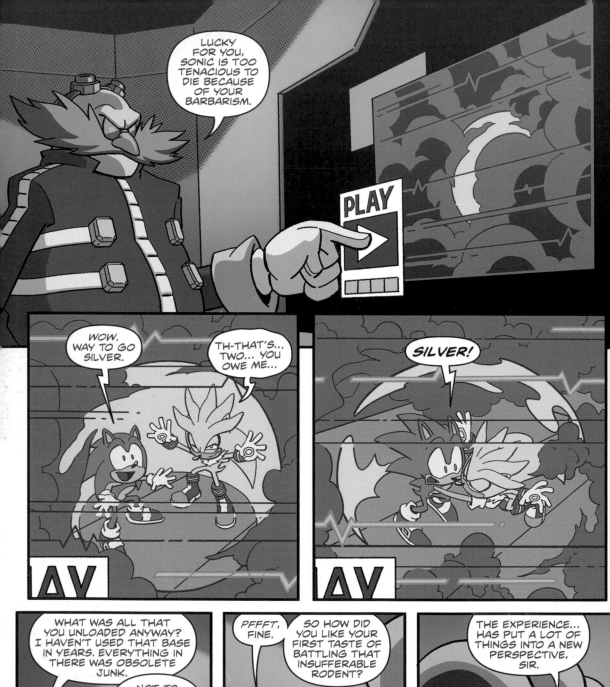

LUCKY FOR YOU, SONIC IS TOO TENACIOUS TO DIE BECAUSE OF YOUR BARBARISM.

PLAY ▷

WOW. WAY TO GO SILVER.

TH-THAT'S... TWO... YOU OWE ME...

SILVER!

WHAT WAS ALL THAT YOU UNLOADED ANYWAY? I HAVEN'T USED THAT BASE IN YEARS. EVERYTHING IN THERE WAS OBSOLETE JUNK.

NOT TO ME. THEY'RE TREASURED COLLECTIBLES OF YOUR LEGACY.

PFFFT, FINE. SO HOW DID YOU LIKE YOUR FIRST TASTE OF BATTLING THAT INSUFFERABLE RODENT?

THE EXPERIENCE... HAS PUT A LOT OF THINGS INTO A NEW PERSPECTIVE, SIR.

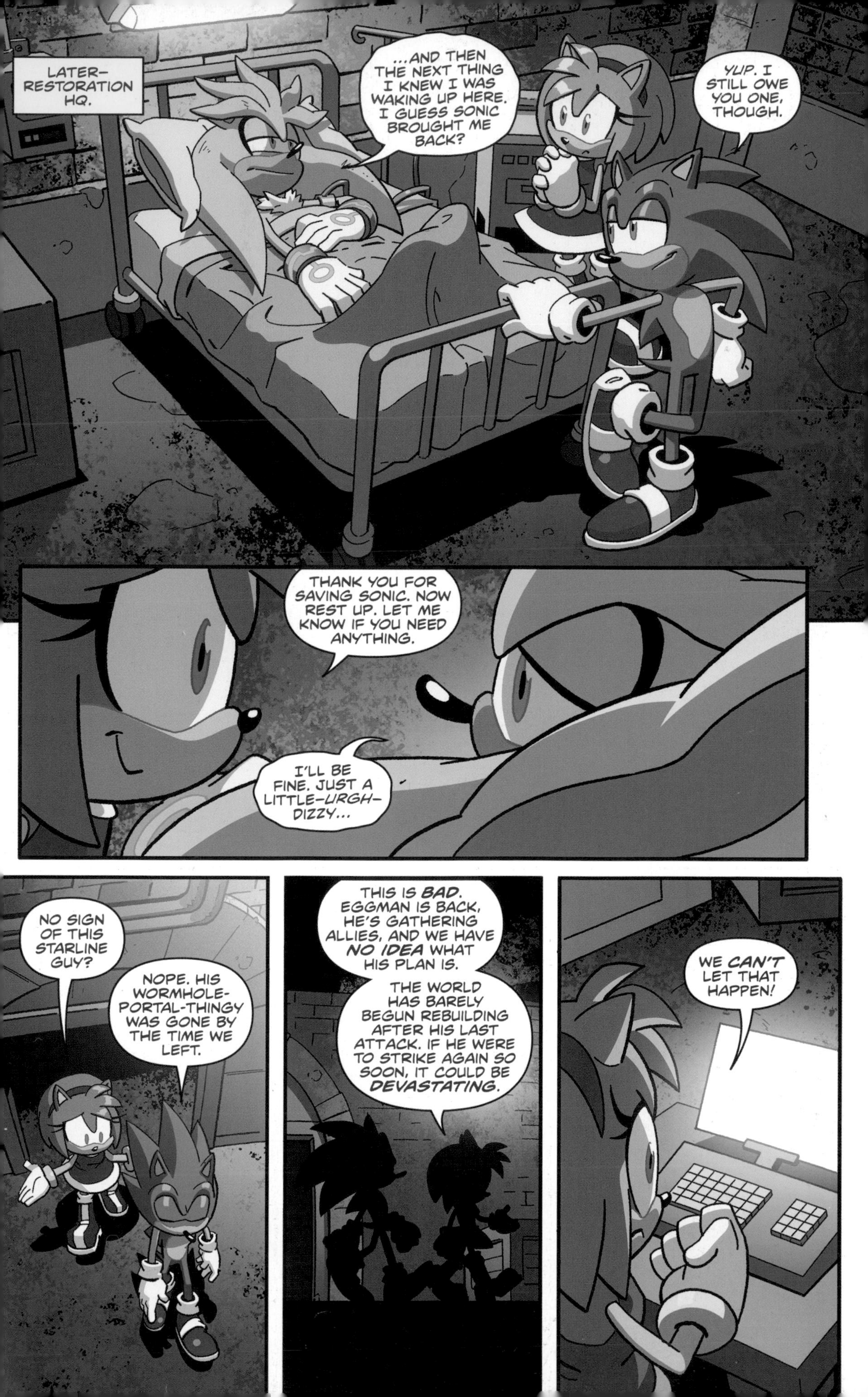

LATER–RESTORATION HQ.
...AND THEN THE NEXT THING I KNEW I WAS WAKING UP HERE. I GUESS SONIC BROUGHT ME BACK?
YUP. I STILL OWE YOU ONE, THOUGH.
THANK YOU FOR SAVING SONIC. NOW REST UP. LET ME KNOW IF YOU NEED ANYTHING.
I'LL BE FINE. JUST A LITTLE–URGH–DIZZY...
NO SIGN OF THIS STARLINE GUY?
NOPE. HIS WORMHOLE-PORTAL-THINGY WAS GONE BY THE TIME WE LEFT.
THIS IS BAD. EGGMAN IS BACK, HE'S GATHERING ALLIES, AND WE HAVE NO IDEA WHAT HIS PLAN IS.
THE WORLD HAS BARELY BEGUN REBUILDING AFTER HIS LAST ATTACK. IF HE WERE TO STRIKE AGAIN SO SOON, IT COULD BE DEVASTATING.
WE CAN'T LET THAT HAPPEN!

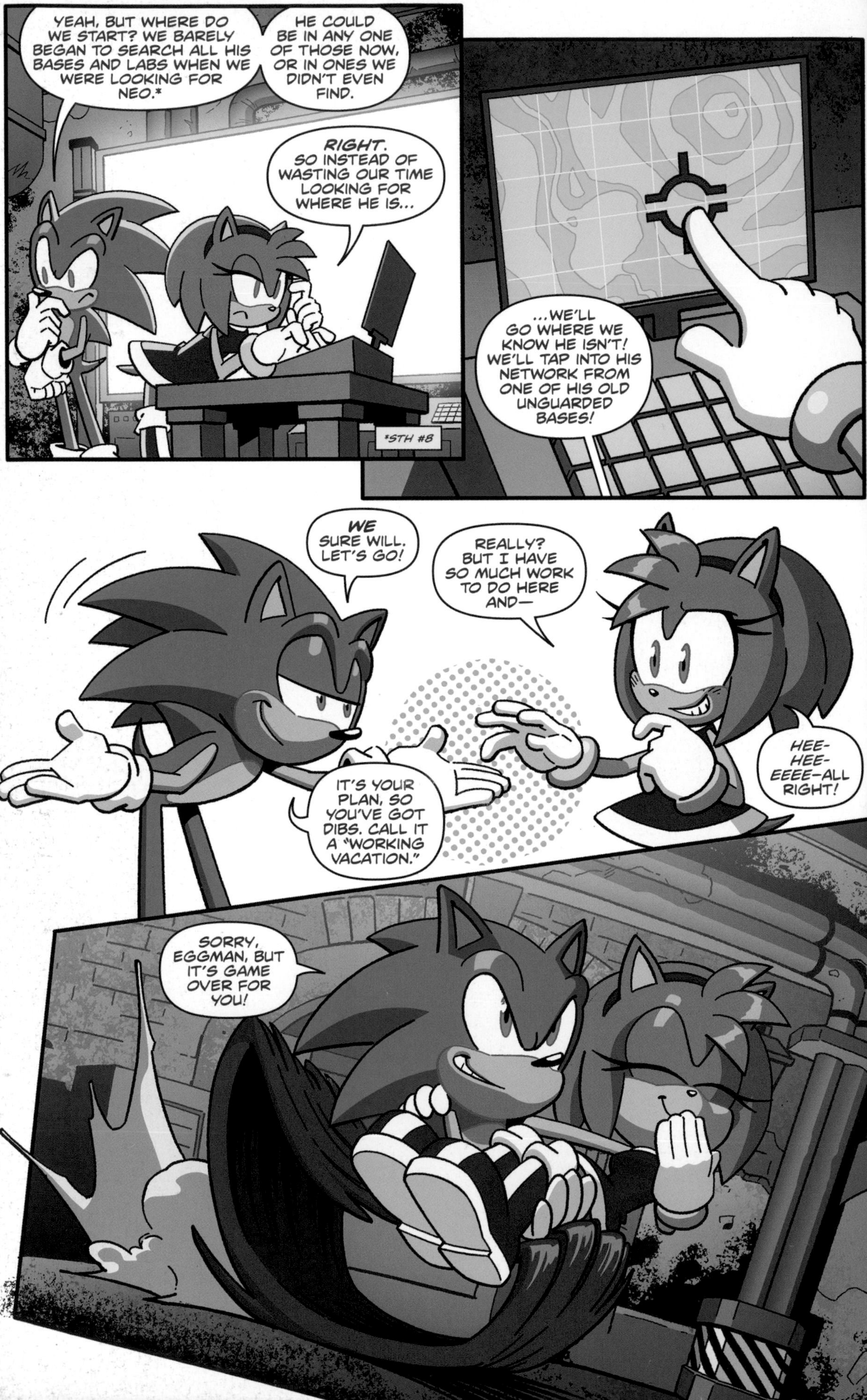
YEAH, BUT WHERE DO WE START? WE BARELY BEGAN TO SEARCH ALL HIS BASES AND LABS WHEN WE WERE LOOKING FOR NEO.*
HE COULD BE IN ANY ONE OF THOSE NOW, OR IN ONES WE DIDN'T EVEN FIND.
RIGHT. SO INSTEAD OF WASTING OUR TIME LOOKING FOR WHERE HE IS...
*STH #8
...WE'LL GO WHERE WE KNOW HE ISN'T! WE'LL TAP INTO HIS NETWORK FROM ONE OF HIS OLD UNGUARDED BASES!
WE SURE WILL. LET'S GO!
REALLY? BUT I HAVE SO MUCH WORK TO DO HERE AND—
IT'S YOUR PLAN, SO YOU'VE GOT DIBS. CALL IT A "WORKING VACATION."
HEE-HEE-EEEE—ALL RIGHT!
SORRY, EGGMAN, BUT IT'S GAME OVER FOR YOU!

ART BY **JACK LAWRENCE** COLORS BY **MATT HERMS**

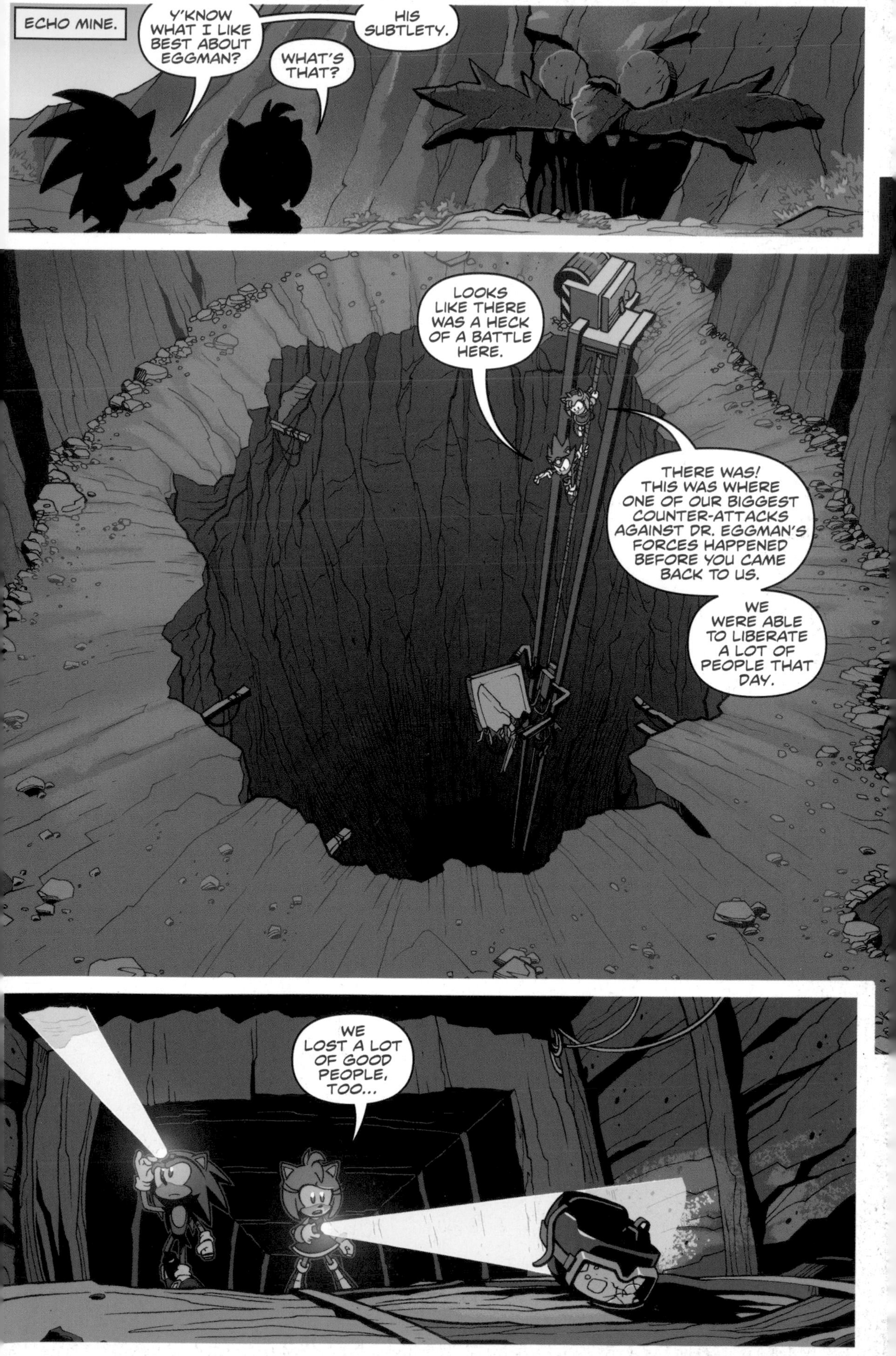
ECHO MINE.
Y'KNOW WHAT I LIKE BEST ABOUT EGGMAN?
WHAT'S THAT?
HIS SUBTLETY.
LOOKS LIKE THERE WAS A HECK OF A BATTLE HERE.
THERE WAS! THIS WAS WHERE ONE OF OUR BIGGEST COUNTER-ATTACKS AGAINST DR. EGGMAN'S FORCES HAPPENED BEFORE YOU CAME BACK TO US.
WE WERE ABLE TO LIBERATE A LOT OF PEOPLE THAT DAY.
WE LOST A LOT OF GOOD PEOPLE, TOO...

HEY— YOU MADE SURE IT WAS WORTH IT.
YOU WON THE WAR FOR US.
WELL, YEAH. SAVING THE DAY IS WHAT I DO.
AND WE'RE HERE TO STOP EGGMAN FROM PERFORMING AN ENCORE. WHICH WAY?
THE COMMAND HUB IS DOWN THIS TUNNEL.
HOPEFULLY THE BACK-UP GENERATOR STILL WORKS.
WITH A LITTLE LUCK, WE'LL BE ABLE TO BOOT UP HIS COMPUTER, ACCESS HIS NETWORK, AND FIND OUT WHAT HE'S PLANNING!
SILVER AND I SAW HIS BADNIKS EMPTYING A DEFUNCT LAB, THOUGH.* HOW DO YOU KNOW HE HASN'T DONE THE SAME THING HERE?
I DON'T. BUT THIS IS THE CLOSEST ABANDONED BASE ON FILE, SO IT'S THE BEST PLACE TO START!
*LAST ISSUE.

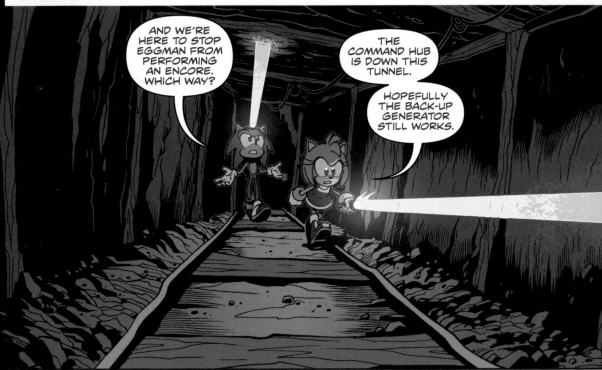

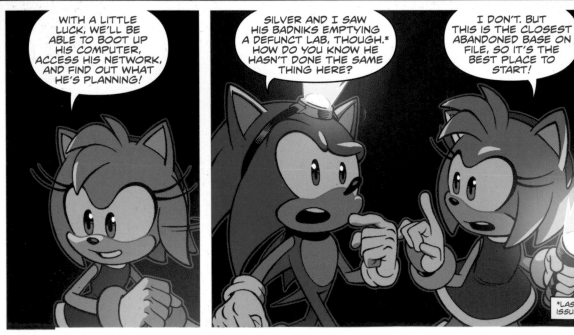

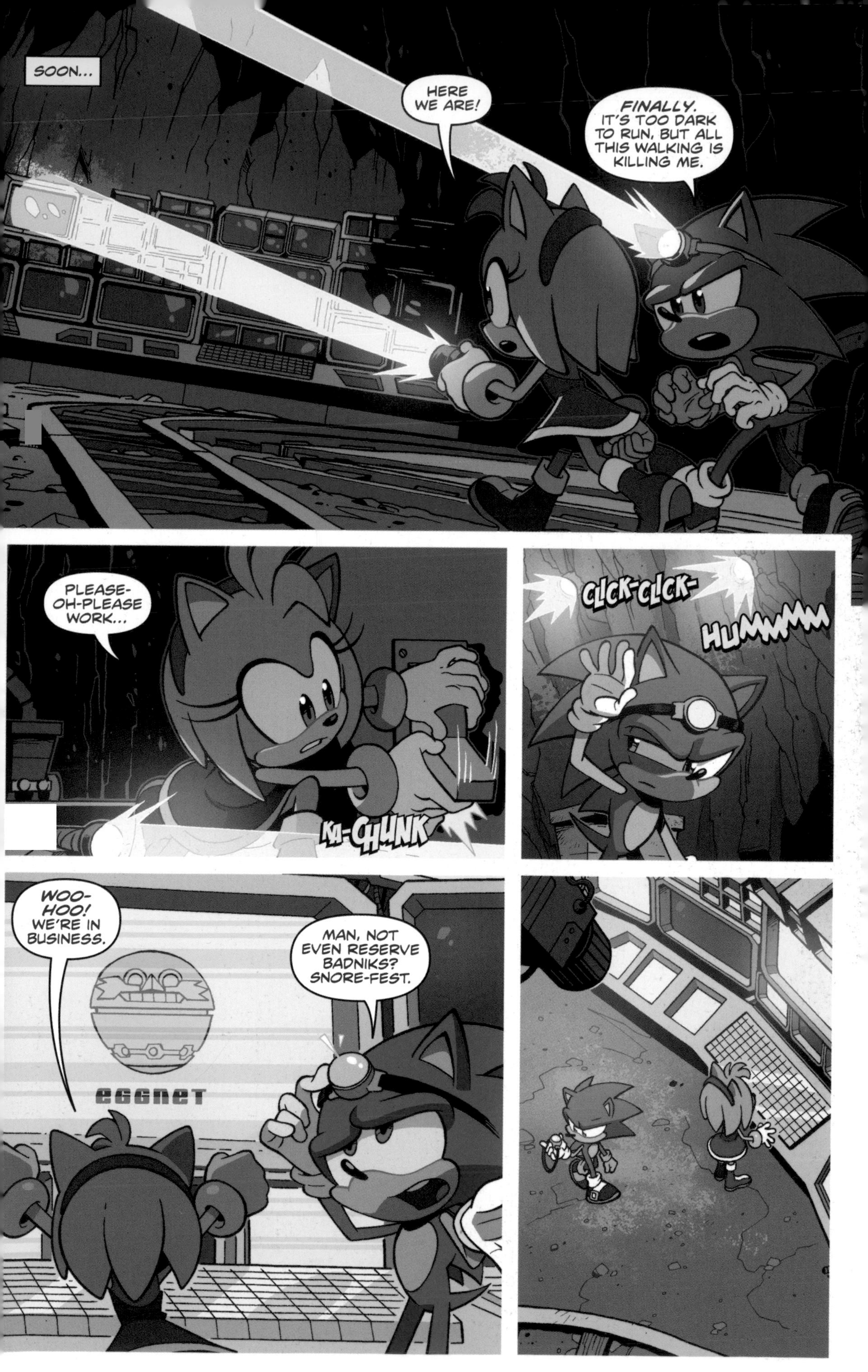
SOON...
HERE WE ARE!
FINALLY. IT'S TOO DARK TO RUN, BUT ALL THIS WALKING IS KILLING ME.
PLEASE-OH-PLEASE WORK...
KA-CHUNK
CLICK-CLICK-
HUMMMM
WOO-HOO! WE'RE IN BUSINESS.
MAN, NOT EVEN RESERVE BADNIKS? SNORE-FEST.
eggnet

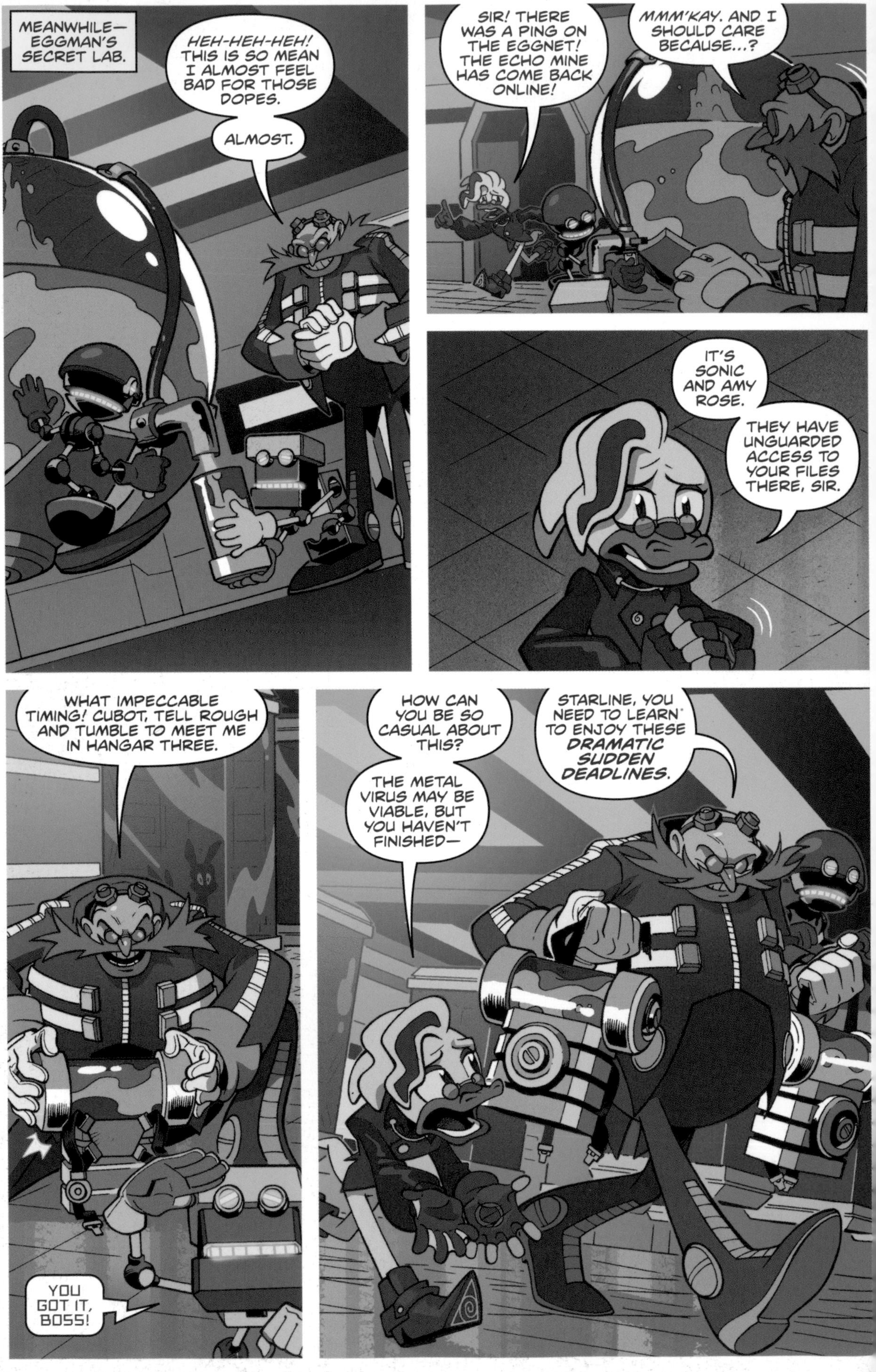
MEANWHILE— EGGMAN'S SECRET LAB.
HEH-HEH-HEH! THIS IS SO MEAN I ALMOST FEEL BAD FOR THOSE DOPES.
ALMOST.
SIR! THERE WAS A PING ON THE EGGNET! THE ECHO MINE HAS COME BACK ONLINE!
MMM'KAY. AND I SHOULD CARE BECAUSE...?
IT'S SONIC AND AMY ROSE.
THEY HAVE UNGUARDED ACCESS TO YOUR FILES THERE, SIR.
WHAT IMPECCABLE TIMING! CUBOT, TELL ROUGH AND TUMBLE TO MEET ME IN HANGAR THREE.
YOU GOT IT, BOSS!
HOW CAN YOU BE SO CASUAL ABOUT THIS?
THE METAL VIRUS MAY BE VIABLE, BUT YOU HAVEN'T FINISHED—
STARLINE, YOU NEED TO LEARN TO ENJOY THESE DRAMATIC SUDDEN DEADLINES.

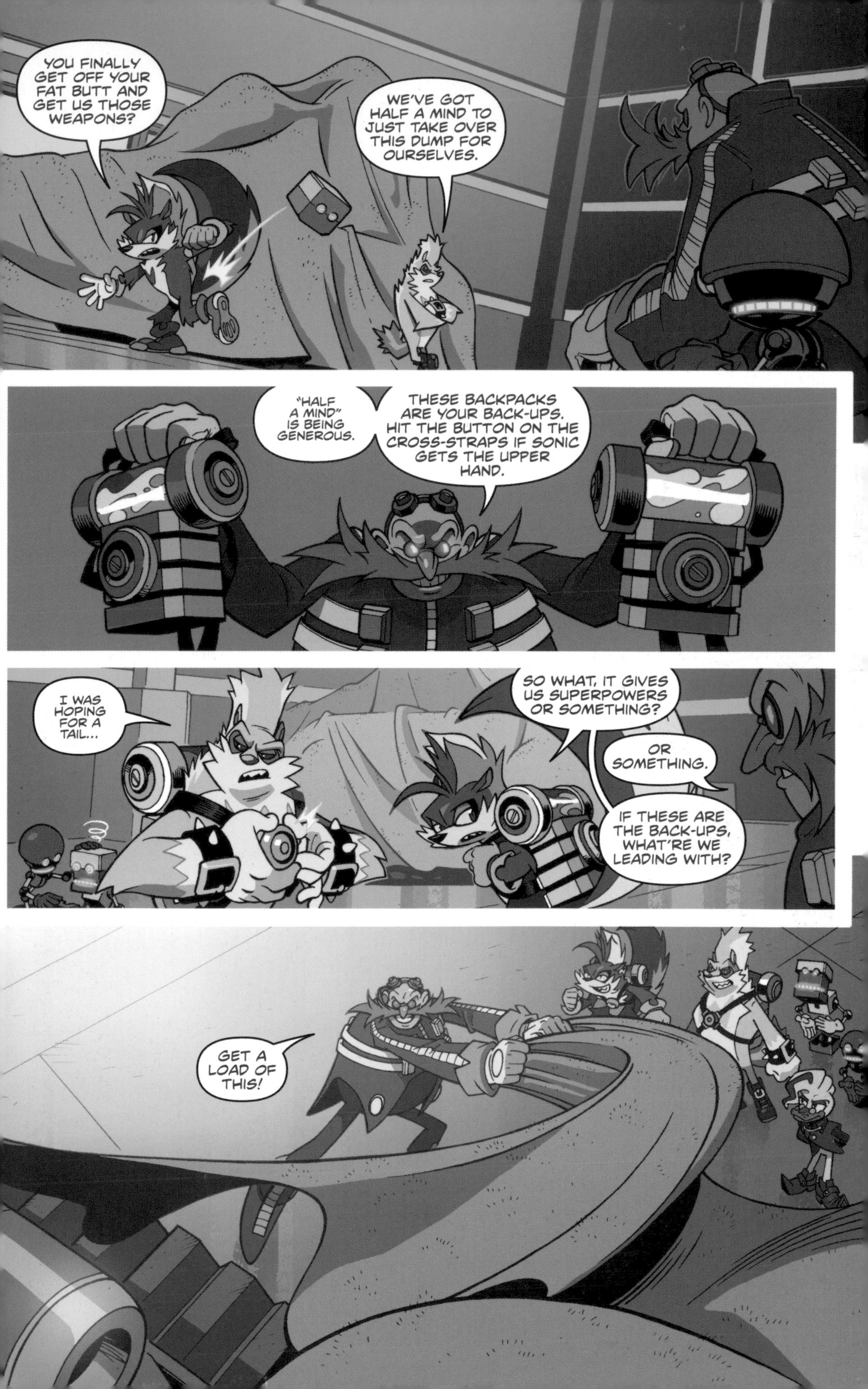
YOU FINALLY GET OFF YOUR FAT BUTT AND GET US THOSE WEAPONS?
WE'VE GOT HALF A MIND TO JUST TAKE OVER THIS DUMP FOR OURSELVES.
"HALF A MIND" IS BEING GENEROUS.
THESE BACKPACKS ARE YOUR BACK-UPS. HIT THE BUTTON ON THE CROSS-STRAPS IF SONIC GETS THE UPPER HAND.
I WAS HOPING FOR A TAIL...
SO WHAT, IT GIVES US SUPERPOWERS OR SOMETHING?
OR SOMETHING.
IF THESE ARE THE BACK-UPS, WHAT'RE WE LEADING WITH?
GET A LOAD OF THIS!

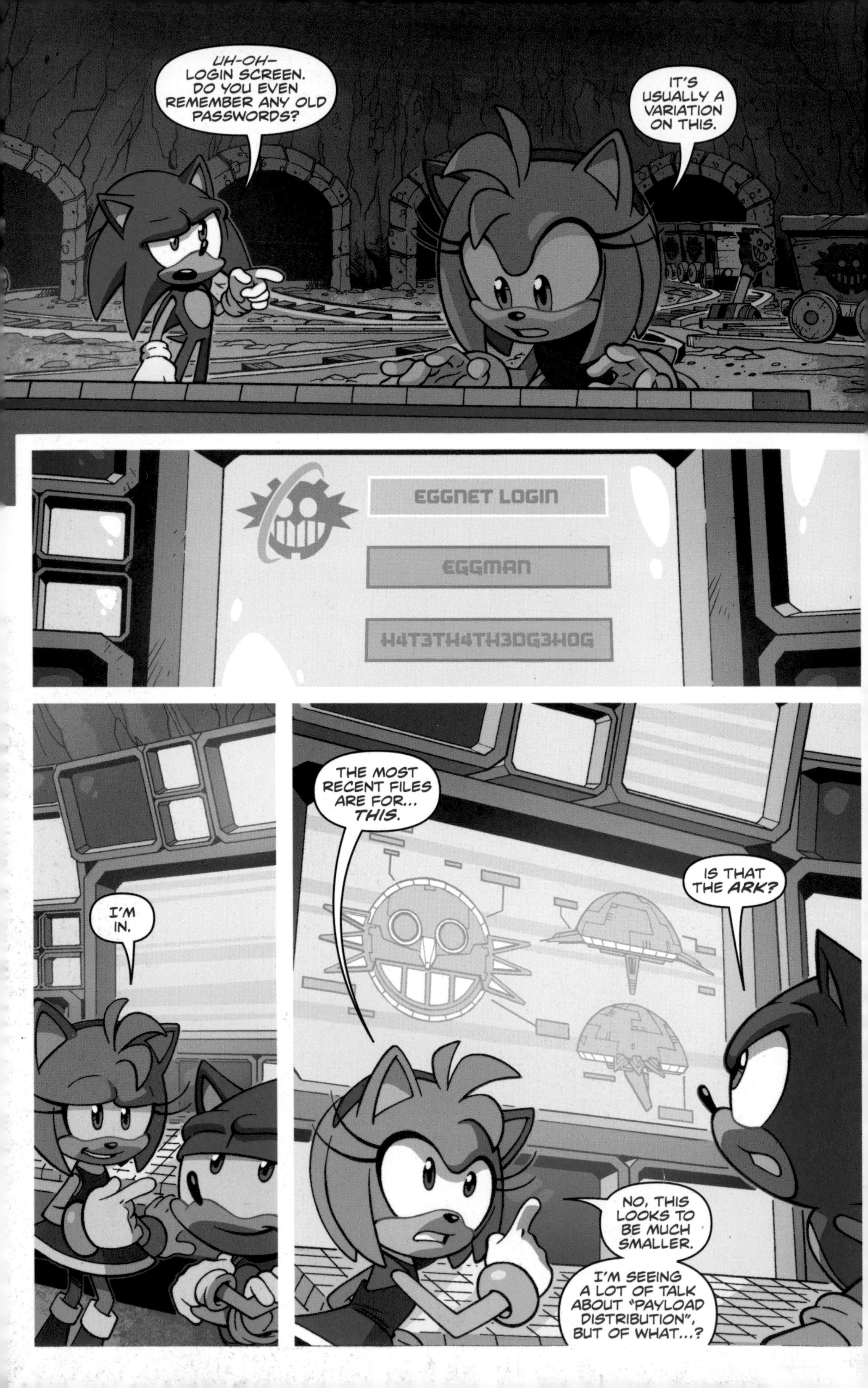

UH-OH— LOGIN SCREEN. DO YOU EVEN REMEMBER ANY OLD PASSWORDS?
IT'S USUALLY A VARIATION ON THIS.
EGGNET LOGIN
EGGMAN
H4T3TH4TH3DG3H0G
I'M IN.
THE MOST RECENT FILES ARE FOR... *THIS*.
IS THAT THE *ARK*?
NO, THIS LOOKS TO BE MUCH SMALLER.
I'M SEEING A LOT OF TALK ABOUT "PAYLOAD DISTRIBUTION", BUT OF WHAT...?

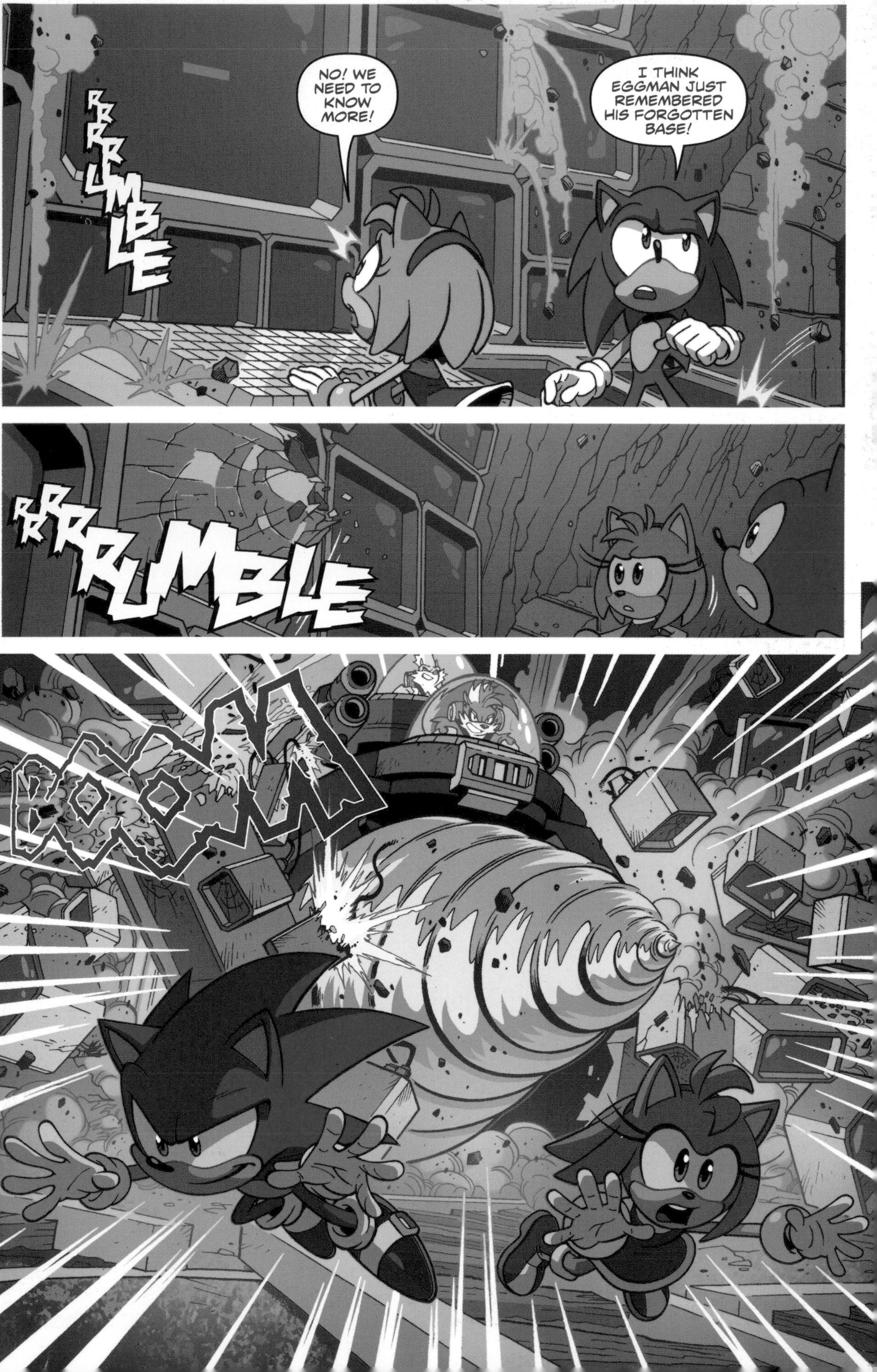
RRRRUMBLE
NO! WE NEED TO KNOW MORE!
I THINK EGGMAN JUST REMEMBERED HIS FORGOTTEN BASE!
RRRRRUMBLE
BOOOM

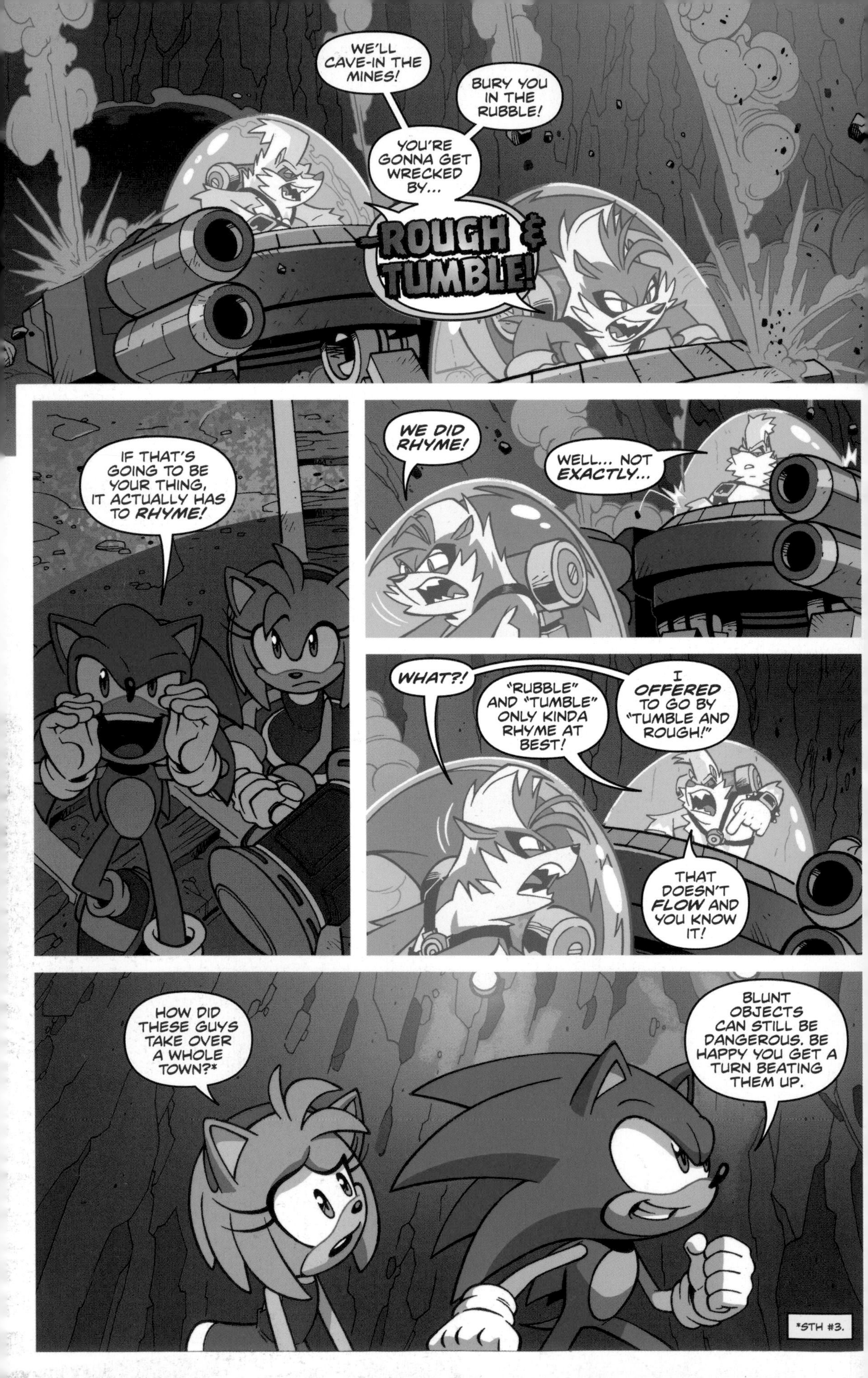
WE'LL CAVE-IN THE MINES!
BURY YOU IN THE RUBBLE!
YOU'RE GONNA GET WRECKED BY...
-ROUGH & TUMBLE!
IF THAT'S GOING TO BE YOUR THING, IT ACTUALLY HAS TO RHYME!
WE DID RHYME!
WELL... NOT EXACTLY...
WHAT?!
"RUBBLE" AND "TUMBLE" ONLY KINDA RHYME AT BEST!
I OFFERED TO GO BY "TUMBLE AND ROUGH!"
THAT DOESN'T FLOW AND YOU KNOW IT!
HOW DID THESE GUYS TAKE OVER A WHOLE TOWN?*
BLUNT OBJECTS CAN STILL BE DANGEROUS. BE HAPPY YOU GET A TURN BEATING THEM UP.
*STH #3.

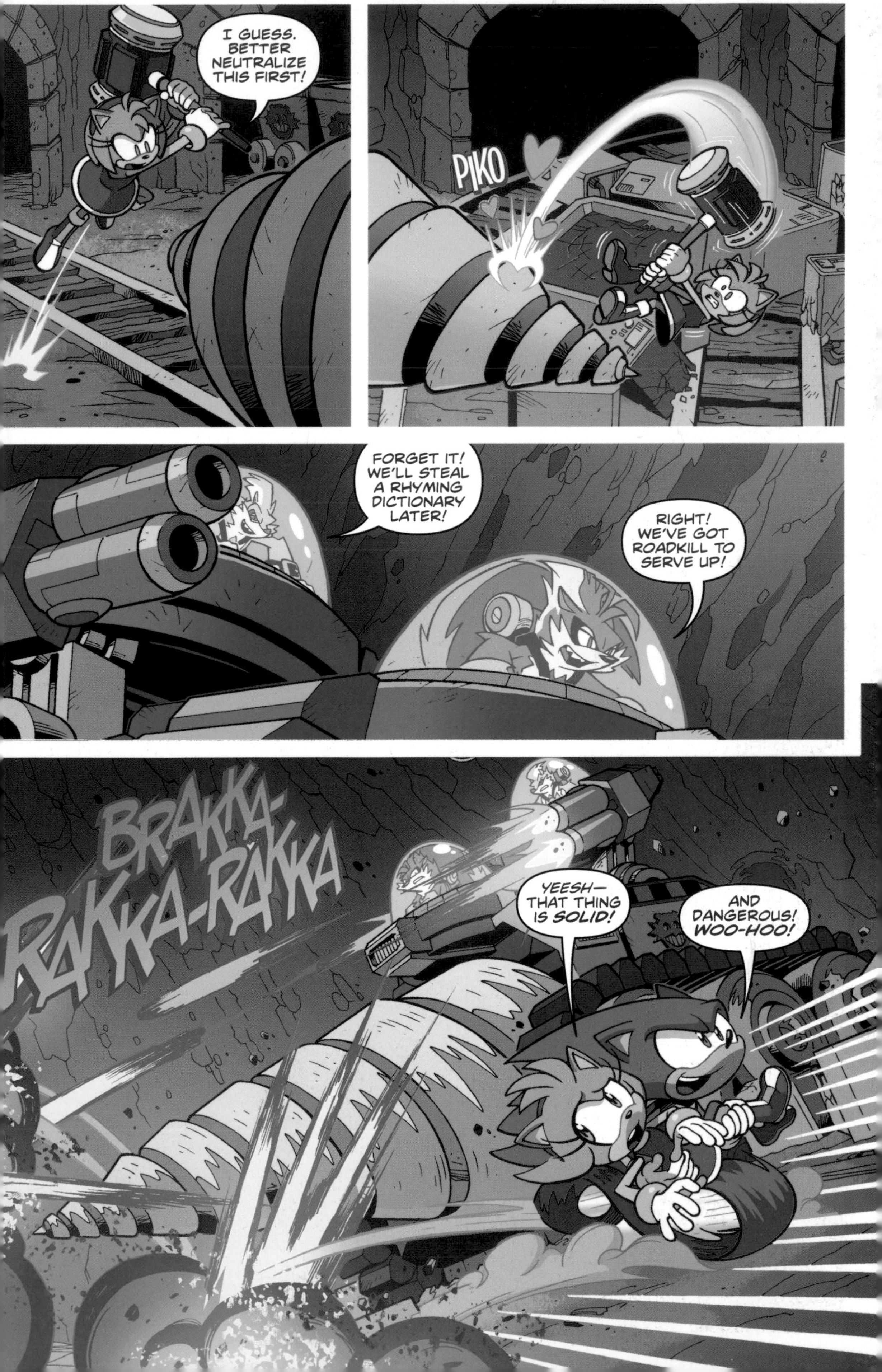
I GUESS. BETTER NEUTRALIZE THIS FIRST!
PIKO
FORGET IT! WE'LL STEAL A RHYMING DICTIONARY LATER!
RIGHT! WE'VE GOT ROADKILL TO SERVE UP!
BRAKKA-RAKKA-RAKKA
YEESH— THAT THING IS SOLID!
AND DANGEROUS! WOO-HOO!

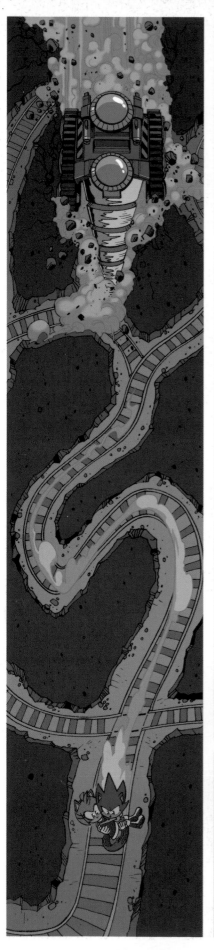

WHOOPS!

CAREFUL!

DEAD END?

IT'S A REFUSE PIT! THE ONLY WAY OUT IS BACK THE WAY WE CAME!

HOLD ON—THIS PATH IS BARELY WIDE ENOUGH FOR THEIR TANK.

IF THEY DROVE OUT HERE, THEY WOULDN'T BE ABLE TO TURN AROUND.

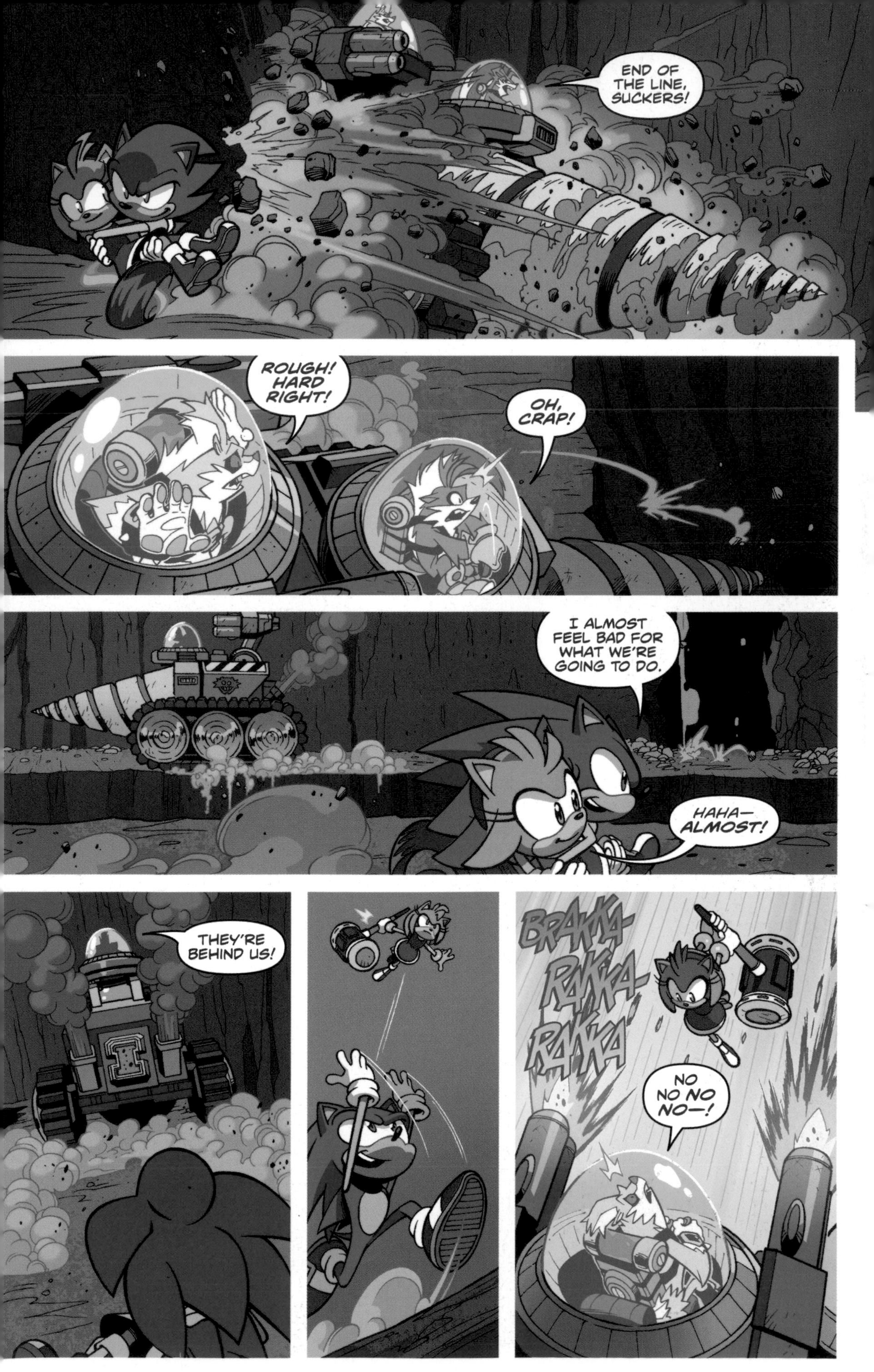
END OF THE LINE, SUCKERS!
ROUGH! HARD RIGHT!
OH, CRAP!
I ALMOST FEEL BAD FOR WHAT WE'RE GOING TO DO.
HAHA— ALMOST!
THEY'RE BEHIND US!
BRAKKA-RAKKA-RAKKA
NO NO NO NO—!

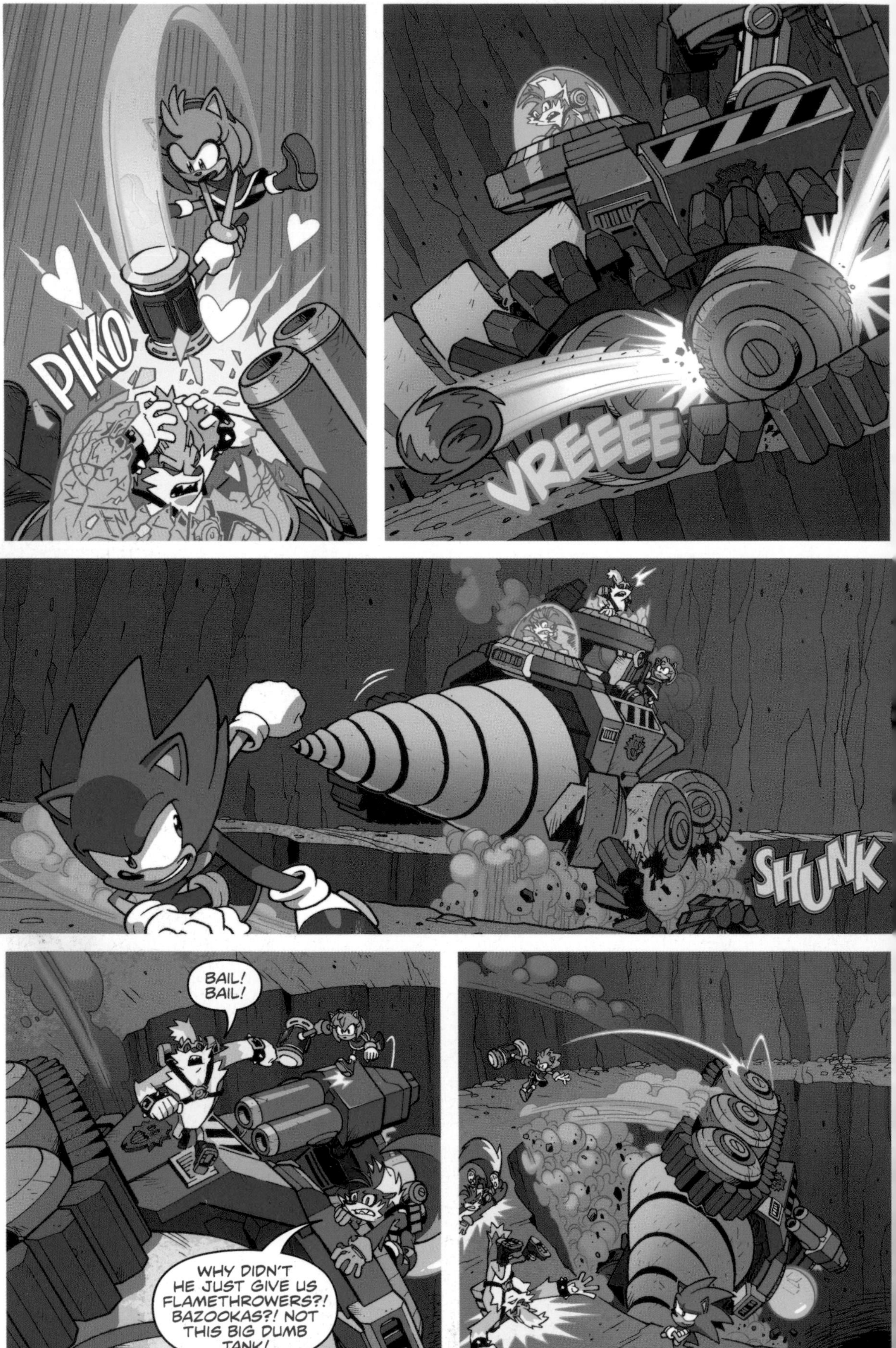
PIKO
VREEEE
SHUNK
BAIL! BAIL!
WHY DIDN'T HE JUST GIVE US FLAMETHROWERS?! BAZOOKAS?! NOT THIS BIG DUMB TANK!

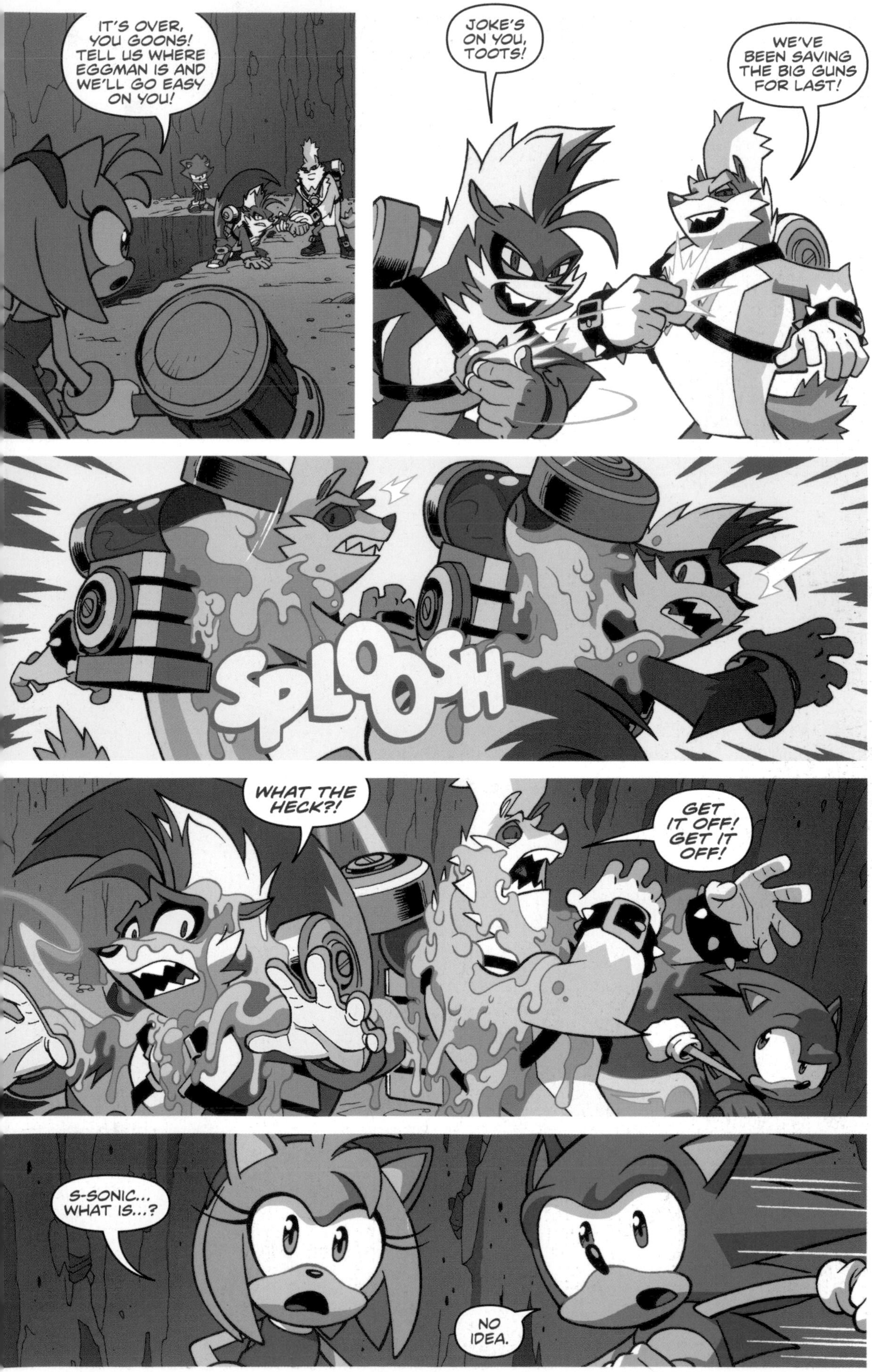
IT'S OVER, YOU GOONS! TELL US WHERE EGGMAN IS AND WE'LL GO EASY ON YOU!
JOKE'S ON YOU, TOOTS!
WE'VE BEEN SAVING THE BIG GUNS FOR LAST!
SPLOOSH
WHAT THE HECK?!
GET IT OFF! GET IT OFF!
S-SONIC... WHAT IS...?
NO IDEA.

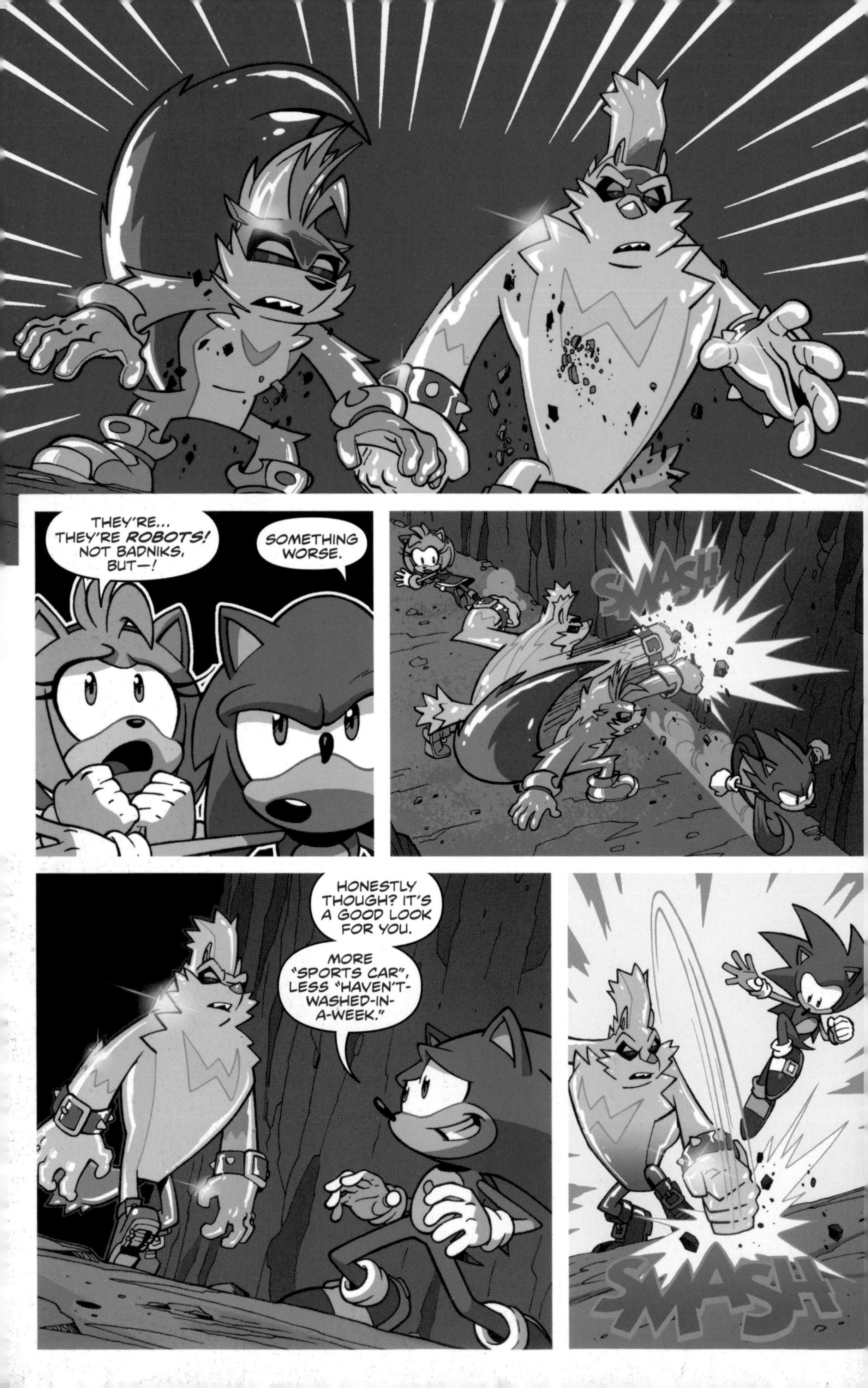
THEY'RE... THEY'RE ROBOTS! NOT BADNIKS, BUT—!
SOMETHING WORSE.
SMASH
HONESTLY THOUGH? IT'S A GOOD LOOK FOR YOU.
MORE "SPORTS CAR", LESS "HAVEN'T-WASHED-IN-A-WEEK."
SMASH

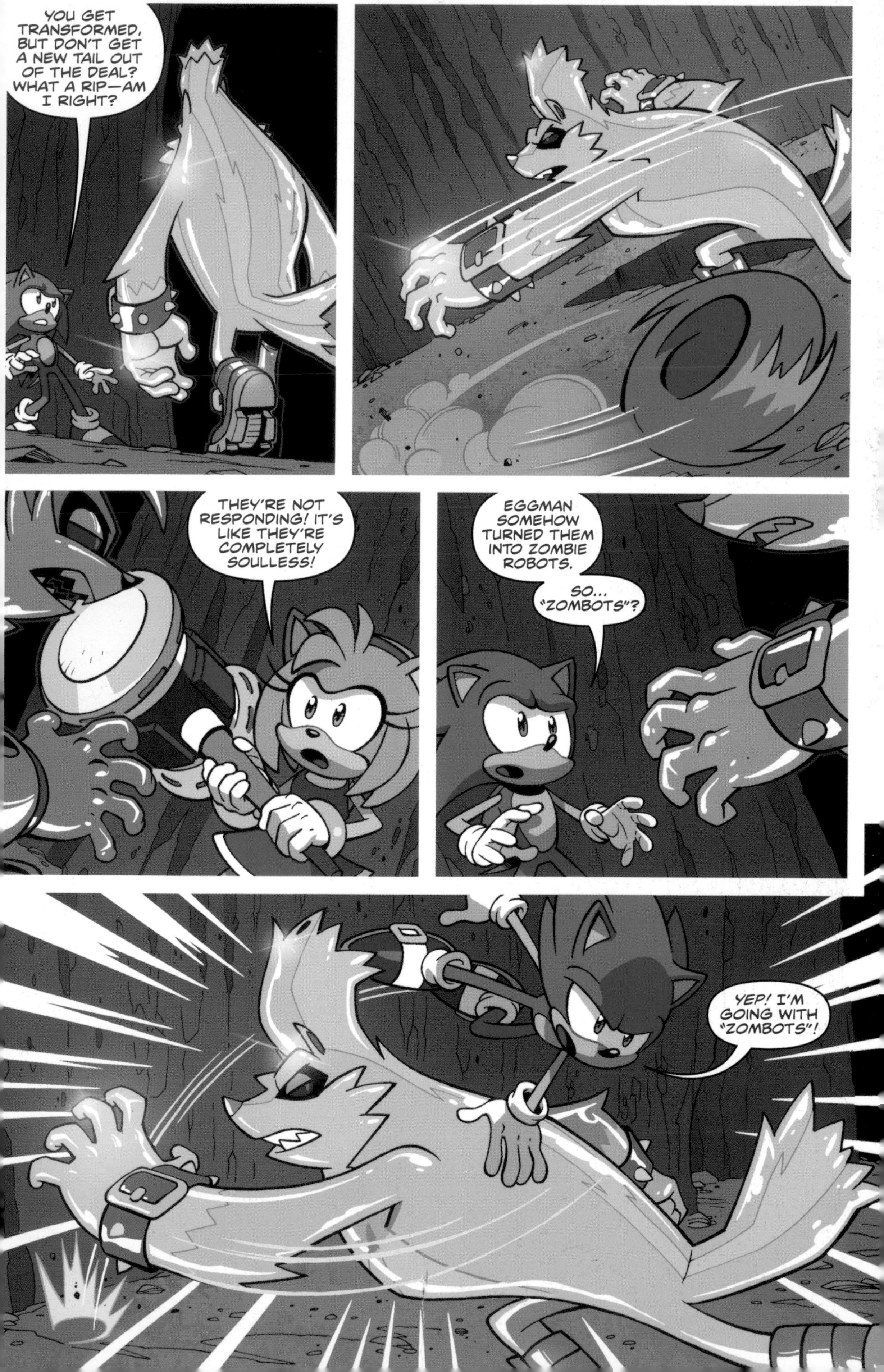
YOU GET TRANSFORMED, BUT DON'T GET A NEW TAIL OUT OF THE DEAL? WHAT A RIP—AM I RIGHT?
THEY'RE NOT RESPONDING! IT'S LIKE THEY'RE COMPLETELY SOULLESS!
EGGMAN SOMEHOW TURNED THEM INTO ZOMBIE ROBOTS.
SO... "ZOMBOTS"?
YEP! I'M GOING WITH "ZOMBOTS"!

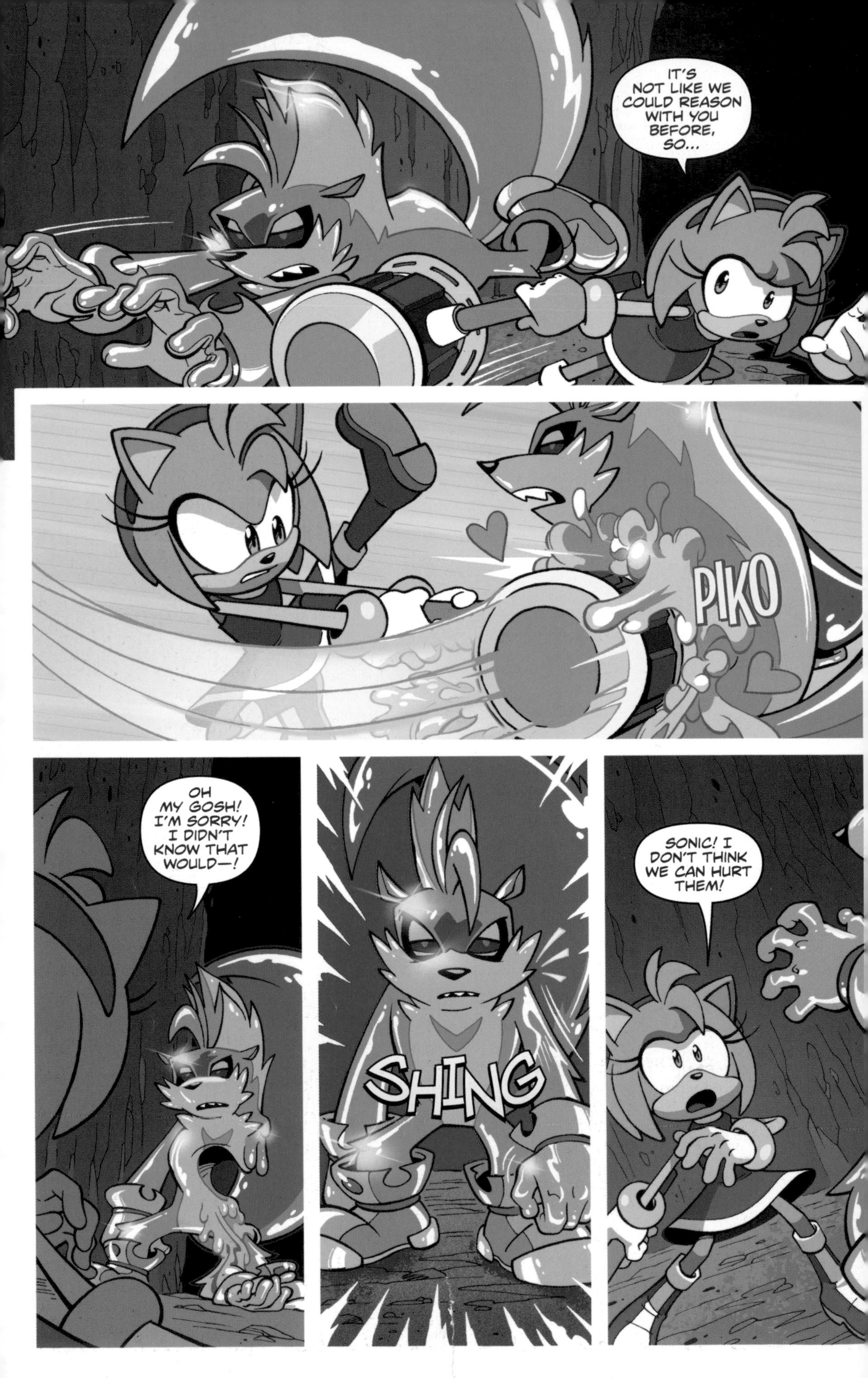
IT'S NOT LIKE WE COULD REASON WITH YOU BEFORE, SO...
PIKO
OH MY GOSH! I'M SORRY! I DIDN'T KNOW THAT WOULD—!
SHING
SONIC! I DON'T THINK WE CAN HURT THEM!

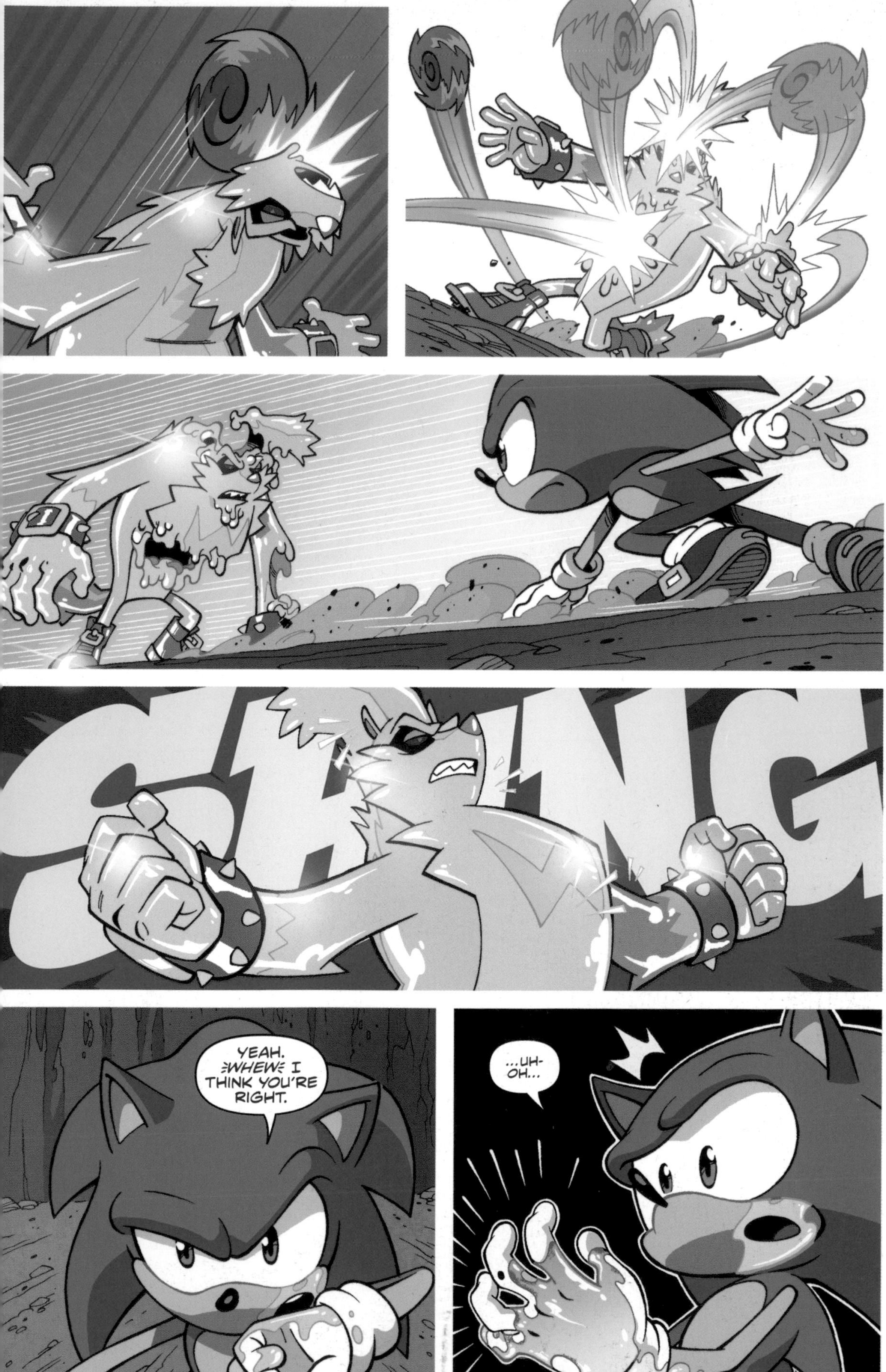
SHING
YEAH. ≡WHEW≡ I THINK YOU'RE RIGHT.
...UH-OH...

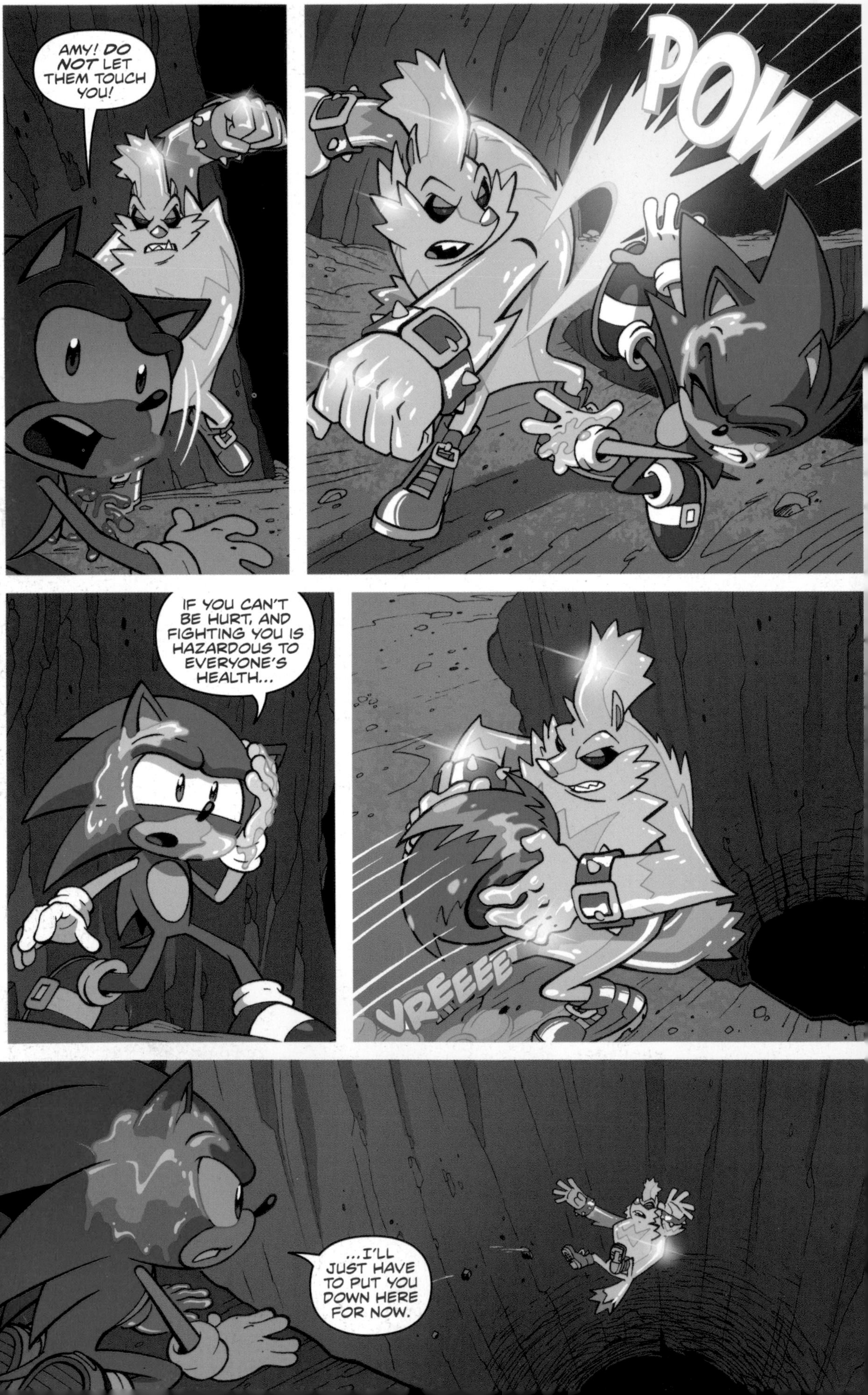
AMY! DO NOT LET THEM TOUCH YOU!
POW
IF YOU CAN'T BE HURT, AND FIGHTING YOU IS HAZARDOUS TO EVERYONE'S HEALTH...
VREEEEE
...I'LL JUST HAVE TO PUT YOU DOWN HERE FOR NOW.

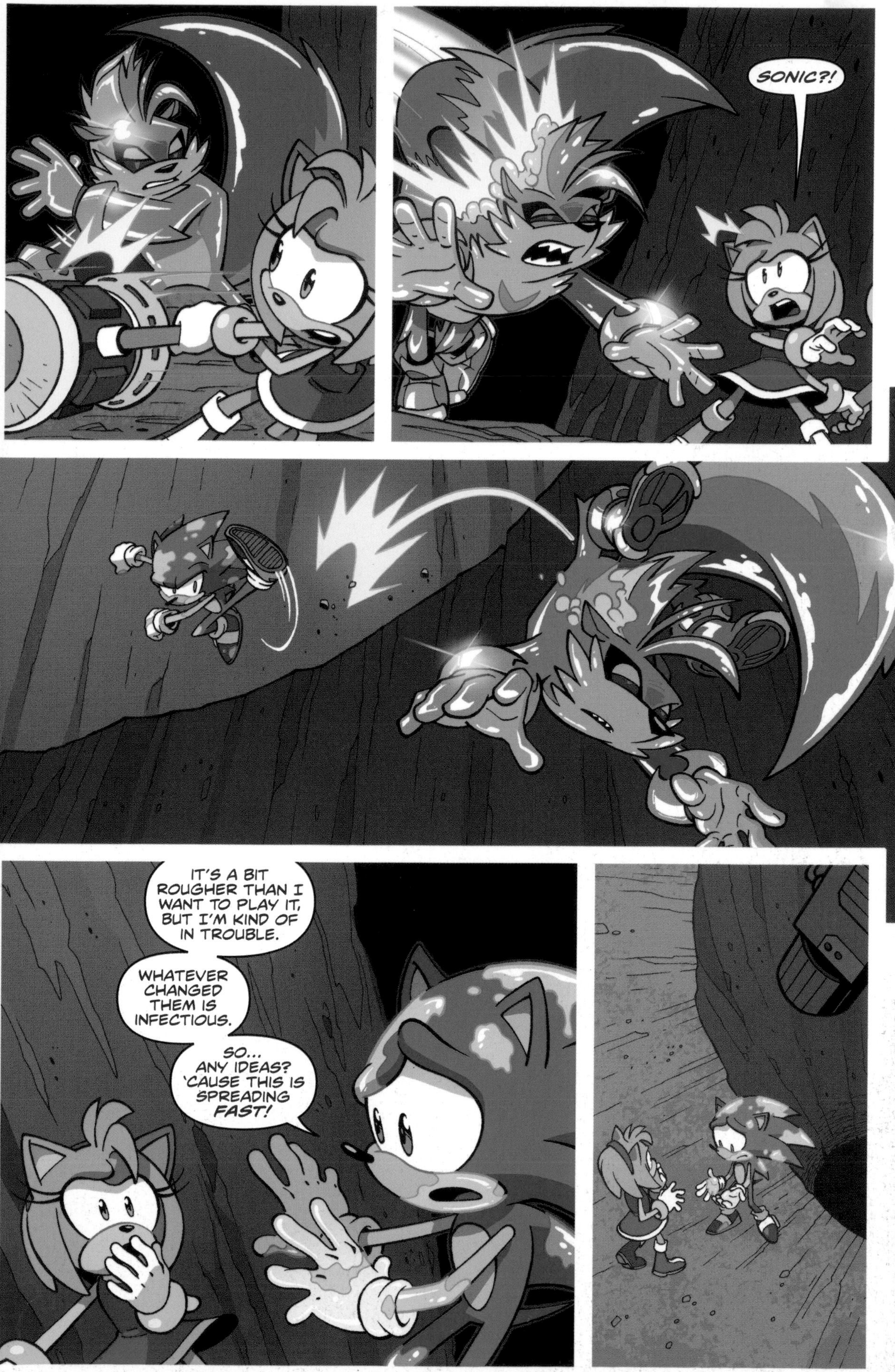
SONIC?!
IT'S A BIT ROUGHER THAN I WANT TO PLAY IT, BUT I'M KIND OF IN TROUBLE.
WHATEVER CHANGED THEM IS INFECTIOUS.
SO... ANY IDEAS? 'CAUSE THIS IS SPREADING FAST!

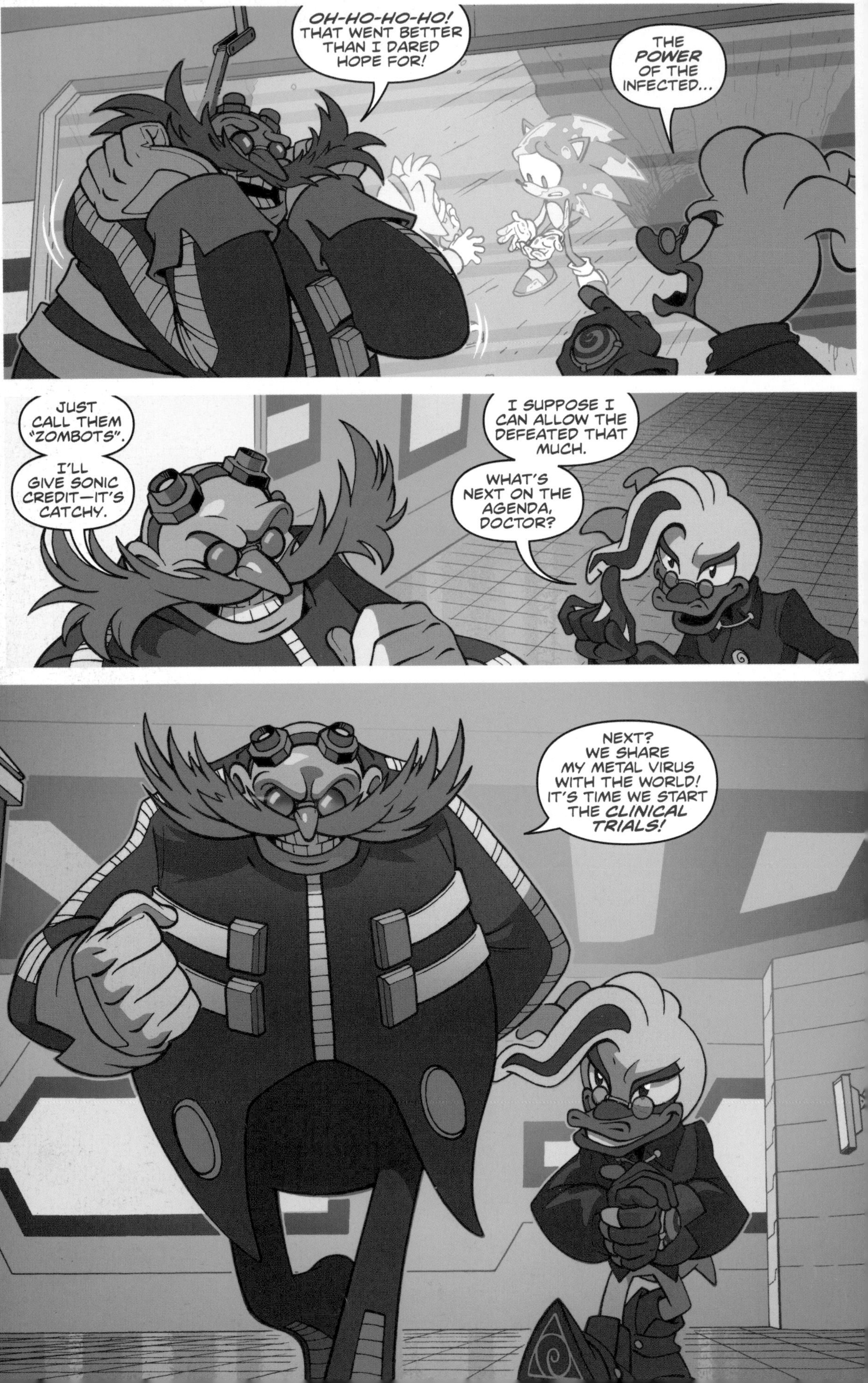
OH-HO-HO-HO! THAT WENT BETTER THAN I DARED HOPE FOR!
THE POWER OF THE INFECTED...
JUST CALL THEM "ZOMBOTS".
I'LL GIVE SONIC CREDIT—IT'S CATCHY.
I SUPPOSE I CAN ALLOW THE DEFEATED THAT MUCH.
WHAT'S NEXT ON THE AGENDA, DOCTOR?
NEXT? WE SHARE MY METAL VIRUS WITH THE WORLD! IT'S TIME WE START THE CLINICAL TRIALS!

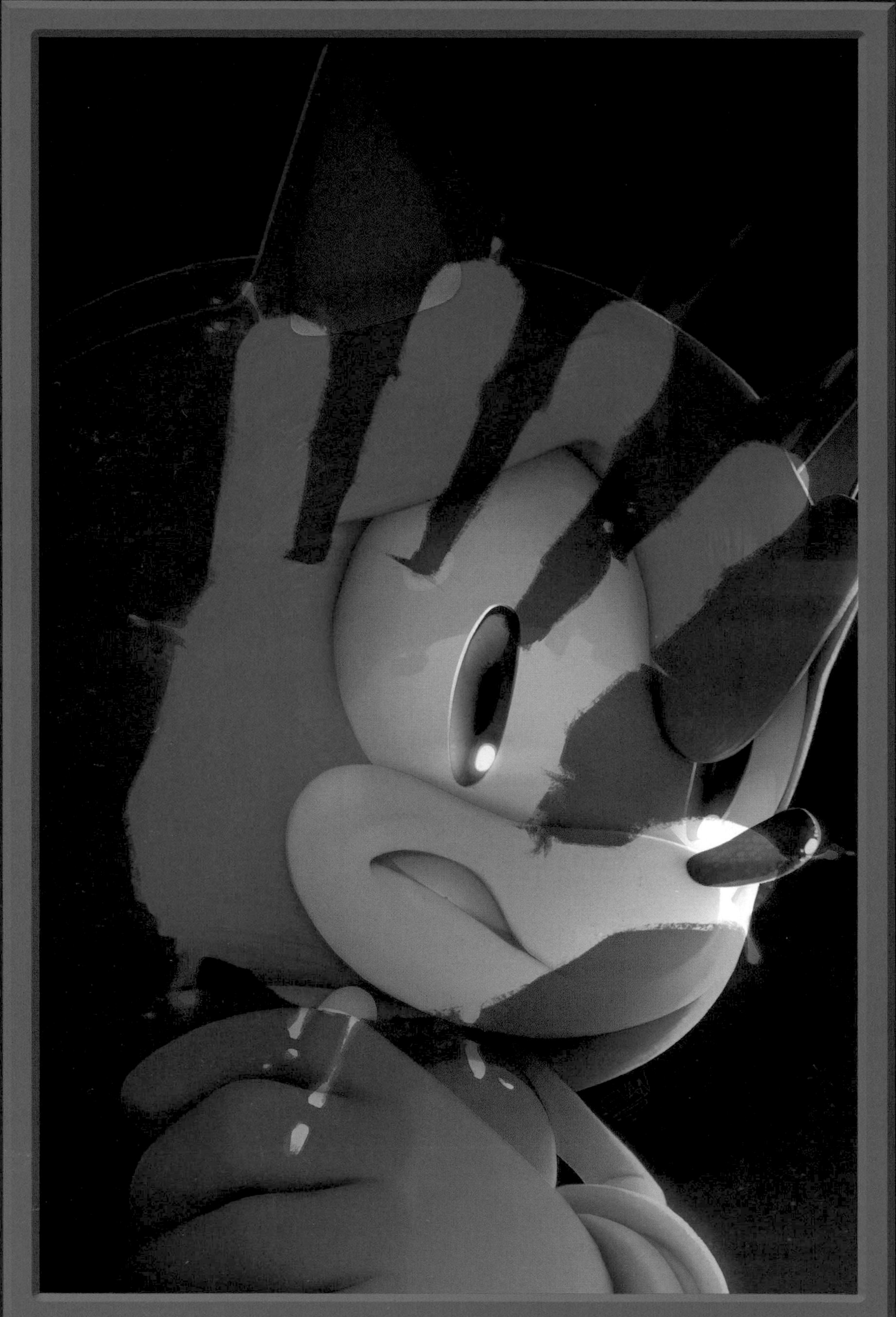

ART BY **EVAN STANLEY**

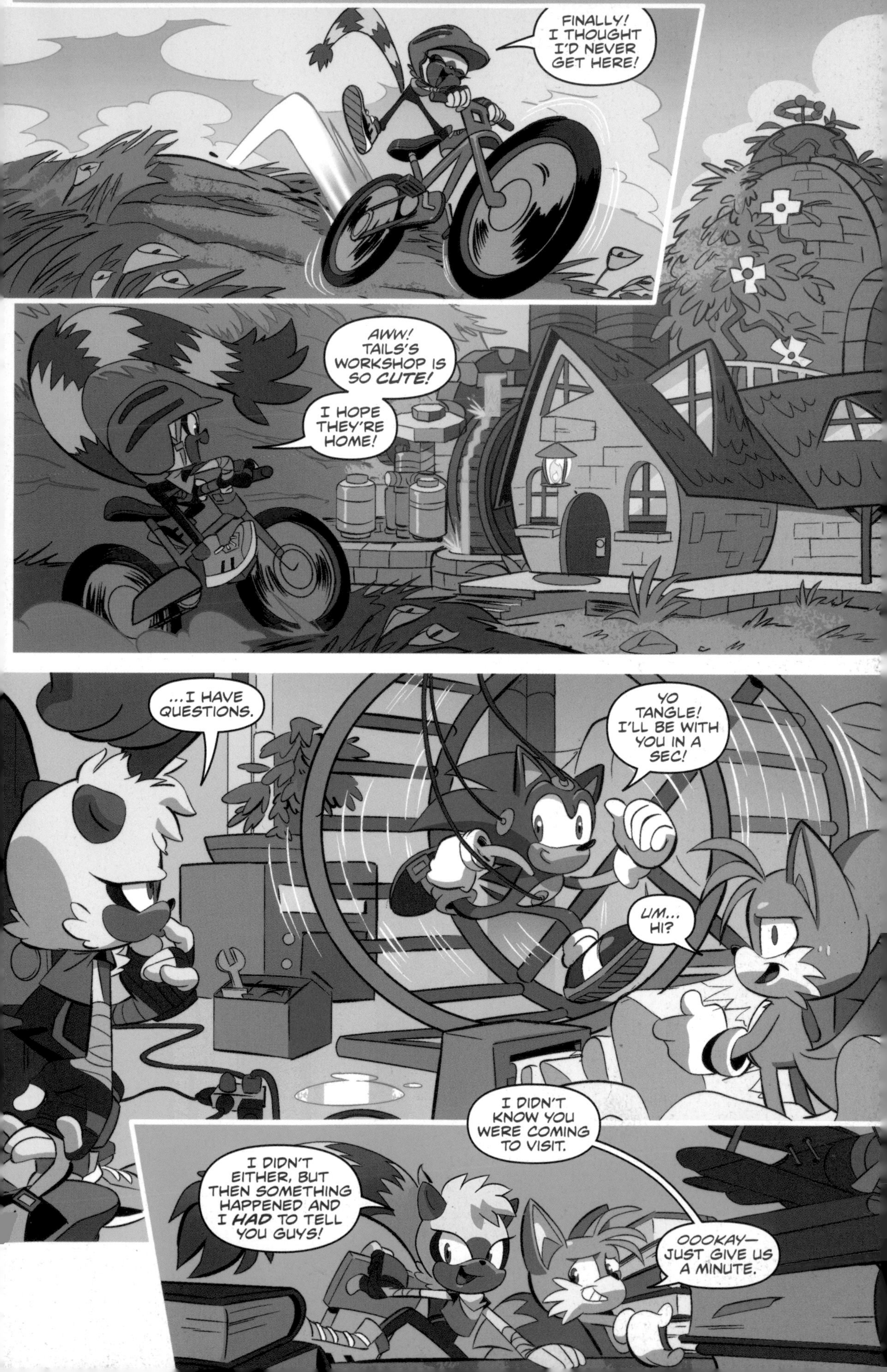
FINALLY! I THOUGHT I'D NEVER GET HERE!
AWW! TAILS'S WORKSHOP IS SO CUTE!
I HOPE THEY'RE HOME!
...I HAVE QUESTIONS.
YO TANGLE! I'LL BE WITH YOU IN A SEC!
UM... HI?
I DIDN'T KNOW YOU WERE COMING TO VISIT.
I DIDN'T EITHER, BUT THEN SOMETHING HAPPENED AND I HAD TO TELL YOU GUYS!
OOOKAY— JUST GIVE US A MINUTE.

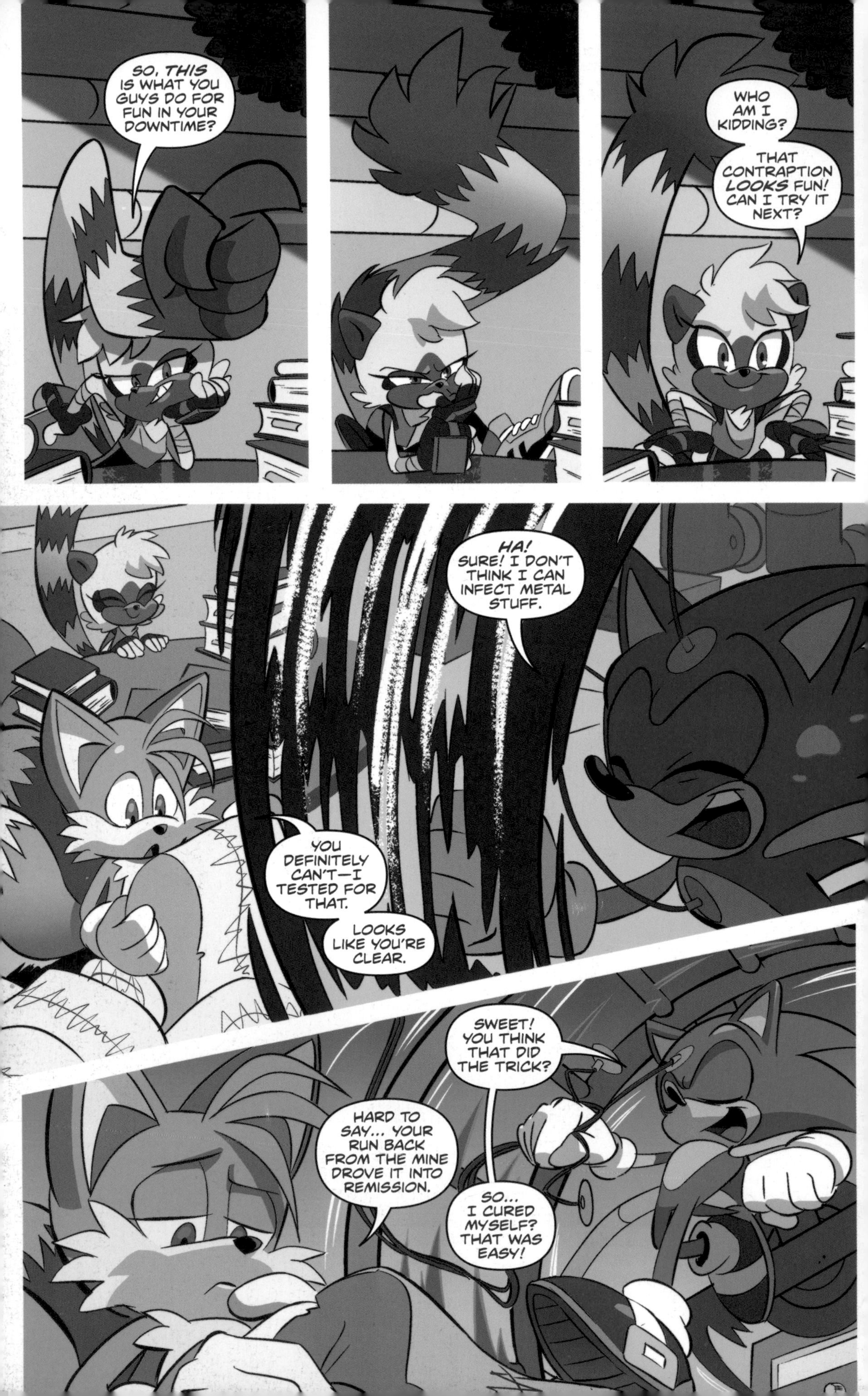

SO, THIS IS WHAT YOU GUYS DO FOR FUN IN YOUR DOWNTIME?
WHO AM I KIDDING?
THAT CONTRAPTION LOOKS FUN! CAN I TRY IT NEXT?
HA! SURE! I DON'T THINK I CAN INFECT METAL STUFF.
YOU DEFINITELY CAN'T—I TESTED FOR THAT.
LOOKS LIKE YOU'RE CLEAR.
SWEET! YOU THINK THAT DID THE TRICK?
HARD TO SAY... YOUR RUN BACK FROM THE MINE DROVE IT INTO REMISSION.
SO... I CURED MYSELF? THAT WAS EASY!

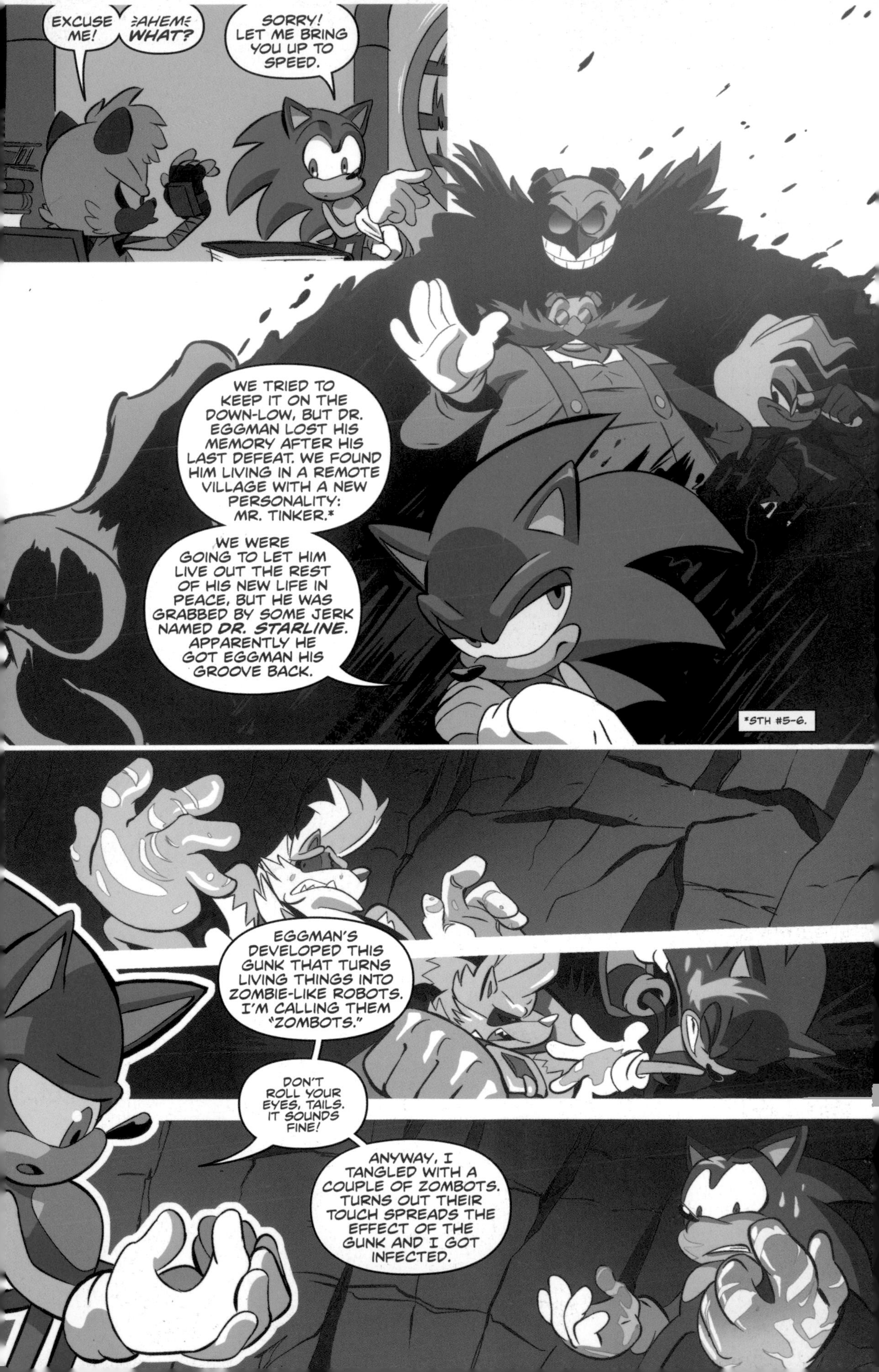
EXCUSE ME!
AHEM WHAT?
SORRY! LET ME BRING YOU UP TO SPEED.
WE TRIED TO KEEP IT ON THE DOWN-LOW, BUT DR. EGGMAN LOST HIS MEMORY AFTER HIS LAST DEFEAT. WE FOUND HIM LIVING IN A REMOTE VILLAGE WITH A NEW PERSONALITY: MR. TINKER.*
WE WERE GOING TO LET HIM LIVE OUT THE REST OF HIS NEW LIFE IN PEACE, BUT HE WAS GRABBED BY SOME JERK NAMED DR. STARLINE. APPARENTLY HE GOT EGGMAN HIS GROOVE BACK.
*STH #5-6.
EGGMAN'S DEVELOPED THIS GUNK THAT TURNS LIVING THINGS INTO ZOMBIE-LIKE ROBOTS. I'M CALLING THEM "ZOMBOTS."
DON'T ROLL YOUR EYES, TAILS. IT SOUNDS FINE!
ANYWAY, I TANGLED WITH A COUPLE OF ZOMBOTS. TURNS OUT THEIR TOUCH SPREADS THE EFFECT OF THE GUNK AND I GOT INFECTED.

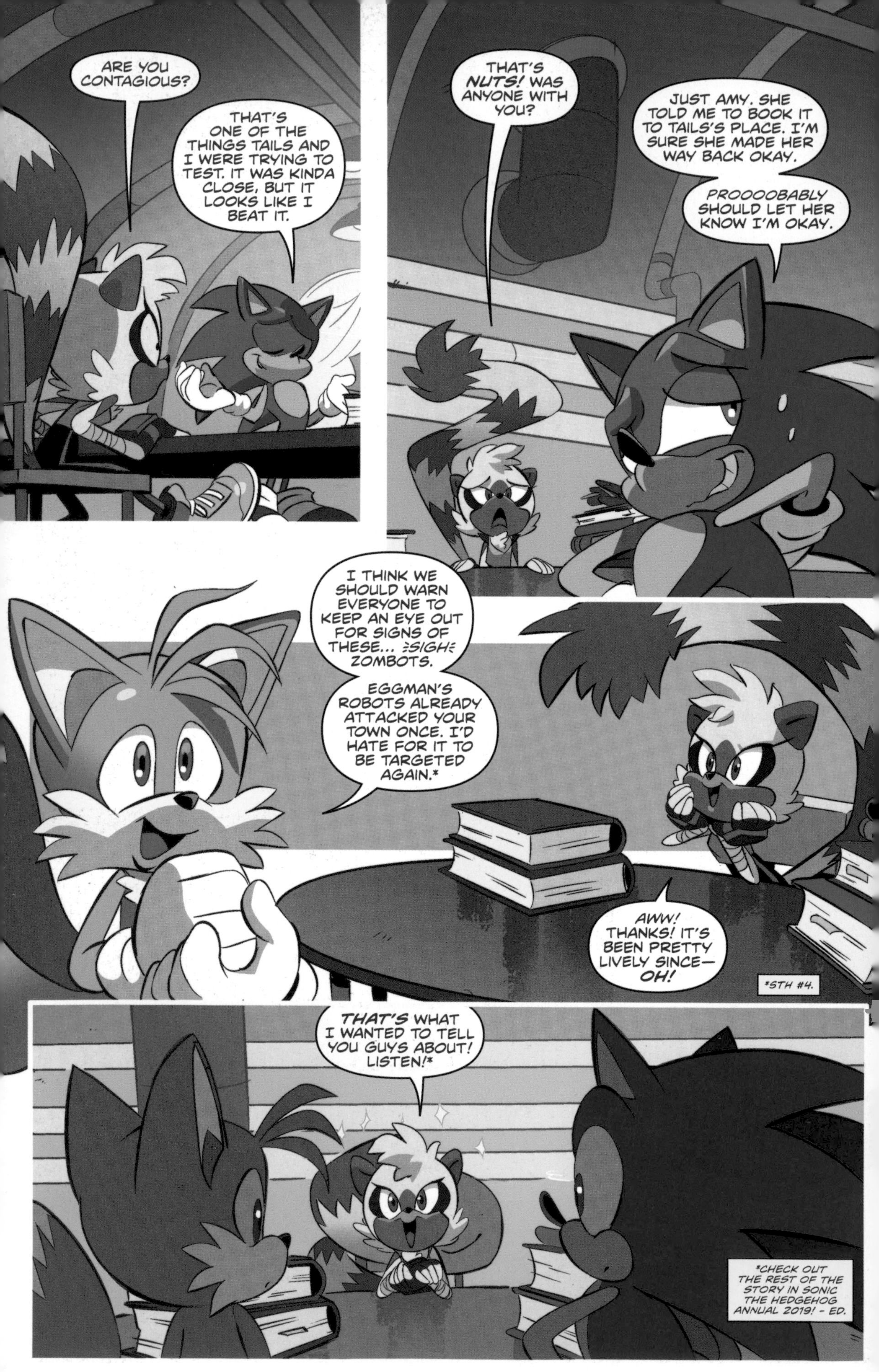
ARE YOU CONTAGIOUS?
THAT'S ONE OF THE THINGS TAILS AND I WERE TRYING TO TEST. IT WAS KINDA CLOSE, BUT IT LOOKS LIKE I BEAT IT.
THAT'S NUTS! WAS ANYONE WITH YOU?
JUST AMY. SHE TOLD ME TO BOOK IT TO TAILS'S PLACE. I'M SURE SHE MADE HER WAY BACK OKAY.
PROOOOBABLY SHOULD LET HER KNOW I'M OKAY.
I THINK WE SHOULD WARN EVERYONE TO KEEP AN EYE OUT FOR SIGNS OF THESE... SIGH ZOMBOTS.
EGGMAN'S ROBOTS ALREADY ATTACKED YOUR TOWN ONCE. I'D HATE FOR IT TO BE TARGETED AGAIN.*
AWW! THANKS! IT'S BEEN PRETTY LIVELY SINCE— OH!
*STH #4.
THAT'S WHAT I WANTED TO TELL YOU GUYS ABOUT! LISTEN!*
*CHECK OUT THE REST OF THE STORY IN SONIC THE HEDGEHOG ANNUAL 2019! - ED.

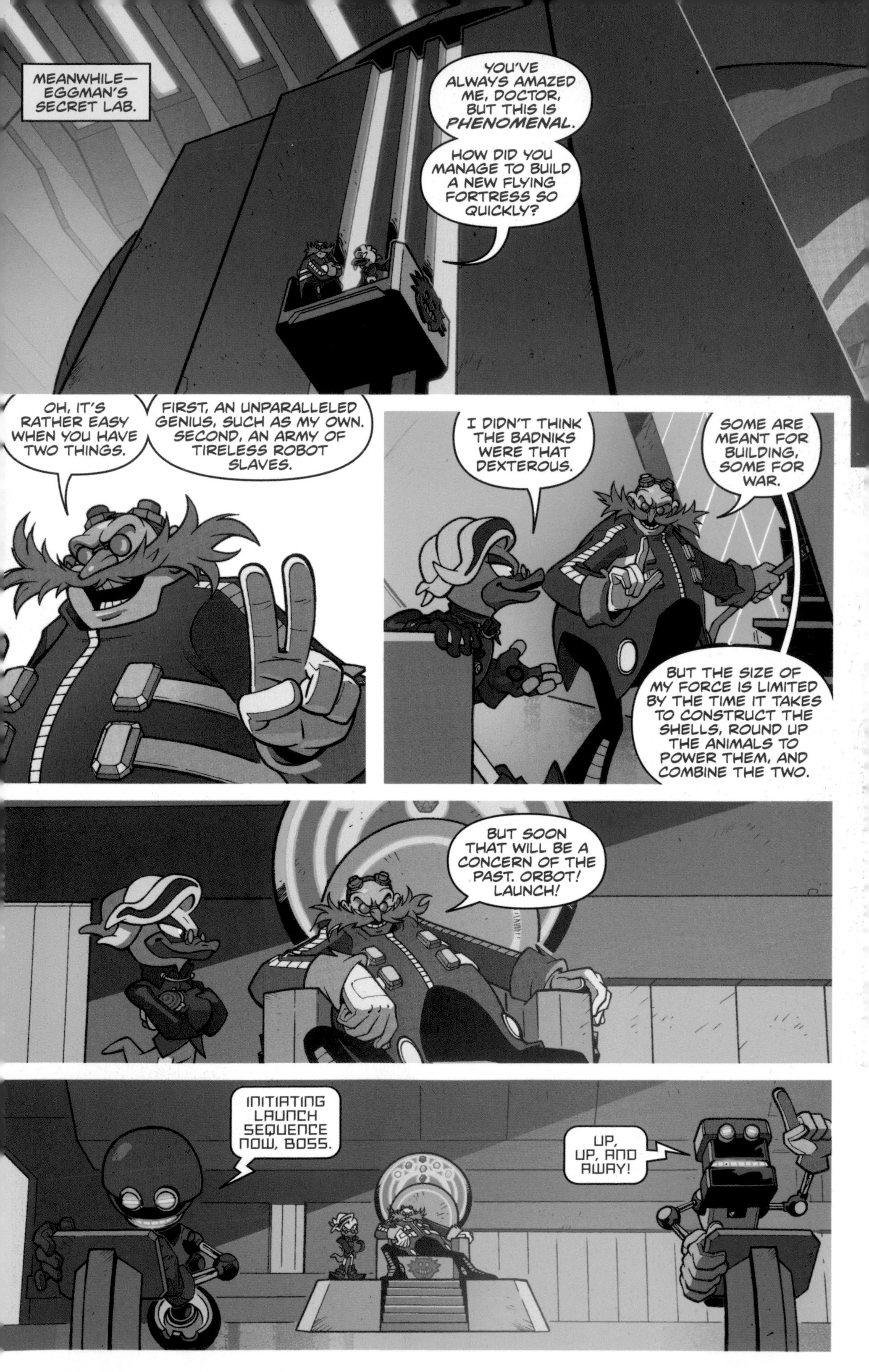
MEANWHILE— EGGMAN'S SECRET LAB.
YOU'VE ALWAYS AMAZED ME, DOCTOR, BUT THIS IS PHENOMENAL.
HOW DID YOU MANAGE TO BUILD A NEW FLYING FORTRESS SO QUICKLY?
OH, IT'S RATHER EASY WHEN YOU HAVE TWO THINGS.
FIRST, AN UNPARALLELED GENIUS, SUCH AS MY OWN. SECOND, AN ARMY OF TIRELESS ROBOT SLAVES.
I DIDN'T THINK THE BADNIKS WERE THAT DEXTEROUS.
SOME ARE MEANT FOR BUILDING, SOME FOR WAR.
BUT THE SIZE OF MY FORCE IS LIMITED BY THE TIME IT TAKES TO CONSTRUCT THE SHELLS, ROUND UP THE ANIMALS TO POWER THEM, AND COMBINE THE TWO.
BUT SOON THAT WILL BE A CONCERN OF THE PAST. ORBOT! LAUNCH!
INITIATING LAUNCH SEQUENCE NOW, BOSS.
UP, UP, AND AWAY!

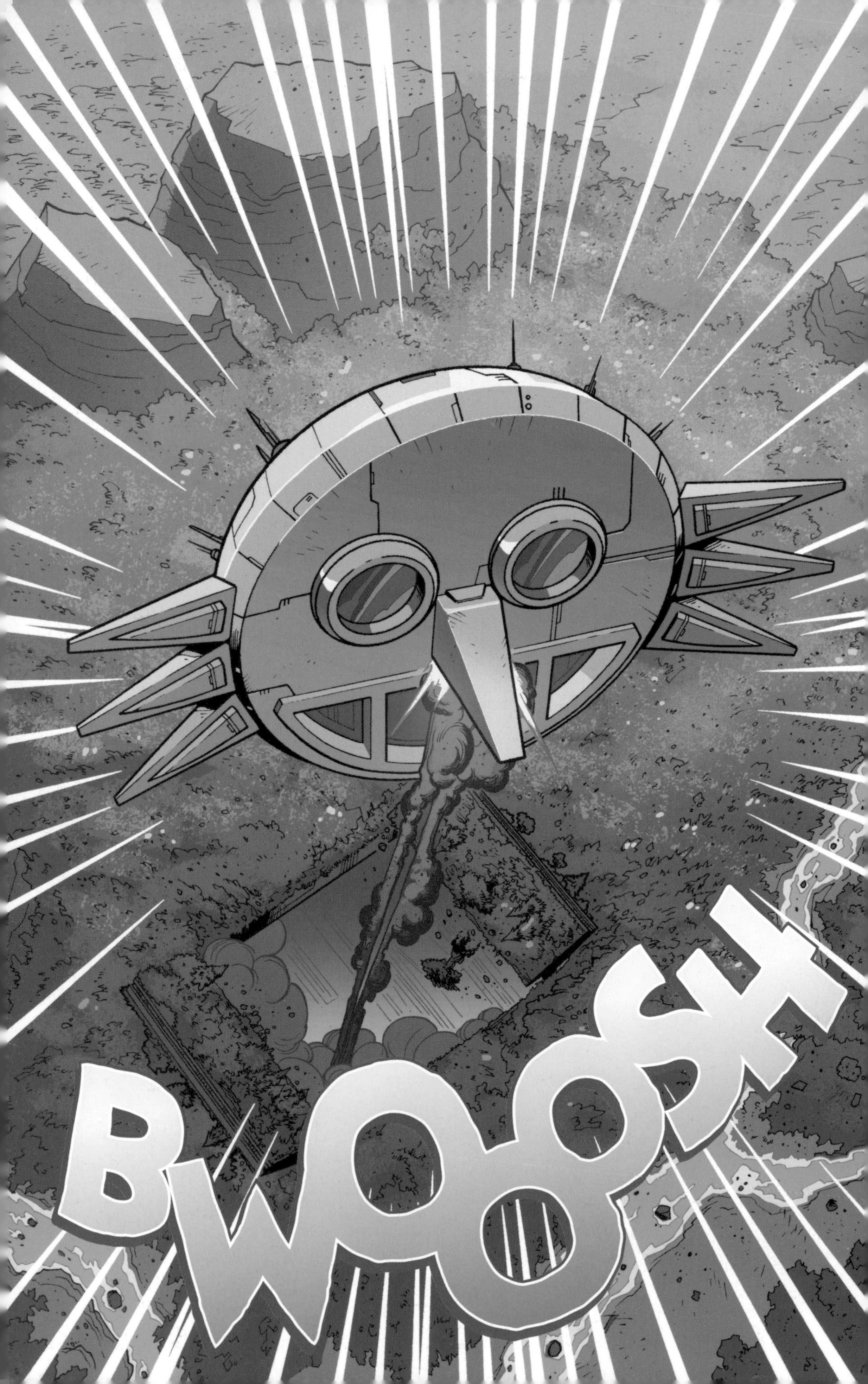
BWOOSH

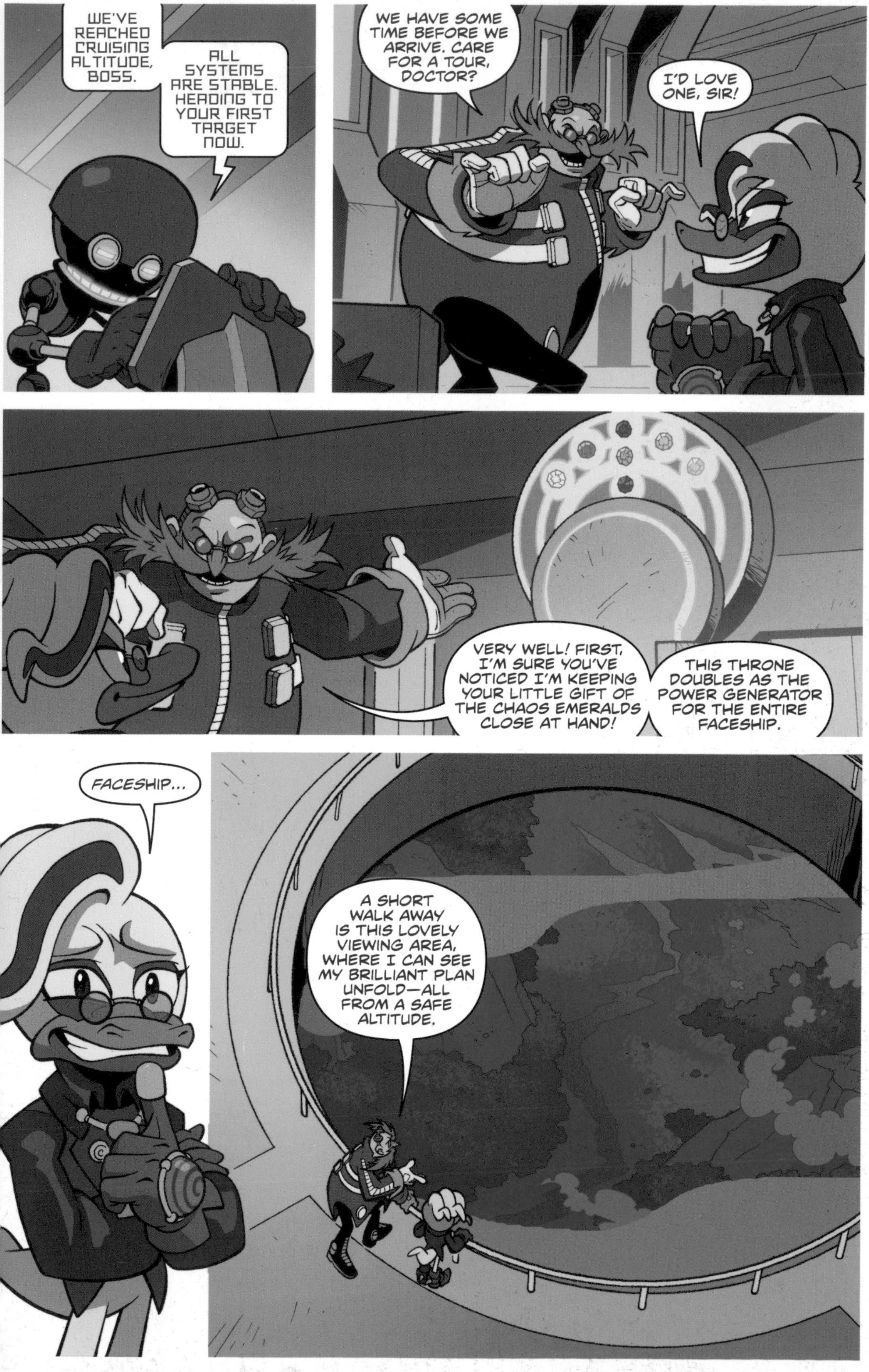
WE'VE REACHED CRUISING ALTITUDE, BOSS.
ALL SYSTEMS ARE STABLE. HEADING TO YOUR FIRST TARGET NOW.
WE HAVE SOME TIME BEFORE WE ARRIVE. CARE FOR A TOUR, DOCTOR?
I'D LOVE ONE, SIR!
VERY WELL! FIRST, I'M SURE YOU'VE NOTICED I'M KEEPING YOUR LITTLE GIFT OF THE CHAOS EMERALDS CLOSE AT HAND!
THIS THRONE DOUBLES AS THE POWER GENERATOR FOR THE ENTIRE FACESHIP.
FACESHIP...
A SHORT WALK AWAY IS THIS LOVELY VIEWING AREA, WHERE I CAN SEE MY BRILLIANT PLAN UNFOLD—ALL FROM A SAFE ALTITUDE.

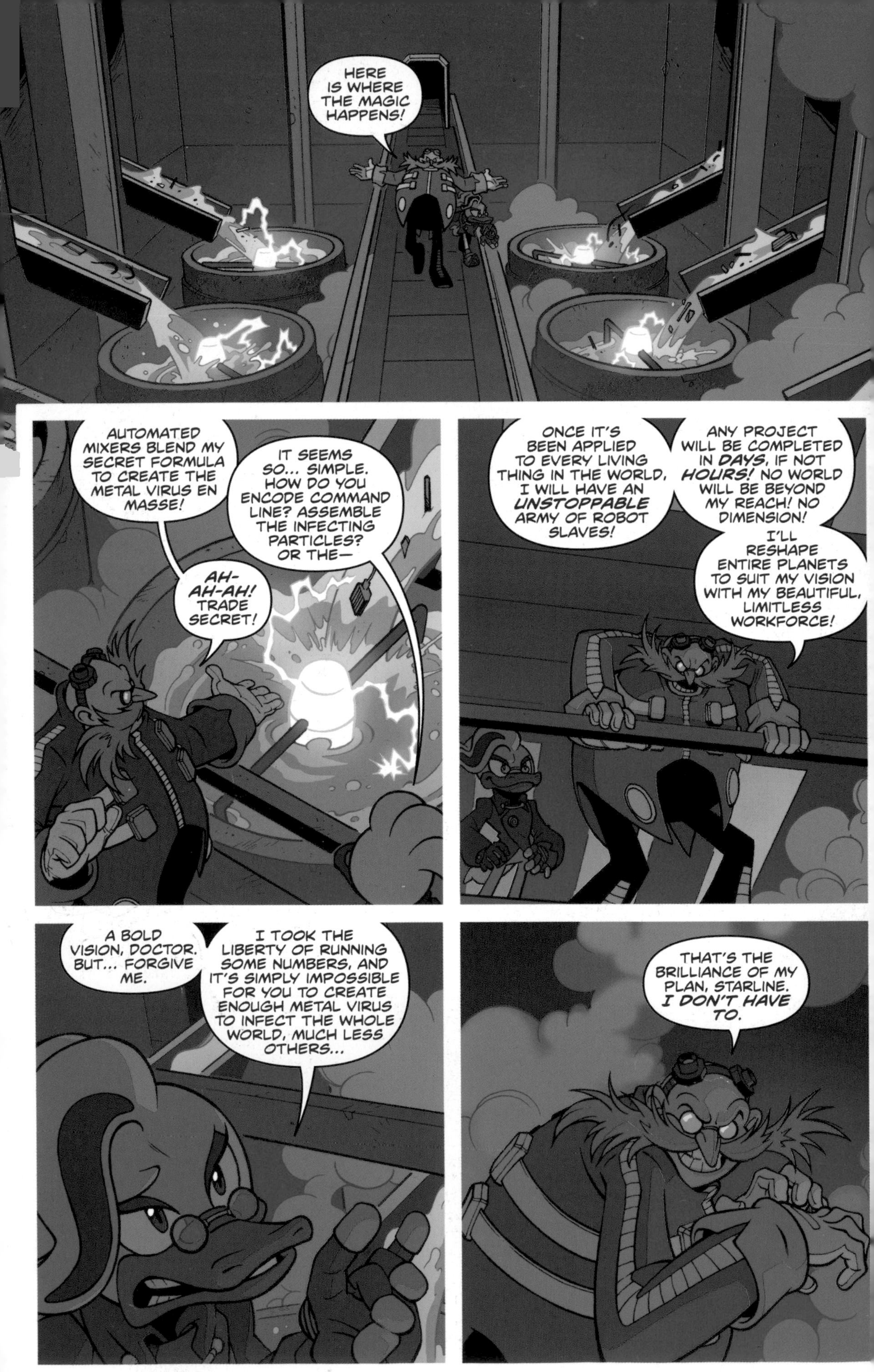
HERE IS WHERE THE MAGIC HAPPENS!
AUTOMATED MIXERS BLEND MY SECRET FORMULA TO CREATE THE METAL VIRUS EN MASSE!
IT SEEMS SO... SIMPLE. HOW DO YOU ENCODE COMMAND LINE? ASSEMBLE THE INFECTING PARTICLES? OR THE—
AH-AH-AH! TRADE SECRET!
ONCE IT'S BEEN APPLIED TO EVERY LIVING THING IN THE WORLD, I WILL HAVE AN UNSTOPPABLE ARMY OF ROBOT SLAVES!
ANY PROJECT WILL BE COMPLETED IN DAYS, IF NOT HOURS! NO WORLD WILL BE BEYOND MY REACH! NO DIMENSION!
I'LL RESHAPE ENTIRE PLANETS TO SUIT MY VISION WITH MY BEAUTIFUL, LIMITLESS WORKFORCE!
A BOLD VISION, DOCTOR. BUT... FORGIVE ME.
I TOOK THE LIBERTY OF RUNNING SOME NUMBERS, AND IT'S SIMPLY IMPOSSIBLE FOR YOU TO CREATE ENOUGH METAL VIRUS TO INFECT THE WHOLE WORLD, MUCH LESS OTHERS...
THAT'S THE BRILLIANCE OF MY PLAN, STARLINE. I DON'T HAVE TO.

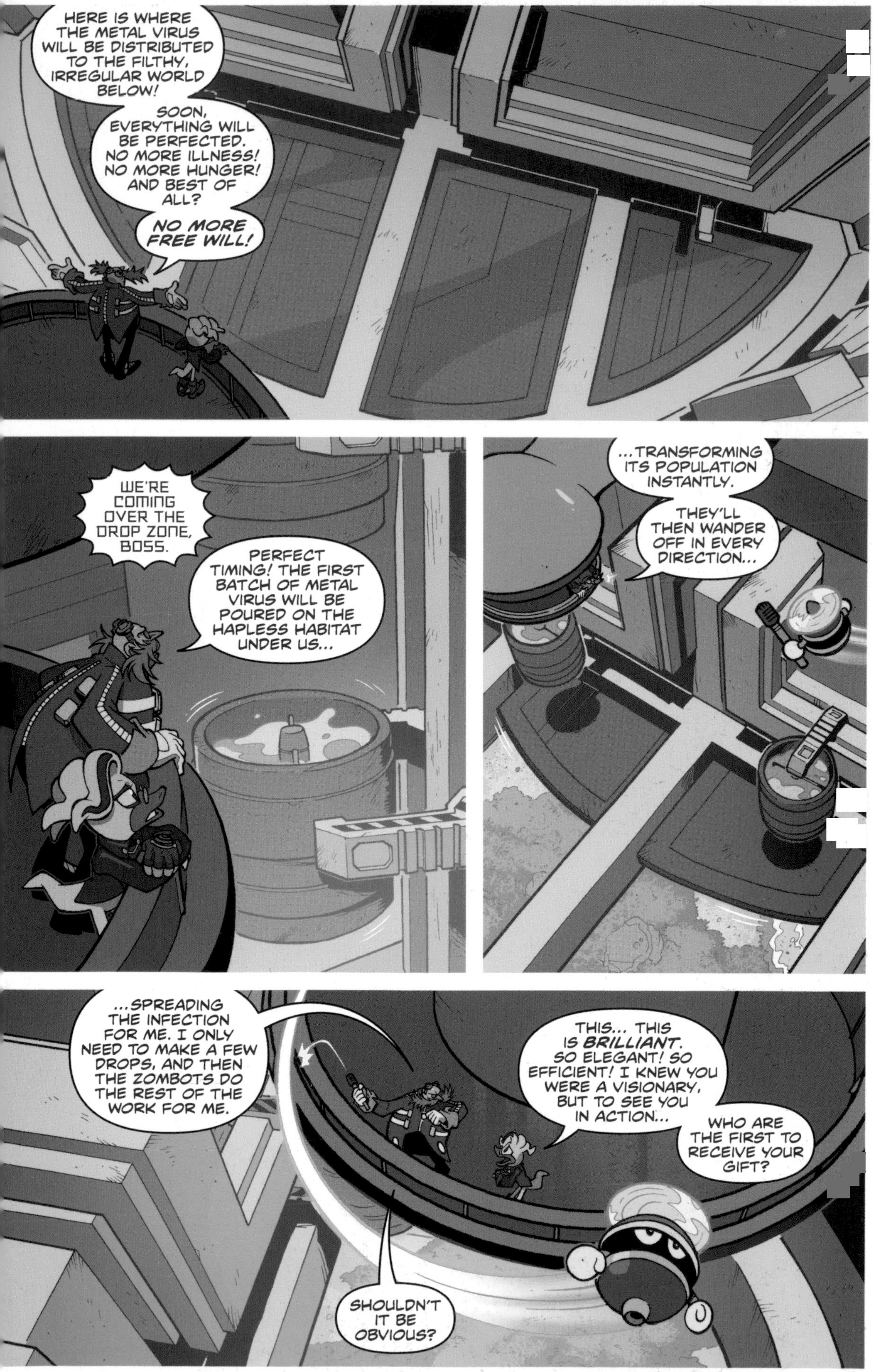
HERE IS WHERE THE METAL VIRUS WILL BE DISTRIBUTED TO THE FILTHY, IRREGULAR WORLD BELOW!
SOON, EVERYTHING WILL BE PERFECTED. NO MORE ILLNESS! NO MORE HUNGER! AND BEST OF ALL?
NO MORE FREE WILL!
WE'RE COMING OVER THE DROP ZONE, BOSS.
PERFECT TIMING! THE FIRST BATCH OF METAL VIRUS WILL BE POURED ON THE HAPLESS HABITAT UNDER US...
...TRANSFORMING ITS POPULATION INSTANTLY.
THEY'LL THEN WANDER OFF IN EVERY DIRECTION...
...SPREADING THE INFECTION FOR ME. I ONLY NEED TO MAKE A FEW DROPS, AND THEN THE ZOMBOTS DO THE REST OF THE WORK FOR ME.
THIS... THIS IS BRILLIANT. SO ELEGANT! SO EFFICIENT! I KNEW YOU WERE A VISIONARY, BUT TO SEE YOU IN ACTION...
WHO ARE THE FIRST TO RECEIVE YOUR GIFT?
SHOULDN'T IT BE OBVIOUS?

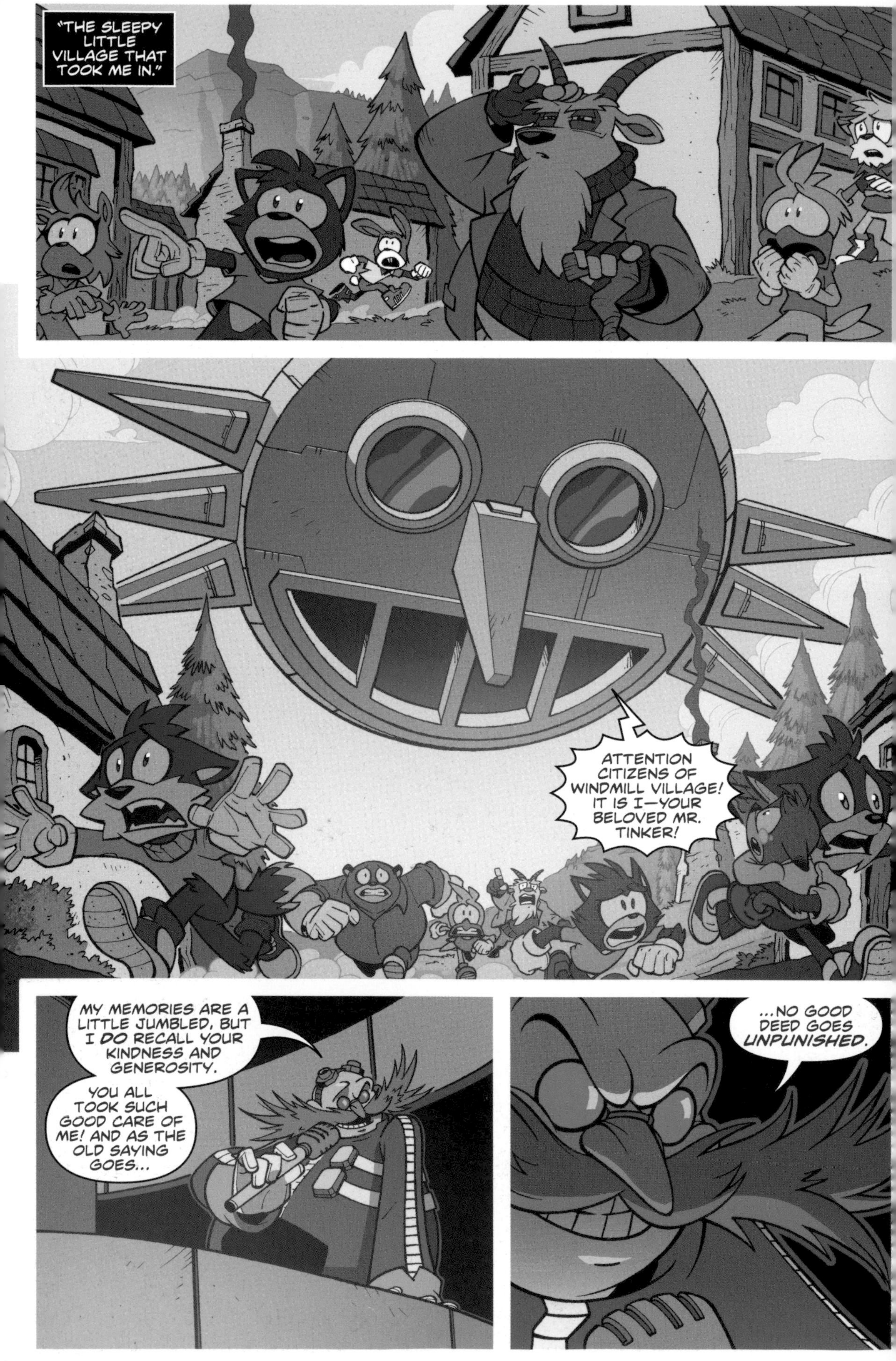
"THE SLEEPY LITTLE VILLAGE THAT TOOK ME IN."
ATTENTION CITIZENS OF WINDMILL VILLAGE! IT IS I—YOUR BELOVED MR. TINKER!
MY MEMORIES ARE A LITTLE JUMBLED, BUT I *DO* RECALL YOUR KINDNESS AND GENEROSITY.
YOU ALL TOOK SUCH GOOD CARE OF ME! AND AS THE OLD SAYING GOES...
...NO GOOD DEED GOES ***UNPUNISHED.***

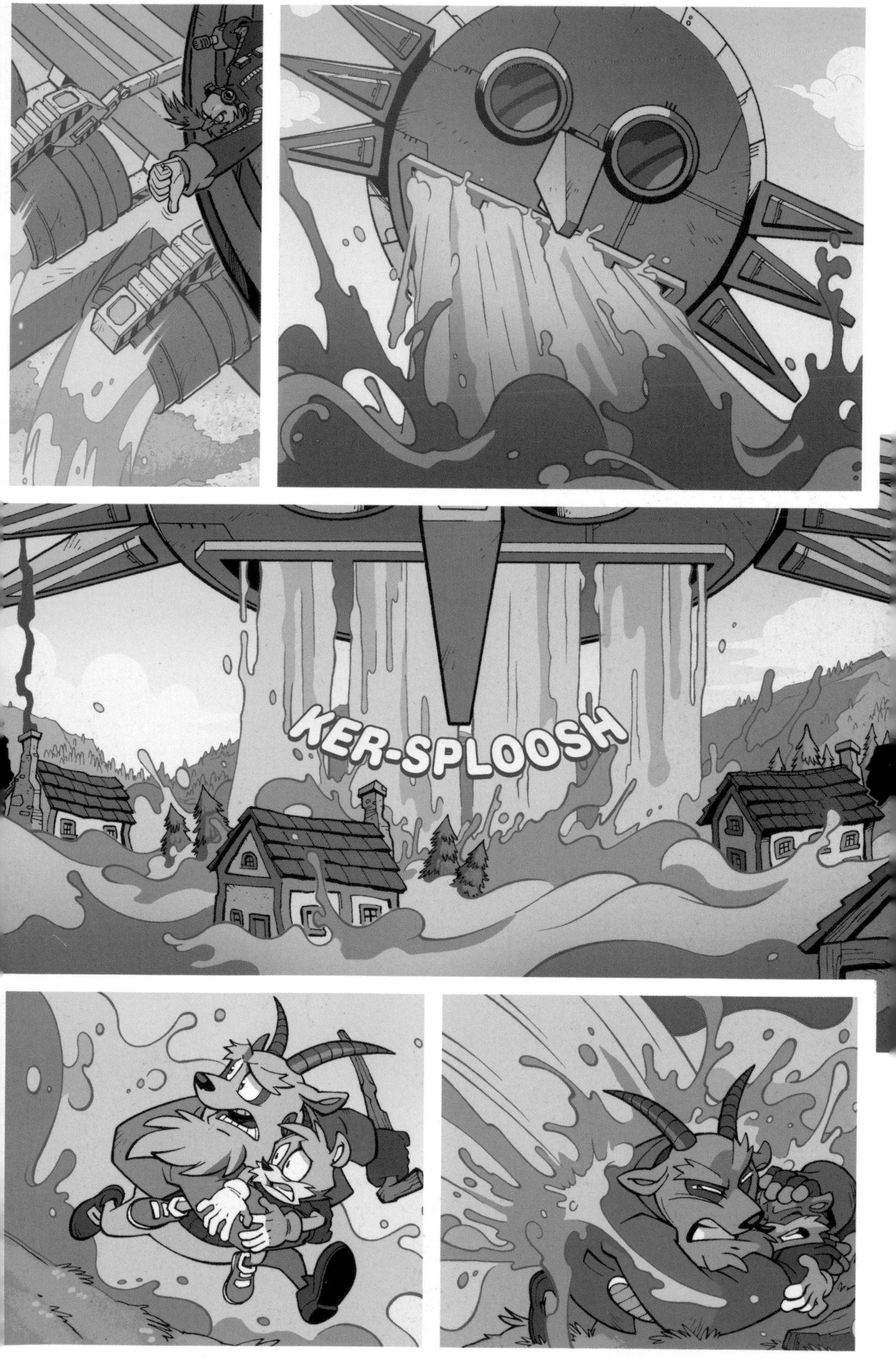
KER-SPLOOSH

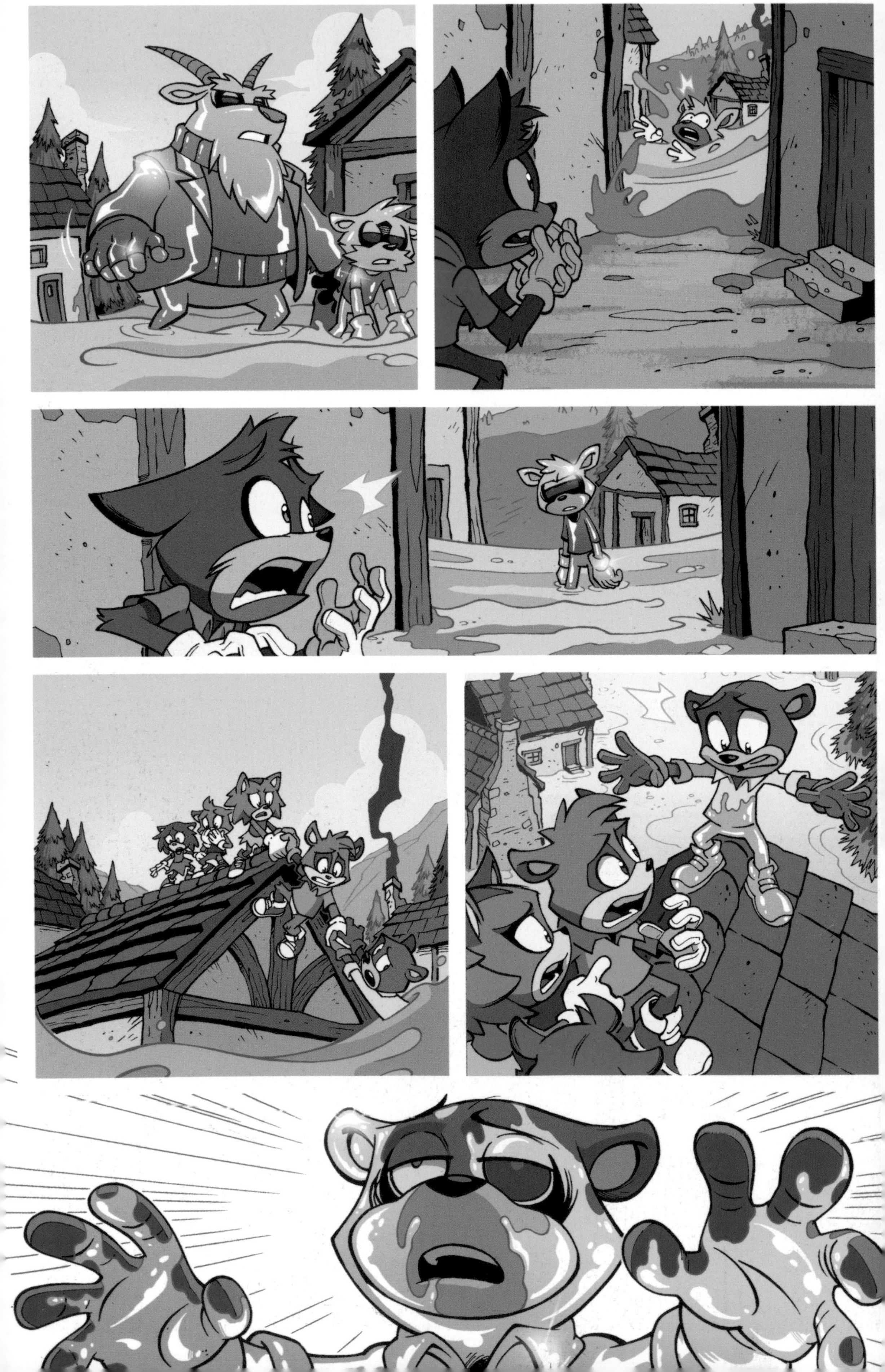

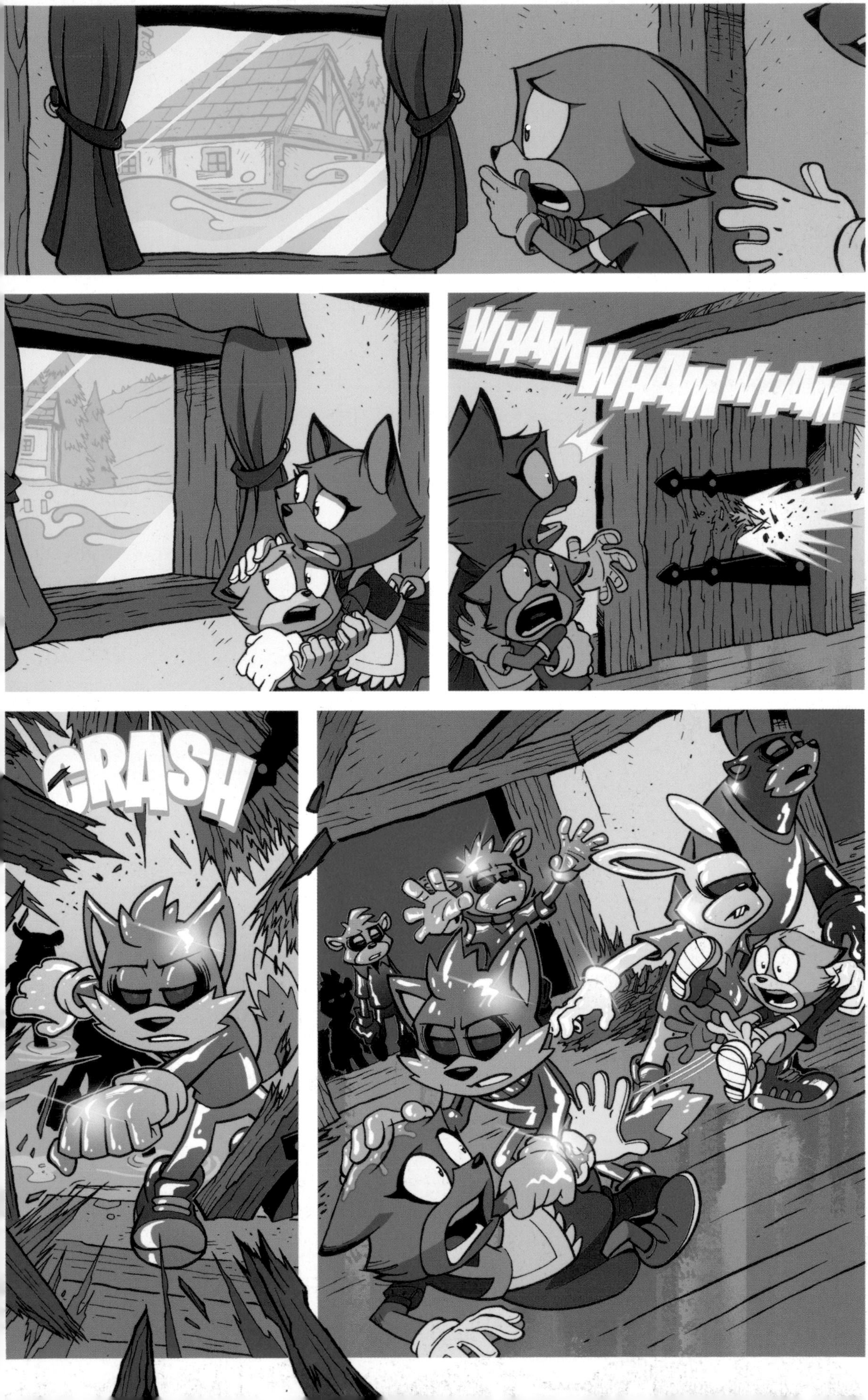
WHAM WHAM WHAM
CRASH

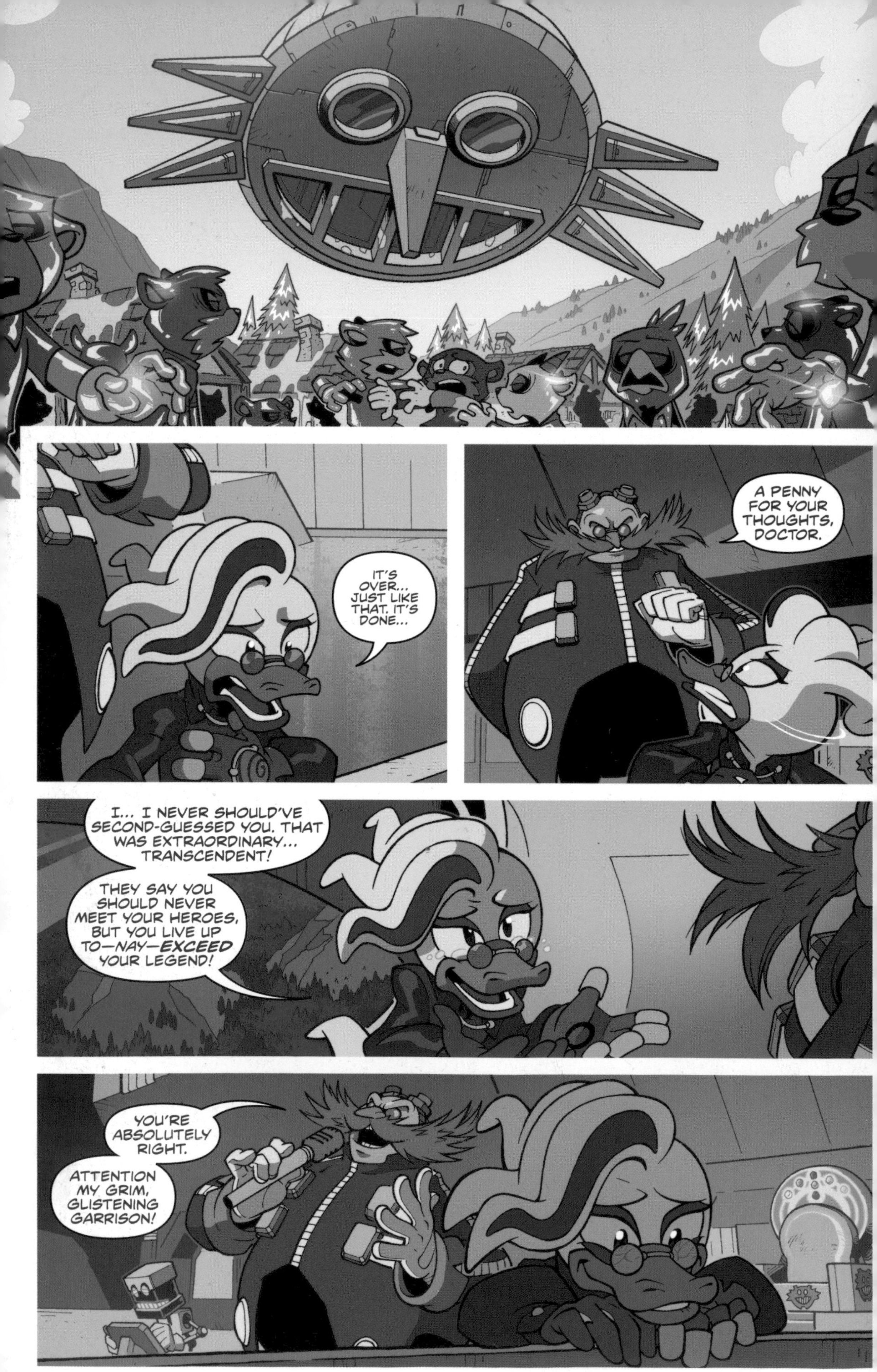
IT'S OVER... JUST LIKE THAT. IT'S DONE...
A PENNY FOR YOUR THOUGHTS, DOCTOR.
I... I NEVER SHOULD'VE SECOND-GUESSED YOU. THAT WAS EXTRAORDINARY... TRANSCENDENT!
THEY SAY YOU SHOULD NEVER MEET YOUR HEROES, BUT YOU LIVE UP TO—NAY—EXCEED YOUR LEGEND!
YOU'RE ABSOLUTELY RIGHT.
ATTENTION MY GRIM, GLISTENING GARRISON!

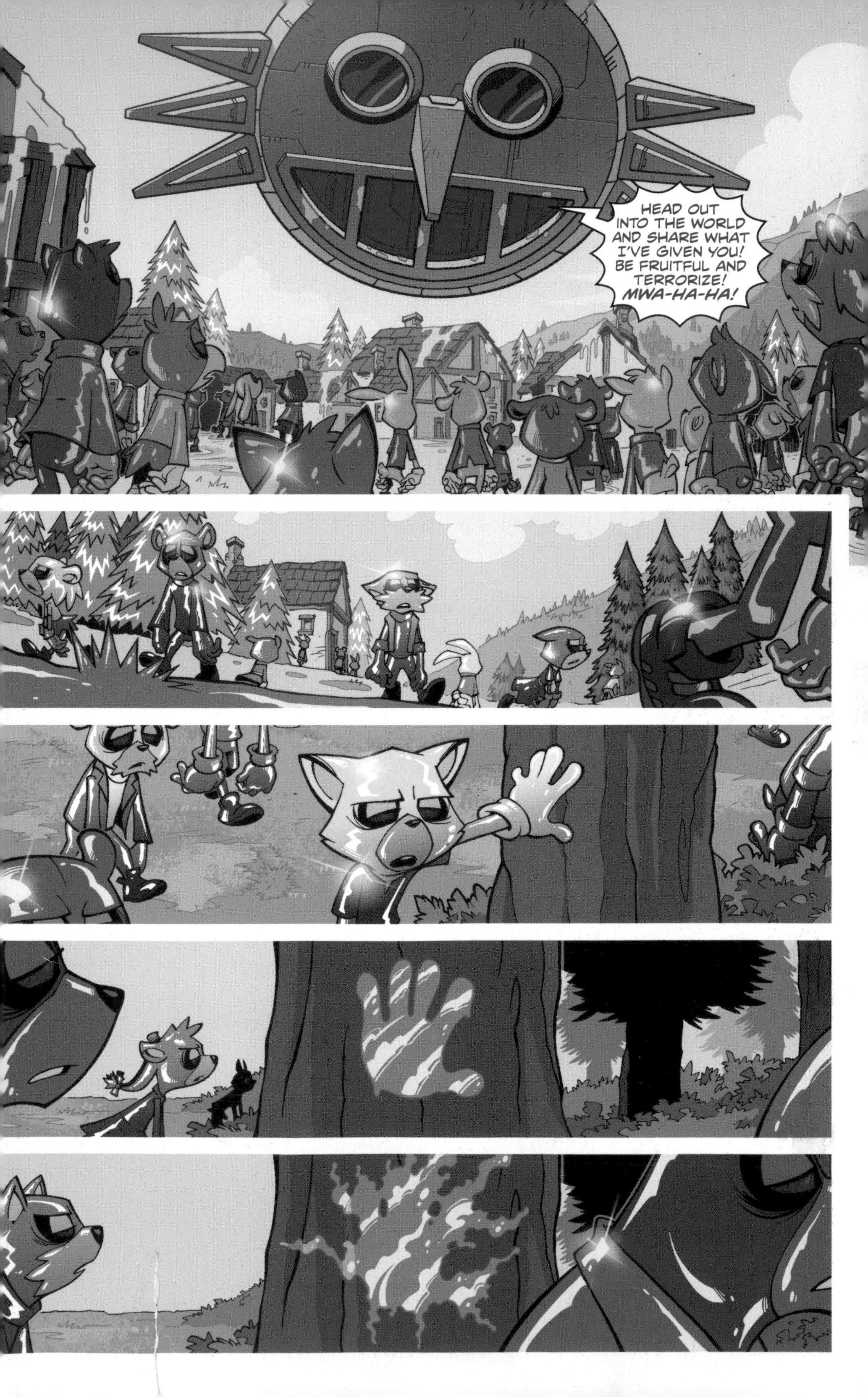
HEAD OUT INTO THE WORLD AND SHARE WHAT I'VE GIVEN YOU! BE FRUITFUL AND TERRORIZE! MWA-HA-HA!

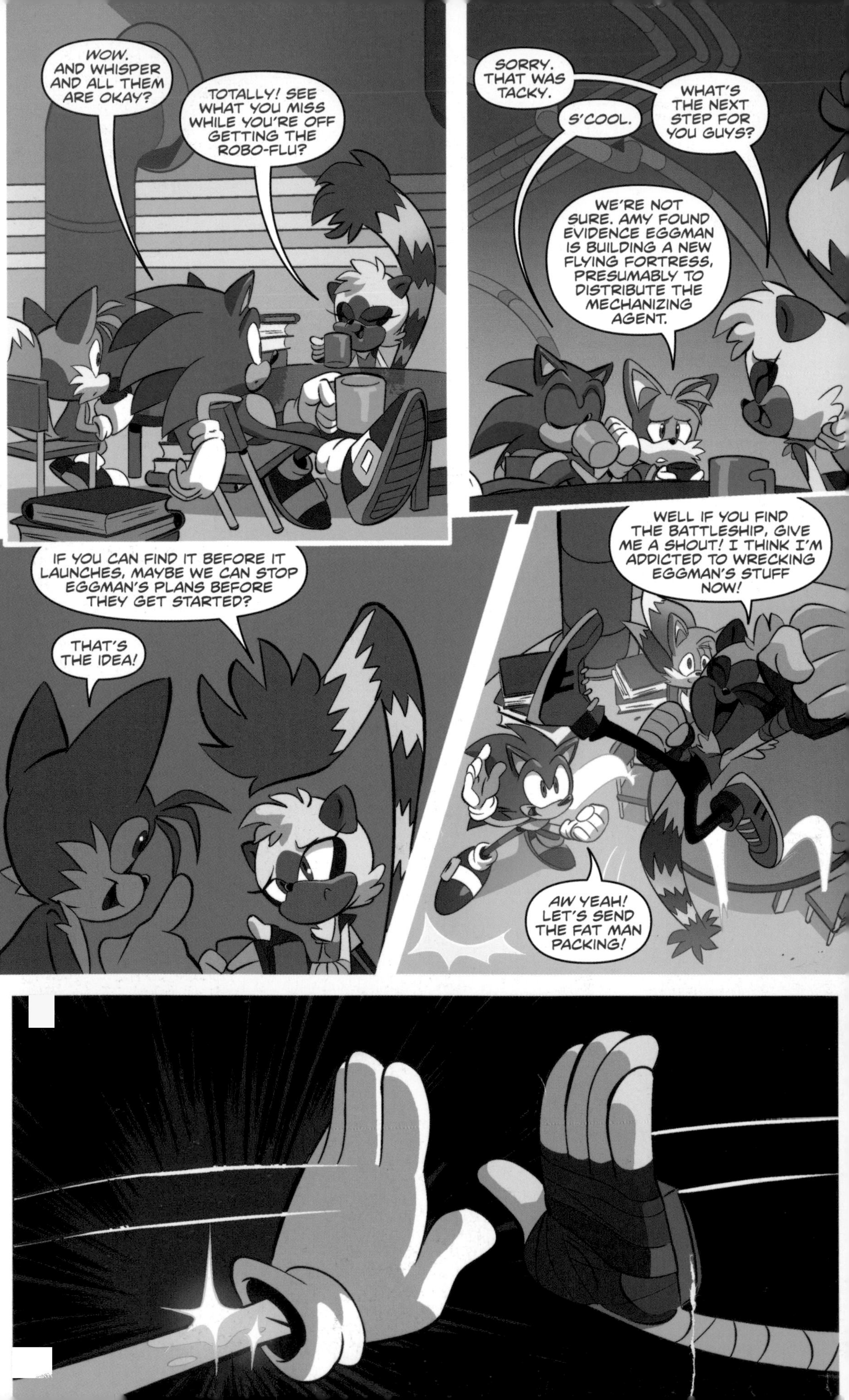
WOW. AND WHISPER AND ALL THEM ARE OKAY?
TOTALLY! SEE WHAT YOU MISS WHILE YOU'RE OFF GETTING THE ROBO-FLU?
SORRY. THAT WAS TACKY.
S'COOL.
WHAT'S THE NEXT STEP FOR YOU GUYS?
WE'RE NOT SURE. AMY FOUND EVIDENCE EGGMAN IS BUILDING A NEW FLYING FORTRESS, PRESUMABLY TO DISTRIBUTE THE MECHANIZING AGENT.
IF YOU CAN FIND IT BEFORE IT LAUNCHES, MAYBE WE CAN STOP EGGMAN'S PLANS BEFORE THEY GET STARTED?
THAT'S THE IDEA!
WELL IF YOU FIND THE BATTLESHIP, GIVE ME A SHOUT! I THINK I'M ADDICTED TO WRECKING EGGMAN'S STUFF NOW!
AW YEAH! LET'S SEND THE FAT MAN PACKING!

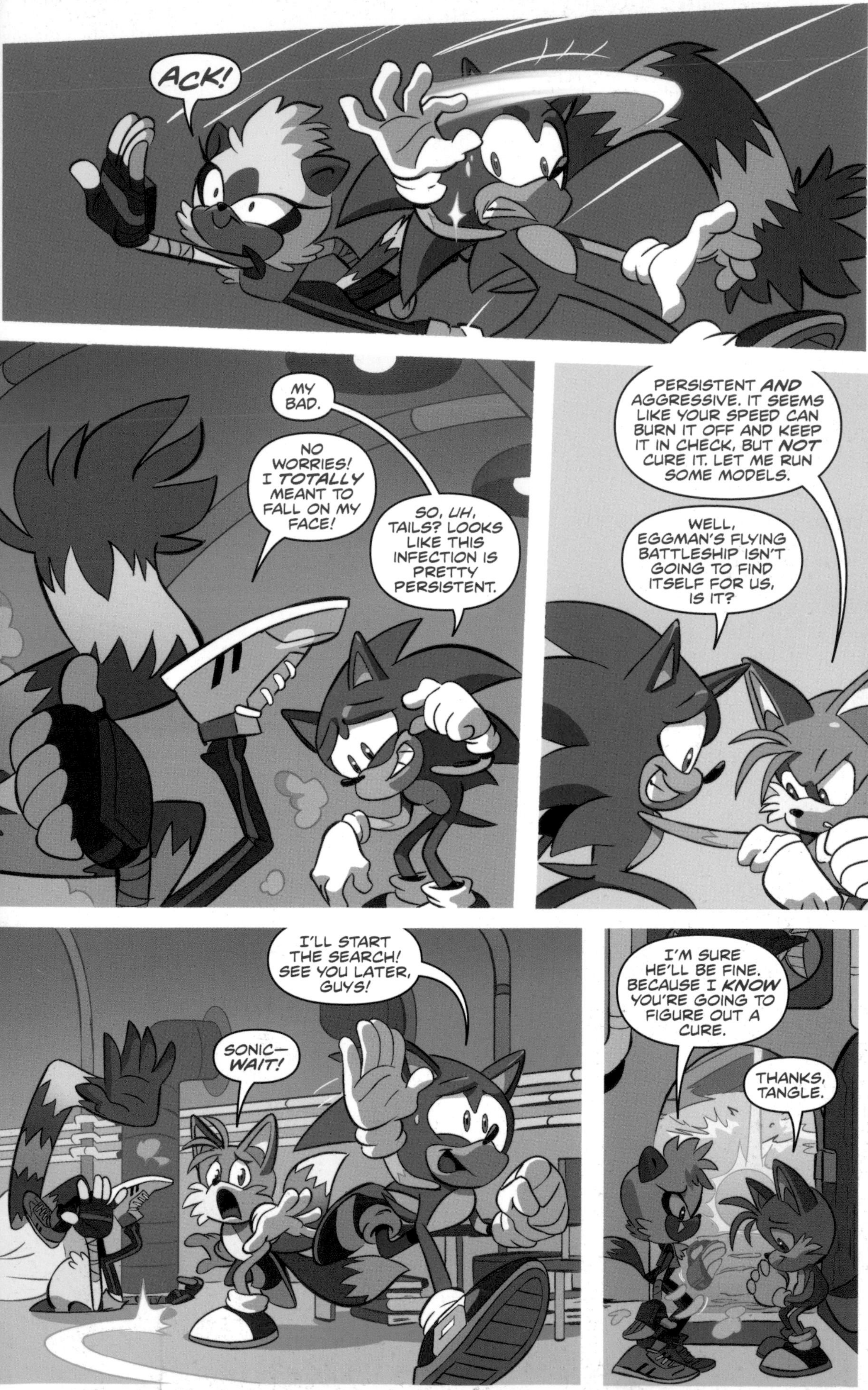
ACK!
MY BAD.
NO WORRIES! I *TOTALLY* MEANT TO FALL ON MY FACE!
SO, UH, TAILS? LOOKS LIKE THIS INFECTION IS PRETTY PERSISTENT.
PERSISTENT *AND* AGGRESSIVE. IT SEEMS LIKE YOUR SPEED CAN BURN IT OFF AND KEEP IT IN CHECK, BUT *NOT* CURE IT. LET ME RUN SOME MODELS.
WELL, EGGMAN'S FLYING BATTLESHIP ISN'T GOING TO FIND ITSELF FOR US, IS IT?
I'LL START THE SEARCH! SEE YOU LATER, GUYS!
SONIC— *WAIT!*
I'M SURE HE'LL BE FINE. BECAUSE I *KNOW* YOU'RE GOING TO FIGURE OUT A CURE.
THANKS, TANGLE.

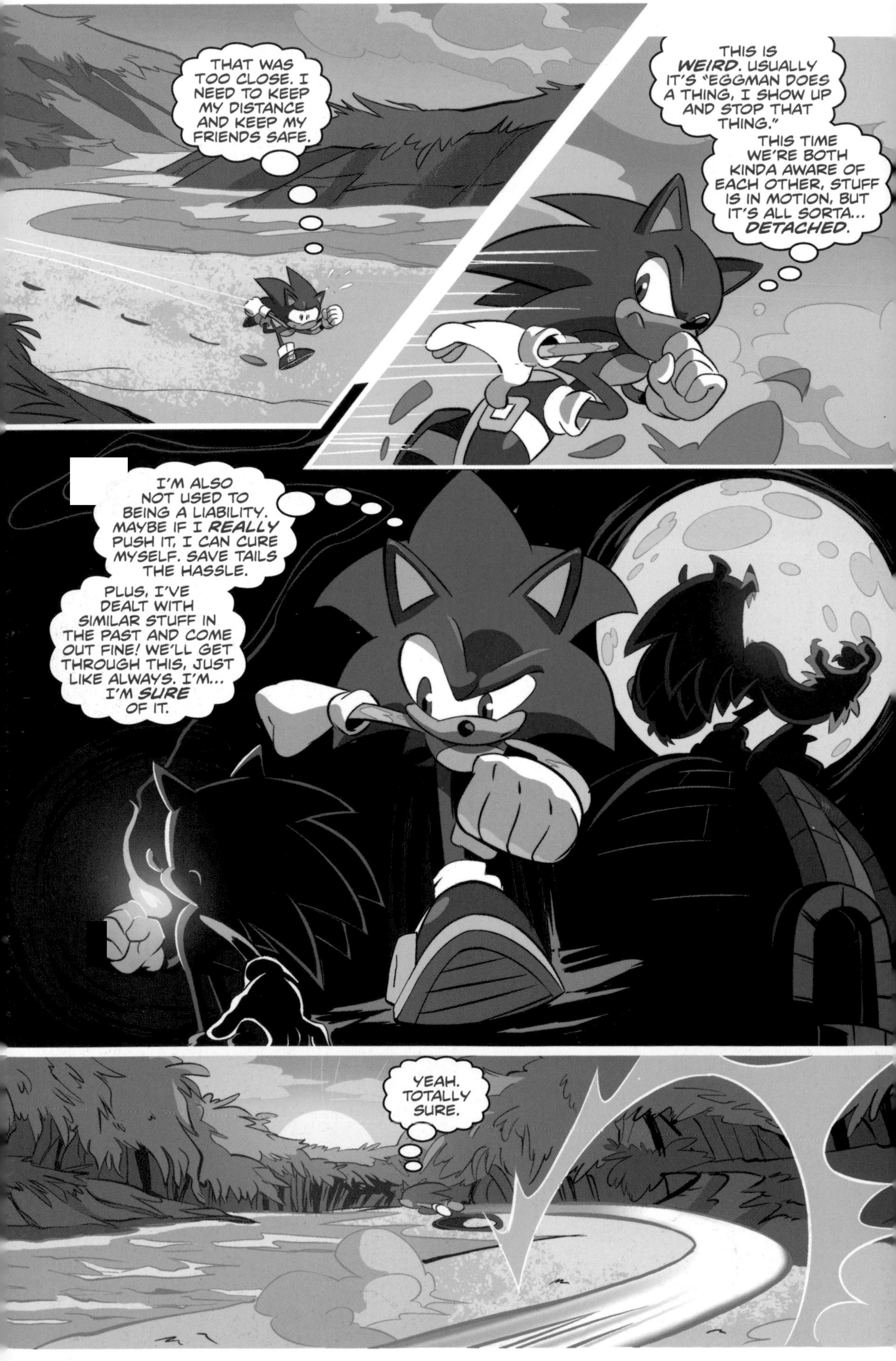
THAT WAS TOO CLOSE. I NEED TO KEEP MY DISTANCE AND KEEP MY FRIENDS SAFE.
THIS IS WEIRD. USUALLY IT'S "EGGMAN DOES A THING, I SHOW UP AND STOP THAT THING."
THIS TIME WE'RE BOTH KINDA AWARE OF EACH OTHER, STUFF IS IN MOTION, BUT IT'S ALL SORTA... DETACHED.
I'M ALSO NOT USED TO BEING A LIABILITY. MAYBE IF I REALLY PUSH IT, I CAN CURE MYSELF. SAVE TAILS THE HASSLE.
PLUS, I'VE DEALT WITH SIMILAR STUFF IN THE PAST AND COME OUT FINE! WE'LL GET THROUGH THIS, JUST LIKE ALWAYS. I'M... I'M SURE OF IT.
YEAH. TOTALLY SURE.

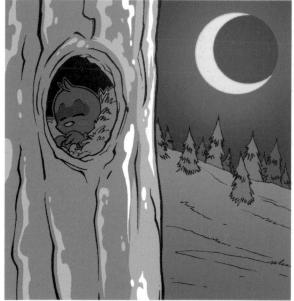

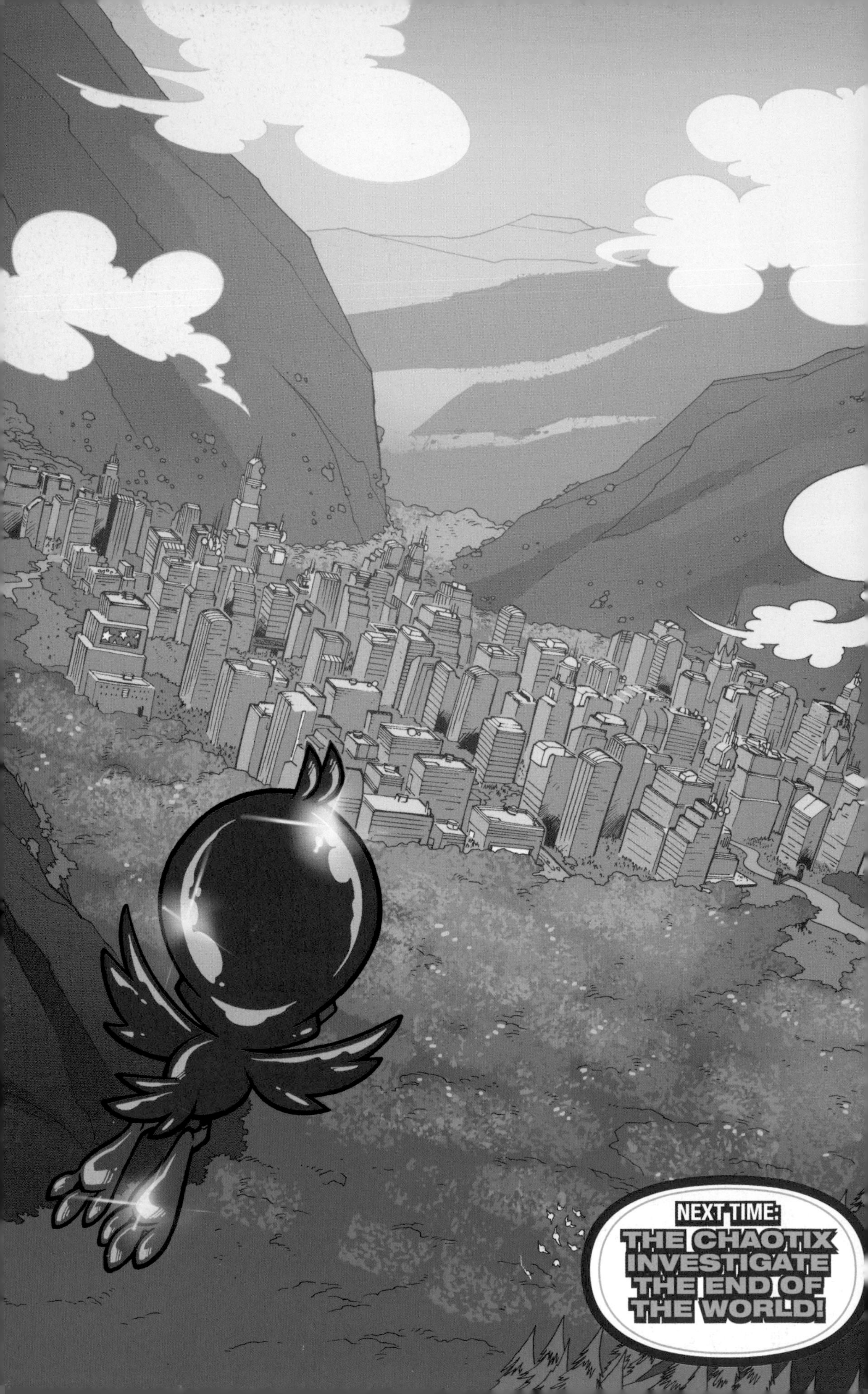
NEXT TIME:
THE CHAOTIX INVESTIGATE THE END OF THE WORLD!

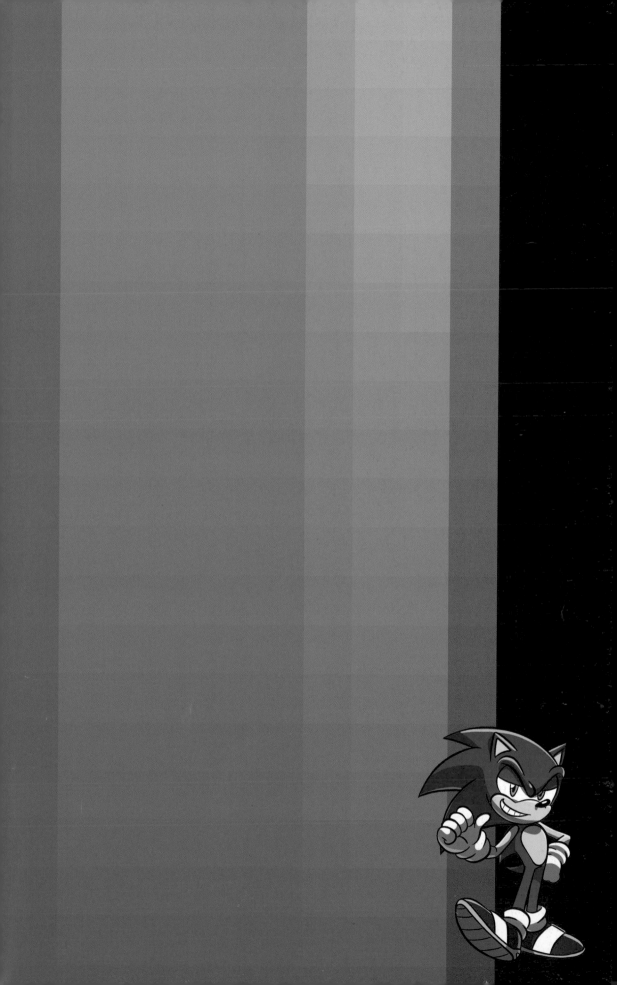

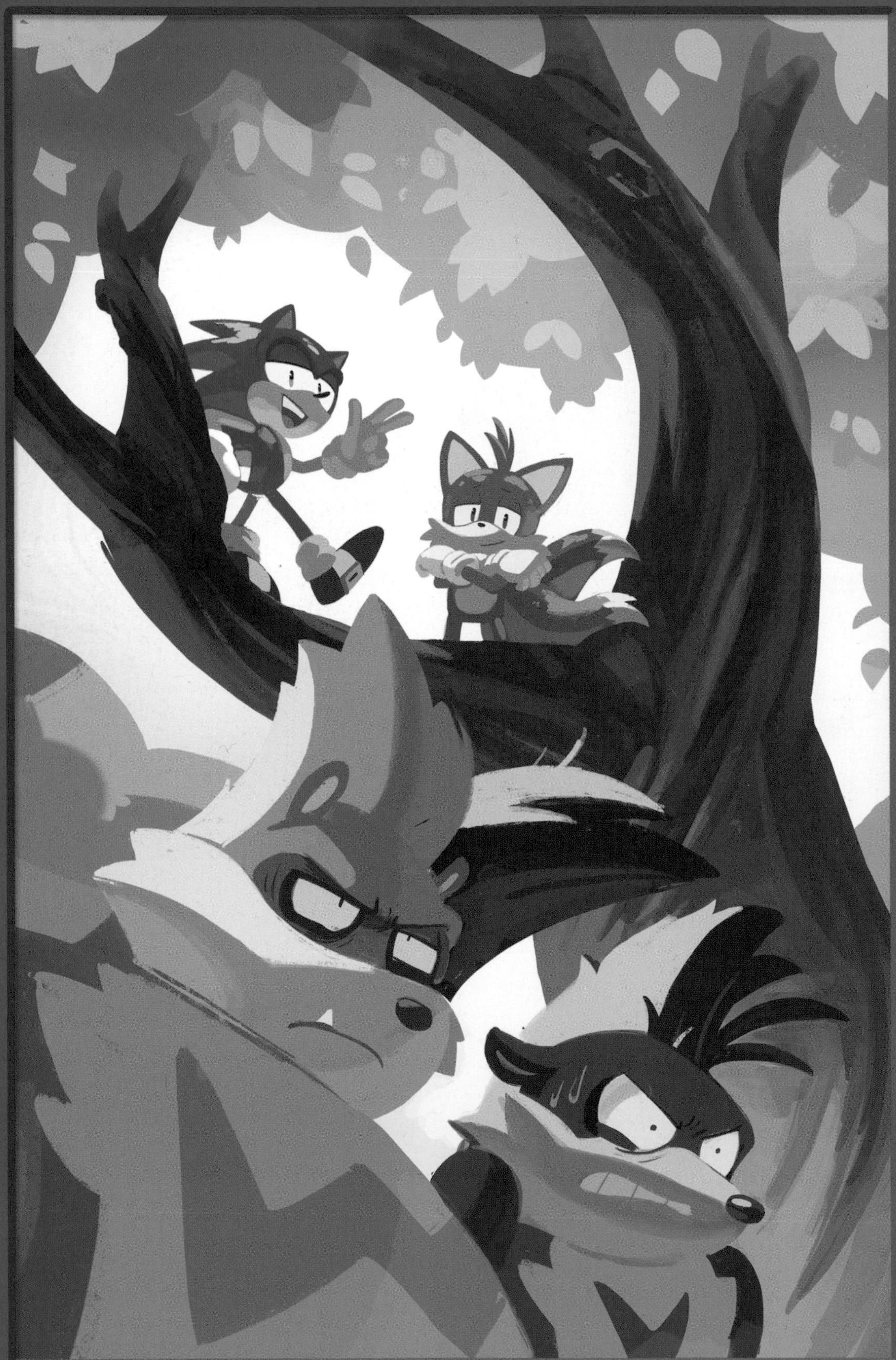

ART BY NATHALIE FOURDRAINE

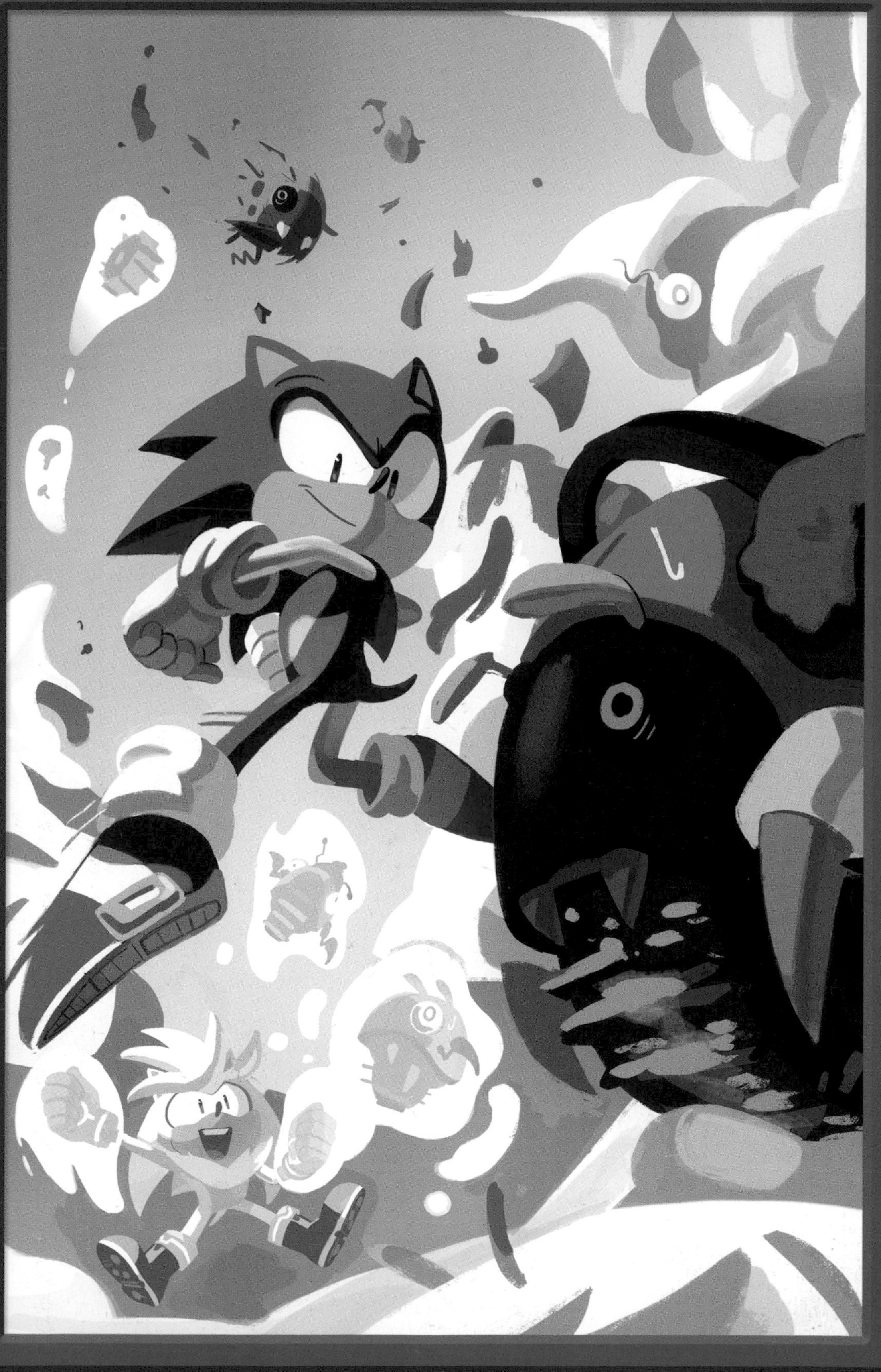

ART BY **NATHALIE FOURDRAINE**

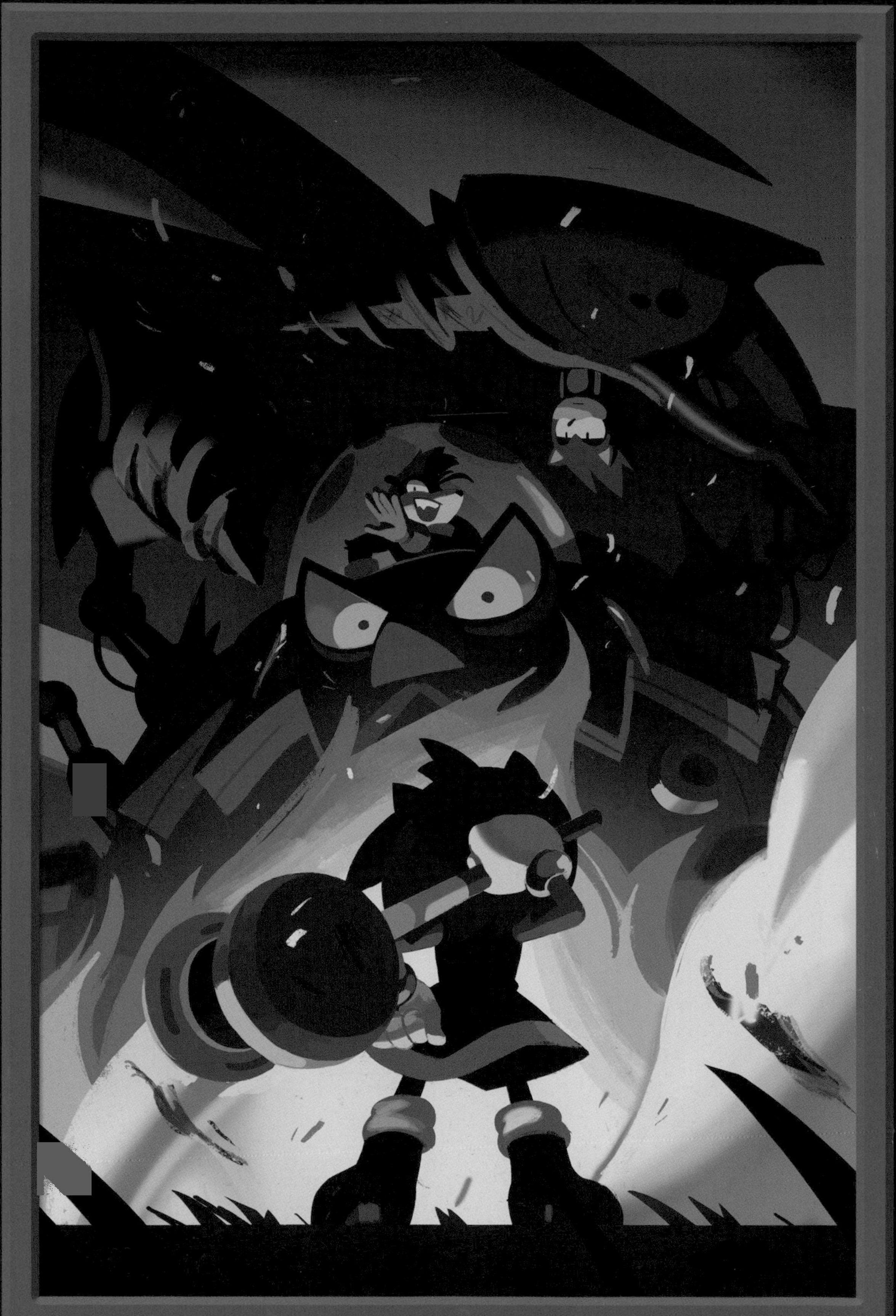

ART BY **NATHALIE FOURDRAINE**

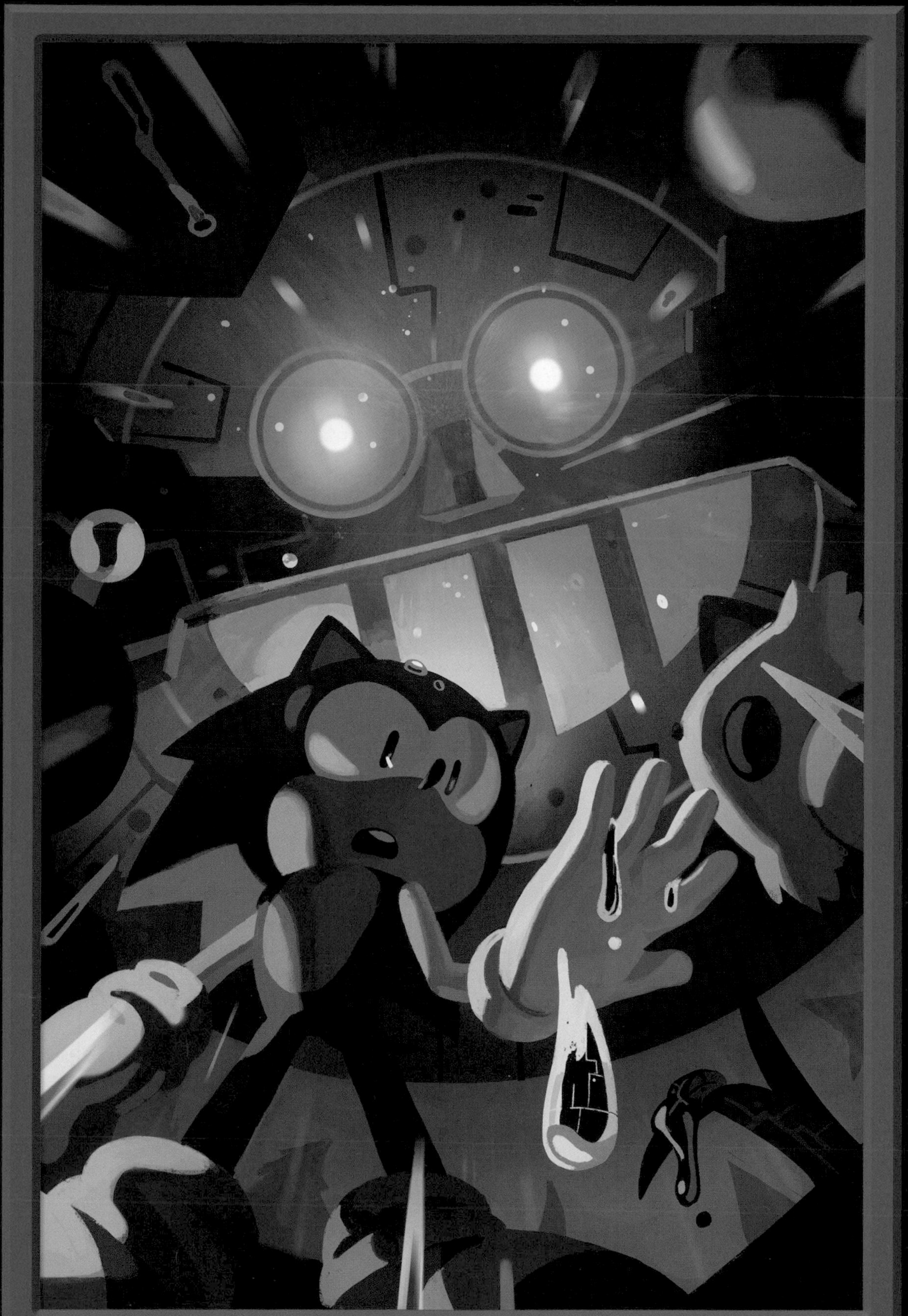

ART BY **NATHALIE FOURDRAINE**

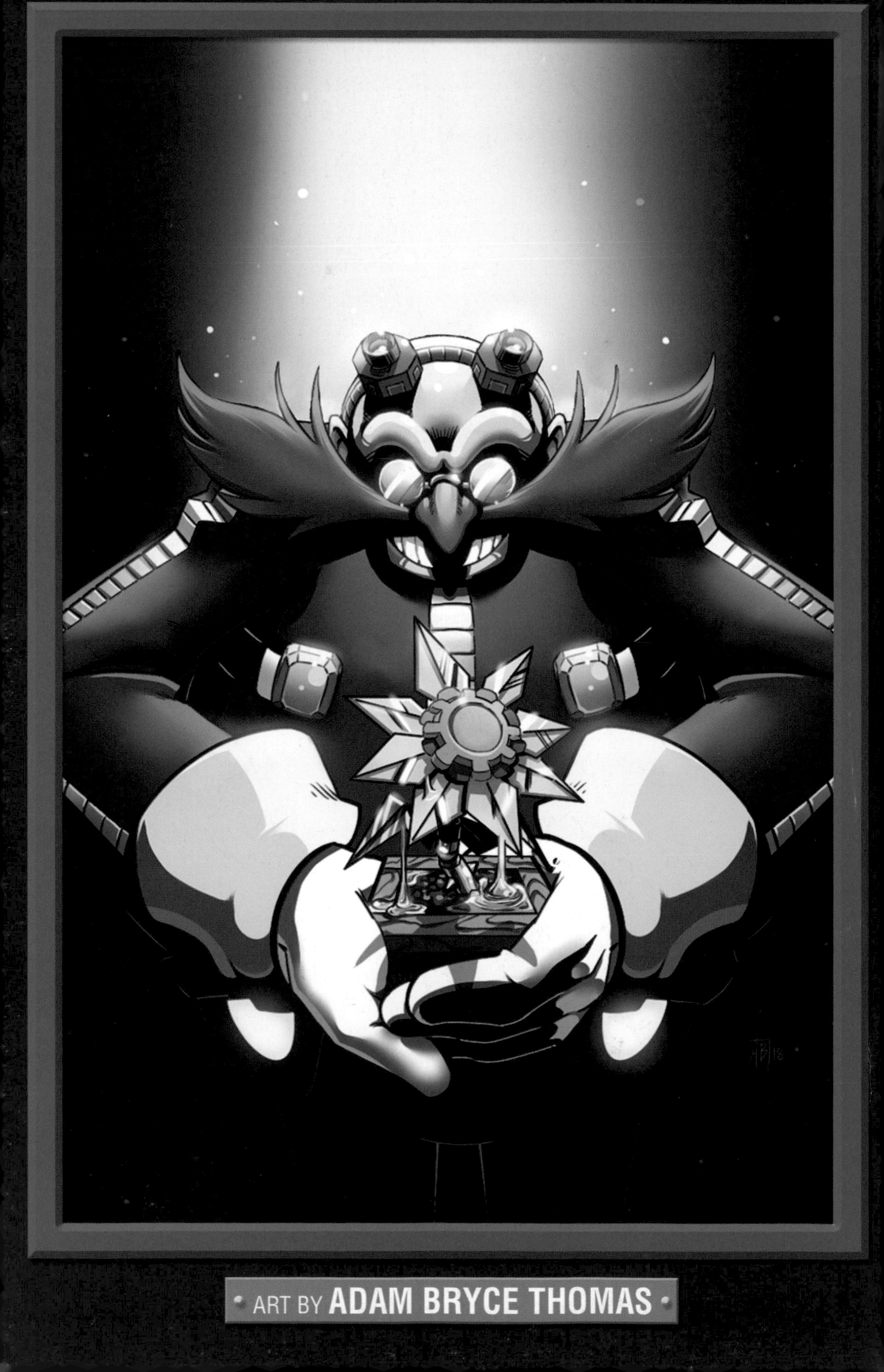

ART BY **ADAM BRYCE THOMAS**

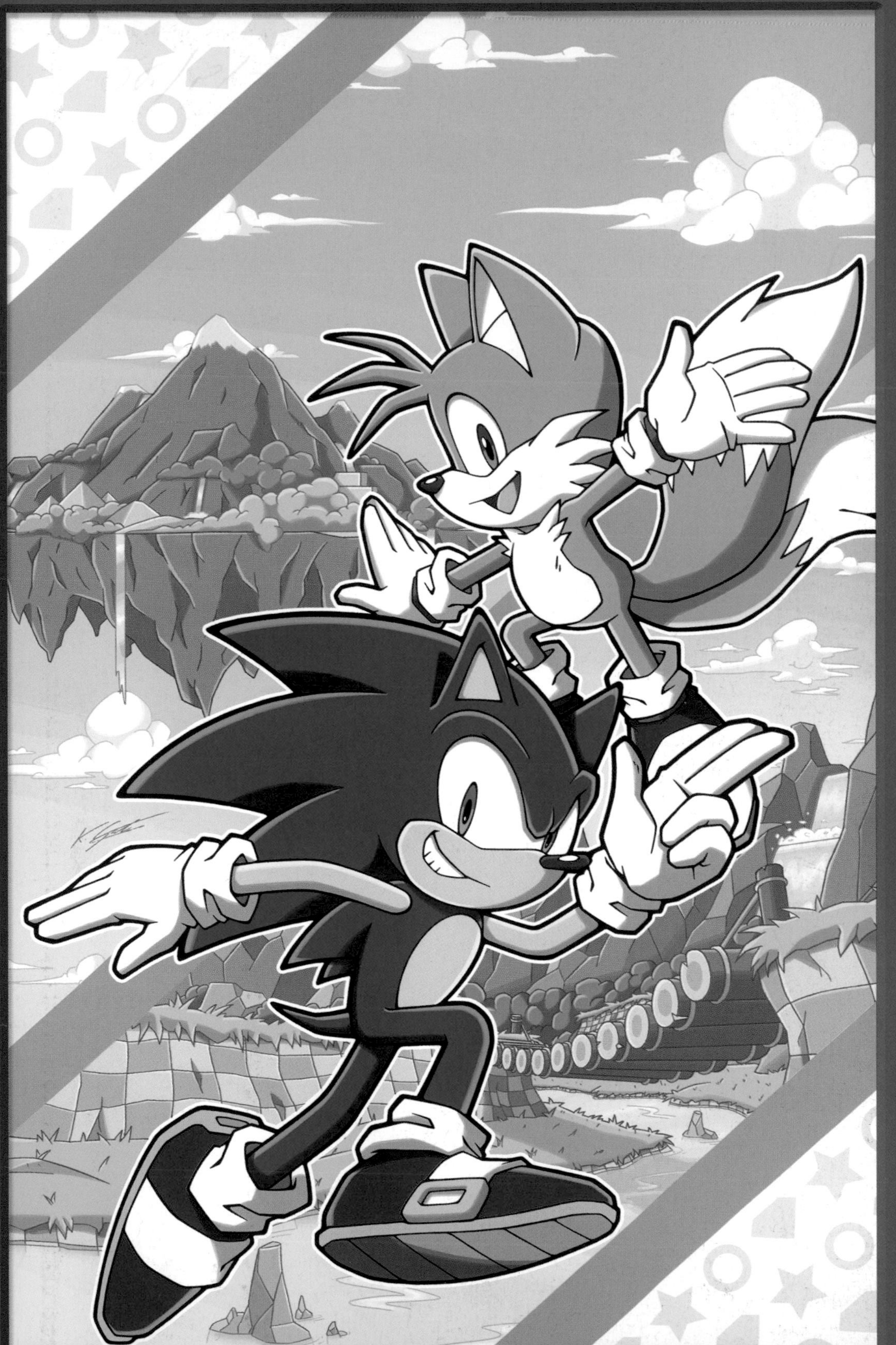

ART BY KIERAN GATES

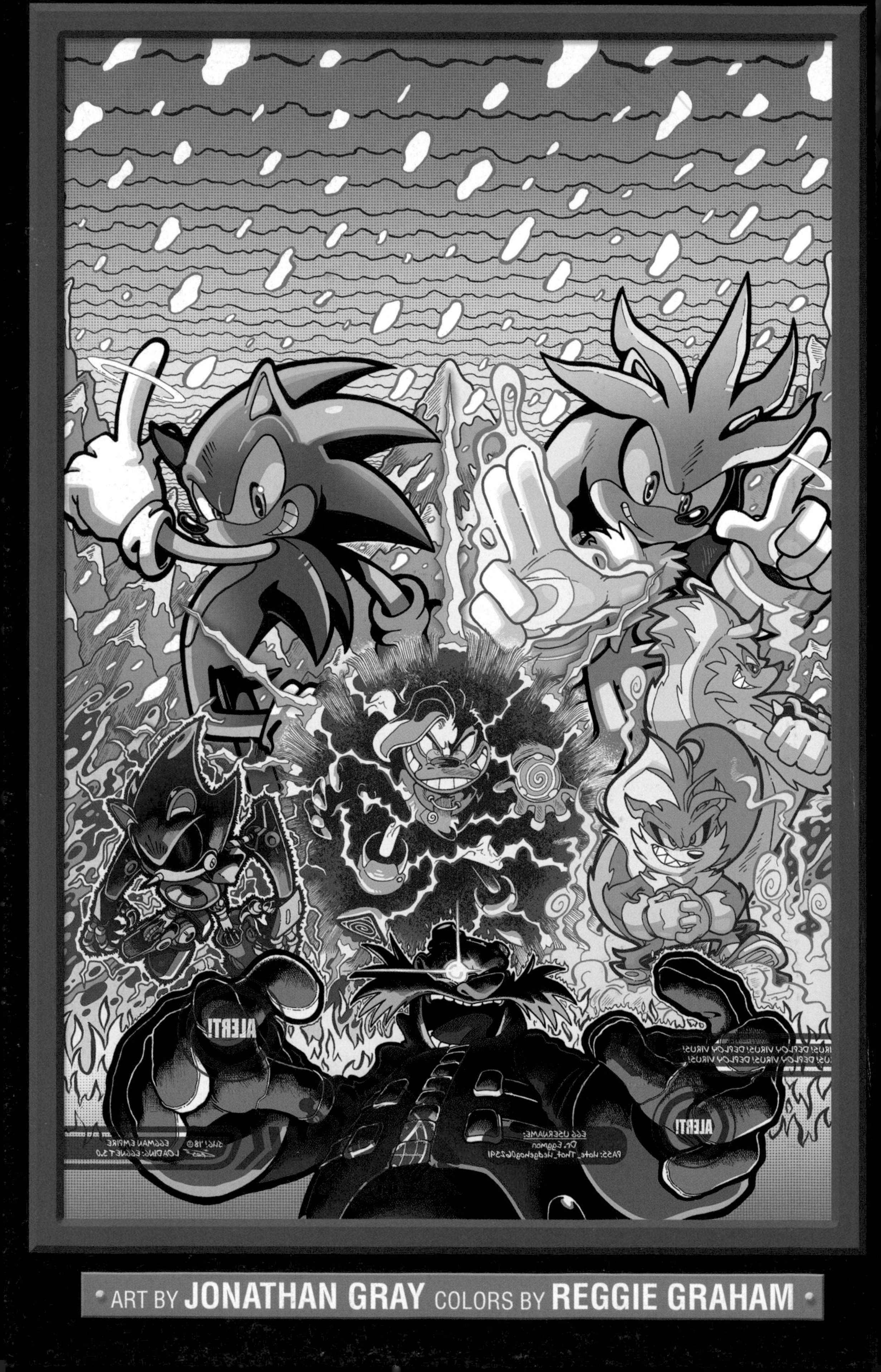
ALERT!
ALERT!

ART BY **JONATHAN GRAY** COLORS BY **REGGIE GRAHAM**

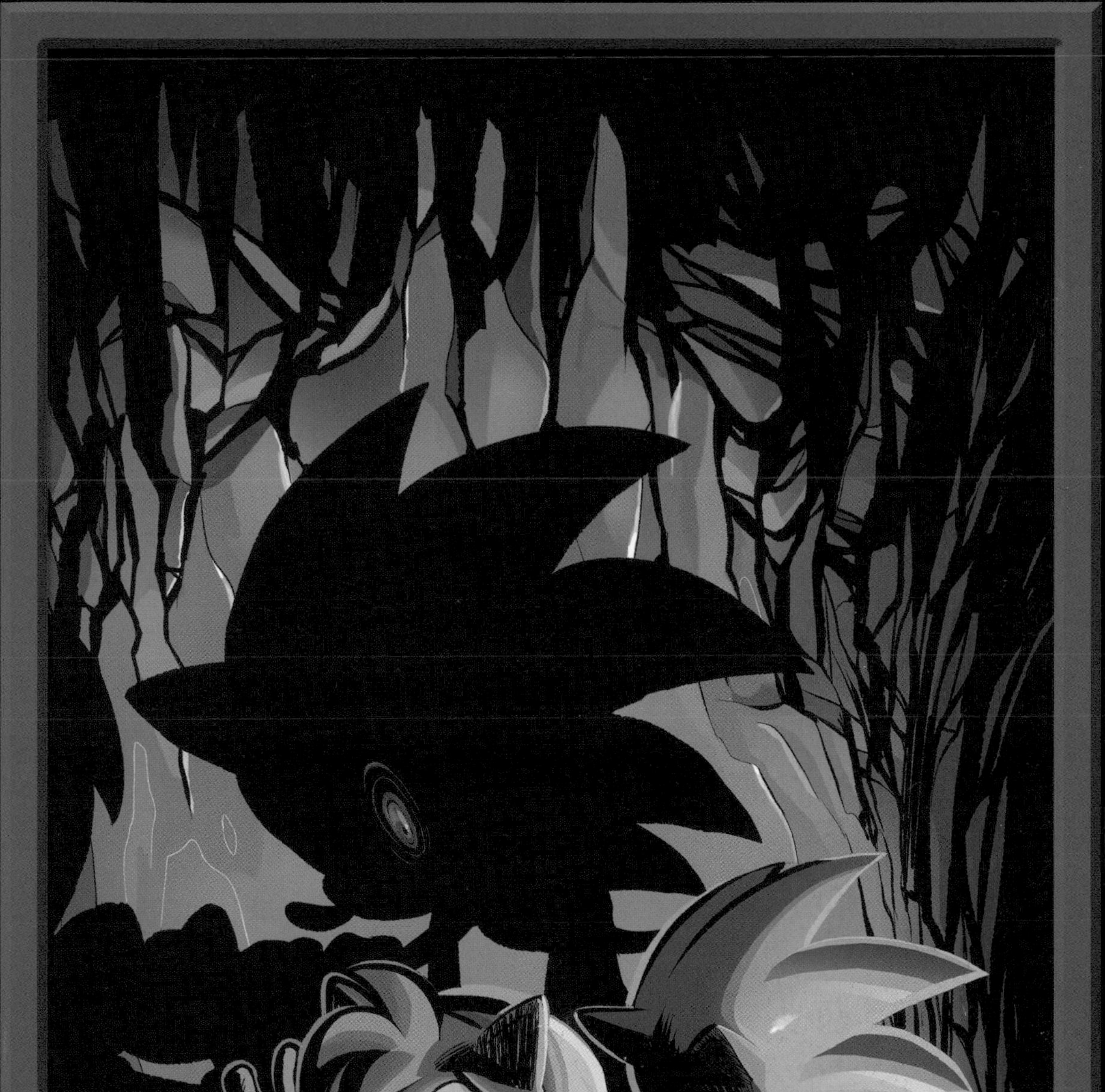

ART BY **DIANA SKELLY** COLORS BY **ELAINA UNGER**

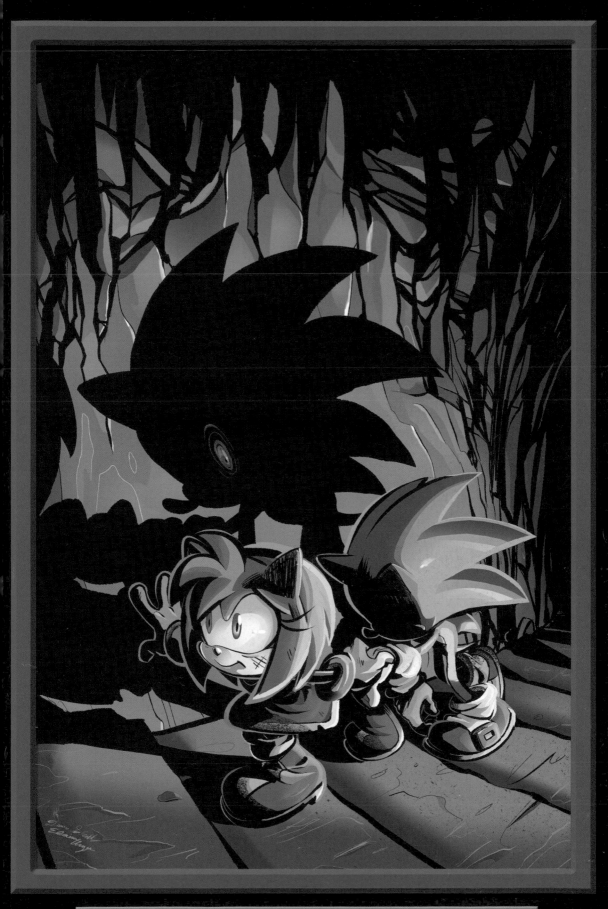

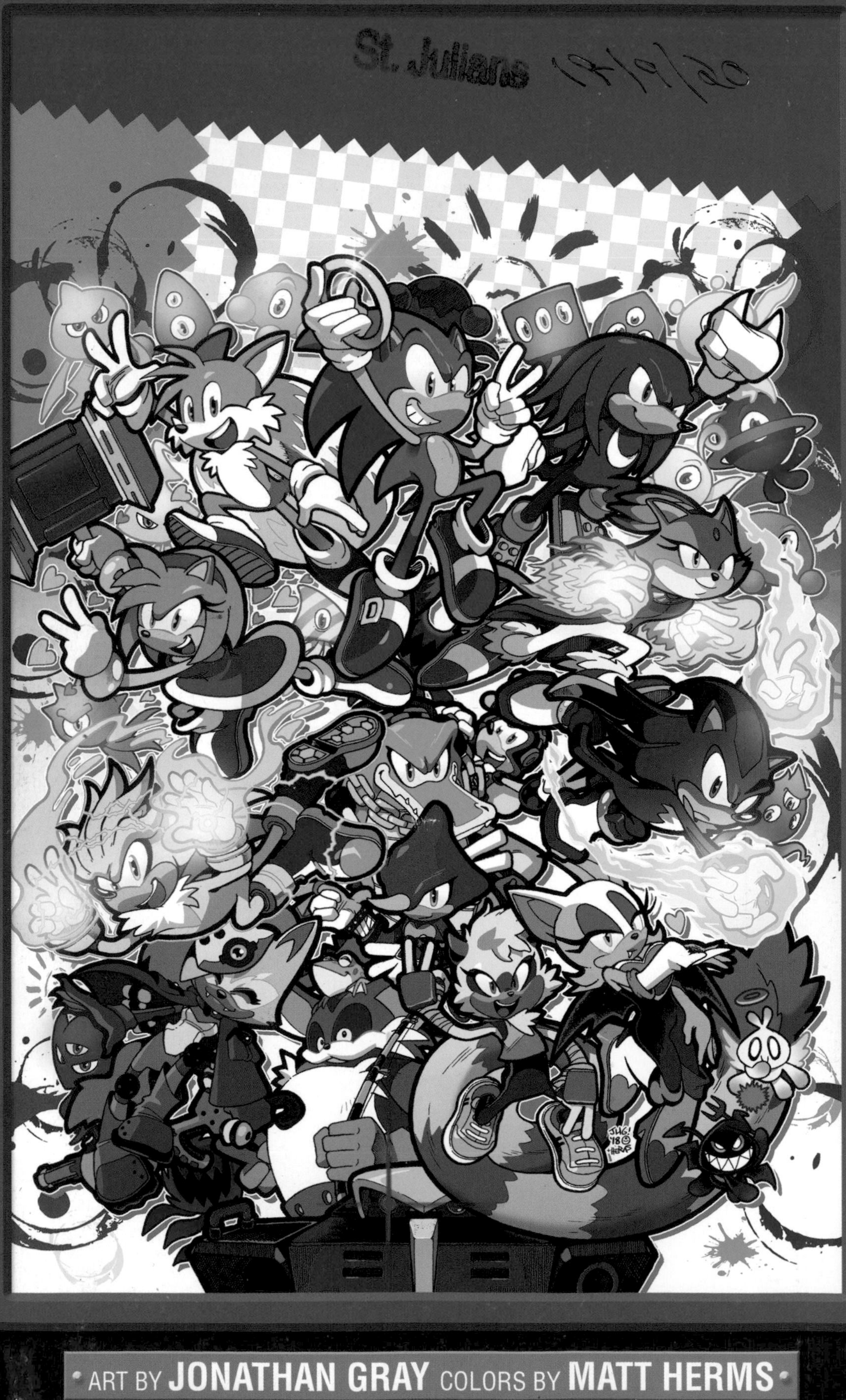

ART BY **JONATHAN GRAY** COLORS BY **MATT HERMS**